SOUND OF MIND

SOUND OF MIND

JIM WALTZER

FIVE STAR

An imprint of Thomson Gale, a part of The Thomson Corporation

Nobles County Library
PO Box 1049
407 12th Street
Worthington, MN 56187

THOMSON
™
GALE

Detroit • New York • San Francisco • New Haven, Conn. • Waterville, Maine • London

THOMSON

GALE

LIBRARY OF CONGRESS CATALOGING-IN-PUBLICATION DATA

Waltzer, Jim, 1950–
    Sound of mind / Jim Waltzer. — 1st ed.
      p. cm.
    "Published ... in conjunction with Tekno Books and Ed Gorman."
    ISBN-13: 978-1-59414-533-9 (alk. paper)
    ISBN-10: 1-59414-533-4 (alk. paper)
    1. Self-actualization (Psychology)—Fiction. 2. Mental illness—Fiction. I.
Title.
PS3623.A368S68 2007
813'.6—dc22
                                         2006034800

First Edition. First Printing: April 2007.

Published in 2007 in conjunction with Tekno Books and Ed Gorman.

Printed in the United States of America on permanent paper
10 9 8 7 6 5 4 3 2 1

ACKNOWLEDGMENTS

Thanks to literary agent Nat Sobel for a critical reading and story ideas, David Youse for plot points, James Rahn for fiction guidance, Detective Kurt Lindelow of the Marple Township (Pa.) Police for some technical information, *Press Newspapers* for computer support and a rooting interest, and most importantly, the unflagging encouragement of family and friends.

PROLOGUE

It's an old dress that he holds out from his chest, the cotton thin and no match for his veiny wrists and hands. He tears off a strip and the sound rips through the small dim room.

"Now don't scream—you won't get hurt."

His voice is subdued, businesslike. She gives him her foot, eases it toward him as if she were submitting it for a pedicure or a shoe fitting. He wraps the cotton strip around ankle and instep, and ties the foot to the bedpost. He is economical in his movements and his knot is tidy, expert even. A square knot, the ends frayed at the tear line. Hunched over her, he looks up and sees a stranger staring back at him from the mirror above the dresser. Forehead sweat crowning soulless eyes.

He snaps open the switchblade and stabs it downward into the wood. Ready position. A gasp catches in her throat; the knife vibrates a trace and a splinter falls to the floor. He tears off another length and ties her other foot to the opposite post so that she is spread-eagled on the bed. Naked.

Now she begins to whimper, a strangled pleading. He yanks the knife free and stabs it into the headboard, which kisses the wall and scratches the bare floor. He is purposeful as he moves about the bed, and now he sits next to her as if he's ready to tell her a bedtime story, but he pauses for only a moment and, as he's tying her arms to the headboard so that she's four-cornered and supremely vulnerable, her mouth opens in a soundless scream. Finally, finally, she understands. Her legs thrash against their restraints, the left one summoning enough terrified energy to undo the knot and break loose, her thigh banging into his back as he works on the final hand. He grunts with the surprise impact, and she screams for as long as it takes him to cover her mouth with his hand. Her free leg flails and she shakes her head furiously and the ridge of his hand slips into her mouth and she opens wide for leverage and bites down as hard as she possibly can, her only weapon, all of her energy concentrated into that little square of intimate horror. He grunts a second time and his eyes water. As long as his hand remains wedged in her mouth, she cannot scream. When he wriggles it out, he forms a fist at once and pounds her with short right-hand punches worthy of a prize fighter. Five consecutive blows, each a split-second apart, cracking fragile bones on the side of her face. She is unconscious.

He gets his breath, stands and withdraws a handkerchief from his pocket, winds it round his bloody hand. For a second or two, he is unsteady on his feet. His eyes fix on the switchblade sticking out of the headboard.

1

Sounds ruled his consciousness. They unnerved him, enchanted him, woke him in the wee small hours, sent him hurtling round street corners to escape, came to his ear like little messengers, singed him like a bullet delivering a flesh wound. He heard more than a human being should. He heard things that dogs could not. He had an earful of the planet.

It had always been so, as far back as he could remember. Kids in the neighborhood said he was strange, freakish. He heard the swish of its tires before the car appeared on the block. Thunder while it was still swallowed in the sky. Preternatural, that's what his mother called his hearing. Spooky, his father said. But they didn't trust him when it mattered most. When he heard it happen. When he was the only one to hear, who *could* hear.

Other than, of course, the little girl herself and her father. They heard it, unless the horror froze their eardrums, her gasping, her petrified whimpering, unearthly cries that came through the walls and permeated his room like steam from a vent. Chilling sounds. Not quite real. Small sounds muted by inches-thick plaster and wood, but loud enough for his ears, those sensitive instruments.

They invaded the sanctuary of his room, right through the wallpaper of cowboys aboard bucking broncos—actually, the same cowboy and bronco repeated several dozen times, each imprint separated from its replica above, below and to either

9

side by blank beige smoothness. He heard and, at first, he didn't know precisely what it meant, but he knew instinctively it was something very wrong. He heard and just lay there, paralyzed and smothered in blankets. He heard and did nothing, didn't even wake his parents. Only later did he tell them. The next day, in the afternoon, when the sun had long since chased the night's fears, but by then it was too late, far too late, and the salt-of-the-earth row-house neighborhood had grasped horror, had seen evil's nocturnal handiwork blanched and sheathed, the little body strapped and sheeted, wheeled on the gurney, the realization all the more terrifying for the sanitizing daylight.

And now, more than two decades later, it was a stain that would not yield to the mind's harshest corrosives, a memory that clung like a spider's gossamer stickiness, a trap not to be escaped.

As surely as the eardrum played to the brain, he was caught in this trap.

It is a three a.m. bugle blast, three nights a week. A delivery truck pulling up alongside the 24-hour Wawa store adjacent to his highrise apartment building, the unloading ramp banging the street, instantly waking him despite the rubber plugs wedged into his ears. Heavy boxes thudding onto the ramp, tossed from inside the truck. Booted feet trampling in the darkness. A half hour of this and then the motor's rumble, and the flurry of warning beeps, a high-pitched piercing staccato that seems injected into his ear. And Richard Keene is wide awake, flinging back the bedcovers, standing and looking out the window, as if his gaze could do anything, could reverse the disturbance that had taken place, or preclude any future such disturbances. Twenty-two floors up and a sheer drop means he can see nothing of his tormentors. But he might raise the miniblinds anyway and have a look at the vast spangled city, glittering at this no-man's hour, its towers empty but lit up like the backdrop of a stage production. He might look beneath him at squatter buildings, where the racket of rooftop compressors is just as likely to interrupt his sleep.

Sometimes he remains under the sheets, eyes shut in defiance, yet ears straining to hear through the plugs, a triumph of instinct.

When he's up and out of bed, prompted by the noise and something far from the surface, something deep in his gut, he switches on the desk lamp and its harsh light staggers him. The room is spare and ordered. Compact, matching oak bureaus stand side by side against one wall; they've been hewn directly from trees, the finish natural, the dovetailing expert and all wood, not a screw or nail anywhere. It reminds him of the knots he learned to make when he was a Boy Scout, all those slip knots and loop knots and square knots, interlaced cord or twine drawn into tight, perfect nodes.

The desk is by the same hand, a Japanese furniture maker discovered in bucolic Bucks County north of Philadelphia by Richard's style-conscious mother, Evelyn. A queen-sized bed and boxspring sit on apartment-standard dishwater carpet, and a single bookcase has volumes lined up like soldiers. History and True Crime titles predominate; presidential biographies, thick studies of the two World Wars, Walt Whitman's *Leaves of Grass,* and several novelistic treatments of small-town murder, especially involving a child. Alone at one end of the top-left shelf, Richard's favorite work of fiction—Camus's *The Stranger*— leans against the varnished wood, its paperback pages billowed from use. He reread it twice during his stay at the clinic.

Richard Keene has just turned thirty, and his world continues to be a fearful place. The milestone passed without notice, except for a card and a phone call from his parents. No acknowledgment from anyone else, but how could there be?

Richard long ago lost touch with the few relatives in his extended family, an aunt here, a cousin there. And he has no close friends, no girlfriend. Sometimes, he's not even sure whether he has *himself*. After the breakdown, after he'd been confined to a room with no mirrors, he'd lie on his bed and relive the sensation of scanning his image in the full-length mirror on his bedroom door at home. He'd discovered the dread in that exercise as a young boy, the out-of-body feeling of it, a fizz of fear like tiny insects inside your skin, the unthinkable notion that you may not exist, at least not as you understand it. He'd stand there and stare at himself and feel the desperation come over him. Nothing scared him more than this sensation, and he could re-create it—even without the mirror's spell—if he concentrated hard enough.

Richard confessed all of this to his doctors, whose mirrorless rooms were intended to discourage more than just imaginary fright. They taught him how to parry his fear through self-distraction, diverting it at or before the onset with unrelated thoughts. It's a technique he has continued to use on the outside. So now, this morning, once the sun has snuck some light into the concrete canyon just beyond his window, Richard stands before the bathroom mirror, mouth unhinged, and gives his teeth a thorough flossing. He is thinking of his dentist and the pretty dental technician who cleans his teeth twice a year. No thoughts of the paranormal at present, no worries that existence is an illusion. He rinses and spits into the sink—not a trace of blood, thanks to his daily rigors. He looks up and eyes like black marbles in an angular face stare back at him. Below the sharp chin, a columnar neck attaches to a bony torso. If he lingers, the strange fears may rise, so he busies himself with movement. Shaving is quick and electric, his beard narrow and light. He applies a wedge of Mennen to his underarms and runs a comb just once through his unruly black hair. He pulls on a

Hanes undershirt and a short-sleeve Arrow, a pair of chinos. For him, dress is casual at the workplace. Pair of Clarks, some days sneakers even.

He grabs the Walkman and jams it in his pants' pocket. Never leaves home without it. He pays no heed to the newer technology.

In the pallid hallway, a tame scent rises from the vacuum-stroked carpet. The elevator requires patience, a wait of three to four minutes. Several floors up, muted chimes distinct to Richard's ear signal stops, the subsequent drone a resumption of the elevator's down-rush. Now a loud chime and the red light, and the door opens, revealing bodies from any one of the twenty higher floors. Richard tries to find a corner or at least some wall space, some breathing room. They all stare straight ahead and don't notice him grind his teeth. The young woman wearing a navy suitcoat and a broad belt cinching her skirt looks up at the panel of floor numbers to monitor the elevator's descent. A stop on sixteen, and a heavyset man gets on, leading with his stomach. As the others press more closely about him, Richard feels his chest tighten, but with the elevator underway once more, and the lobby rushing up to meet them, he knows that release is imminent. When the elevator reaches ground-level and Richard bolts off, he takes a gulp of air.

The polished tile of the lobby floor reflects light beams from the bulbs recessed in the ceiling, as do the mirrored wall panels that flank the elevator doors. Now tethered to his Walkman by earphones, Richard walks past the front desk, through the automatic, sliding-glass doors and into the sunshine of a mid-September Tuesday morning.

Richard's new home, the "42s" (hiply named for the number of stories it rises above Locust Street), races upward toward a docile sky. Summer has only a week to run, but it is in no hurry to depart. The city is warm and sticky, Locust Street crammed with faces expectant, blank or disconcerted. Cell phones, cupped by hands, bloom out of ears. Richard turns up 15th Street and dodges trash cans, no-parking signs, and foot-walkers too oblivious or arrogant to give way. Through his headset he hears the clarion tones of a Chopin polonaise on an FM classical station, as the city's muffled cacophony swirls about him. Clamped down in a Walkman world, Richard can still hear the outside fury, in nuance and volume, better than the unencumbered. His other senses, too, are quite sharp, if not as exceptional as his hearing. In the alleyway outside a restaurant on one corner of Sansom Street, a stuffed Dumpster emits the scent of sour milk. The morning's creased light outlines every object he sees. At Market Street, the number of traffic lanes doubles, and Richard moves smartly across when the "walk" icon beckons. He's a reflex quicker than everyone else, as he strides down the steps to the subway concourse leading to the stop below City Hall.

Once on the underground platform, he spies the light in the distance burning a hole through the black tunnel, and braces himself for the onrushing train and its deafening roar. He steps back as it blurs past, closing his eyes, inhaling the dankness. Chopin's crystal notes rain down on him, bursting through the train's thunder.

Inside, the seats are all occupied, and Richard stands, grasping a shiny metal pole. At the Race/Vine, Fairmount, and Girard stops, more people get on than off, and the tide engulfs Richard, pressing him against his gleaming pole, his life raft. As the train lurches back into motion, he is sweating, the world closing in on him, but he takes two deep breaths and, slowly, convinces himself not to panic. He is beginning to deal with this phobia, he senses, at least to the point where he can function.

The radio program host speaks to him in a resonant baritone.

He gets off at Olney Avenue and surfaces through the soiled

passageways and stairs. Preston Medical Tower is right across a perilous intersection, where multi-car crackups are commonplace, participants seemingly encouraged by the convenience of Einstein General Hospital in the next block of Broad Street. In the Preston lobby, Richard enters a waiting elevator, and retreats to the rear when two uniformed nurses arrive, giving him their backs. He removes the Walkman from his ears and stashes it in his pocket.

Rosen & Wallingford ENT Associates has a suite on the fifth floor. Kathy, the front-office secretary, wears clinging sweaters, blouses, or T-shirts that showcase a pair of breasts too ample for her slender frame. Her forehead is still trying to chase stubborn acne. Richard has thought about her once or twice, but the connection's not there; they're civil to each other, that's all. He nods as he passes the broad front counter.

"Morning, Kathy."

"Oh, Richard, there's a change in your schedule. Your ten o'clock, Mrs. O'Hanlon, canceled, so I stuck in Mrs. Campbell."

"Who?"

"Loretta Campbell. Doctor wants a complete workup for dizzy spells . . . And Mister Caracappa can't make it this afternoon at three, so I rescheduled for tomorrow morning."

Richard shrugs. "Thanks." Campbell, O'Hanlon, Caracappa, it's all the same in the life of an audiometric technician. Plug 'em in, turn the dials, and they either hear the thin, high-pitched tones or they don't. At first, it was a novel task to run the contraption and conduct the tests; he was a kind of Master-of-the-Machine who could exercise dominion over all sounds in the universe, the faintest of which could not escape his astounding acuity. But now, after several years on the job, it has grown routine. Once he gathers a few extra dollars and musters sufficient stamina, he'll study to be an audiologist, and then things will get a bit more interesting; he'll be qualified to administer an Electronystagmography and an Auditory Brainstem Response, tests that may defy pronunciation, but do evaluate the balance mechanism and central nervous system. For now, though, he has to be content with his audiometer, and merely assisting on the ETMs and ABRs.

It is ironic—Richard is quick to detect irony—that the boy with super hearing has grown up to be a tester of other people's hearing, as if searching for a fellow traveler. He simply gravitated to audiology, his arena. Who better to make the call than Richard Keene? But, of course, it's the machine that does the work.

The day is uneventful, as most of them are. One woman actually has a sense of humor—she professes to have better hearing than her Chihuahua—but the others sit there glumly and raise their hands when they hear something or think they do. The good technician doesn't telegraph the sounds, varies the rhythm, looks away from the patient to avoid prompting. A raised hand is easy enough to pick up without making direct eye contact; it's amazing how many technicians don't grasp that. Limited peripheral vision in some cases, but mostly stupidity. Richard prides himself on technique and producing reliable results.

This day, in addition to his regular customers, he has a personal health matter that needs attention. During his lunch break, he takes the stairs to the sixth floor to see the osteopath, Melvin Natrol. Natrol is rostered on Richard's HMO, and you can't beat the convenience; if he knows his job, it's a bonus. Richard's right knee has been bothering him the last couple of years, and now the soreness has become a stabbing. Still, he pounds the treadmill nightly at his apartment building's fitness center, driving his weight onto the tender knee, kneading it like mad afterward to lessen the pain.

"Maybe it's time you got an MRI," says Natrol, rather grave

as he flexes Richard's leg dangling aside the padded table, the patient seated there, a papery surgical gown bunching at his shoulder blades. Richard grimaces more at the doctor's suggestion than his probing hands. Natrol notices.

"You OK?"

"Yeah."

Natrol manipulates the knee some more, thumbs it.

"Can you breathe in those things?" Richard asks.

Natrol looks at him, begins to understand. "Usually."

Richard manages a weak smile.

"A little claustrophobia?" asks Natrol. Richard nods.

"I'll get you into one of the newer machines," says the doctor. "It's like flying first class."

The subway ride home is decidedly less than first class, but Richard is getting used to this cramped subterranean passage. It is a kind of training regimen, as he attempts to blunt his claustrophobia. This trip, he finds a seat smack up against the window and stares at his photographic negative in the tunnel-blackened glass, as the train hurtles through the darkness. The Walkman parries the sonic insult with soothing strings, the burnished sound of the Philadelphia Orchestra. He closes his eyes and floats on the rise and swell of melody, the train's clatter and hollow roar receded to a far corner of the stage. Six weeks on his own, he's a man of the world now. He's getting the hang of it. His mission is to rejoin the human race. The doctors told him it was high time and he accepted their recommendations. Time to move out of his parents' suburban home, where he'd been forever, a halfway house following his six-month stay at the mental health clinic, the health farm, a place of beige walls and restful gardens and rooms with no mirrors and shatterproof Plexiglass windows, where he had his books to read and jigsaw puzzles to solve but was denied the rope or string he requested for practicing his knots, an old skill, a therapeutic activity.

At 15th and Market, the City Hall stop, Richard emerges from the depths into a jamboree world. Skateboarders dodge hard-soled, grim foot-walkers in the plaza dwarfed by the gray gothic tower conceived and built in another era, topped by the city's historic benefactor, Quaker-garbed William Penn memorialized in black bronze. Richard approaches the river of traffic on Market Street, and the blare of car horns bounces off his earphones, but enough of it filters through to make him cringe a bit. When the traffic light signals him to walk, he scoots across the street to the concrete apron at the foot of the highrise offices of Centre Square. In front of a twenty-five-foot-high sculpture of a clothespin, a pale man points to a homemade chart propped on an easel. The words "tension" and "peace" and "happiness" claim most of the space on the chart. "Everybody is looking to get rid of their loneliness," the man says, the giant, chocolate-brown clothespin pinched at the top by an oversize metal clasp. The sidewalk is thick with the day's center-city work crowd careening for the exits, anxious to escape from the place where they make their livelihood. The city is emptying itself of the daytime white-collar horde, turning the streets over to the twilight people, a mix of stragglers, incense peddlers and clubhoppers.

Richard's refuge, he hopes, is a building a few blocks down on Locust Street, and in daylight, the monolith that is the 42s arches skyward, poking cottony clouds.

The sliding-glass doors part and Richard is home. He passes the front desk, where attendant-in-chief Frank is speaking with an elderly couple, and heads straight to the mailroom. Tarnished metal slot-doors, like miniature crypts, fill the walls. Richard keys one open and eyes a narrow cylinder of space between wraparound magazines and large manila envelopes. He tries to remove the whole wedge with one tug, but it stalls on the edges of the compartment. He re-grips and tries again in vain. Finally, he yanks the mass toward him and, with a small rip, it spurts from its cloister, out of his hand and onto the tiled floor, scattering at his feet. There's a yellow "call at the desk" slip among the fallen.

Richard gathers up his pile, marches back to the front desk, and extends the slip to Frank, a gregarious fellow who has manned this post for several years and likes the idea of running the building's nerve center.

"2207," Richard says without expression. He dislikes small talk, and is not a big fan of Frank, who strikes him as one more concerned with his own image than the welfare of the tenants.

Frank reaches under the U-shaped counter, selects an item and hands it to Richard. It is a book parcel, too rigid for the mail compartment.

"There you go, my man."

Richard takes it, mutters "thanks," and moves away quickly to the elevator, another piece of his training regimen to combat claustrophobia. He stays to the rear as others board, imploring the door to close and set the conveyance in motion, closing his eyes momentarily. The elevator pulls upward and Richard waits. The little light on the panel above the door is on the move, hopping floors. The side panel shows four floors lit, only one lower than Richard's. A woman gets off at fourteen and Richard feels the lift in his chest, the readiness to rid himself of this closed-in shuttle. The next chime is his release, and he's off the elevator, into the hallway, and across it at a modest angle to the first apartment on the left, number 2207, home.

Inside, he sorts through his mail, deems most of it useless and tosses, opens the parcel (the historical documentary *Sky-scrapers* ordered through his video club), and checks for telephone messages. There are two, the first in a familiar nasal voice.

"Richard, it's your mother. Your father and I would like to come over for dinner one night, if you'd be so kind as to extend an invitation. You know, we haven't even seen your place yet—it's been at least a month, hasn't it? We have a birthday present, housewarming gift for you all wrapped up in one. Anyway, call me and let's schedule. Hope you're all settled in and having a ball . . . Lotsa love."

Six weeks, to be exact, since leaving home just shy of his thirtieth birthday. His parents are helping him with the rent (good of them, but not a huge sacrifice since they had to be just a little happy to get him out of the house); center city isn't cheap. Comes the liberation, finally, the doctors' latest prescription more than two years after the "illness." But the cure is not immediate, the same fears move right along with him, dwell with him in his new apartment.

"Second message," says the female-approximate, computer voice followed by a prerecorded pitch for a center-city singles group, something about a Friday night "bash" at a pub on Walnut Street. Richard erases it. There must be a constantly updated file of every newcomer to every place in the world. By phone or mail or browser, they get you; there's no hiding. But he didn't come here to hide—quite the opposite. He's here to make a new start, blend in, reconstruct a life. He yearns for solitude and silence, but can't trust that impulse either. Which way does freedom lie?

He spends nearly a half-hour in the bathroom, dousing his face with cold water, sending streams of saline spray up each nostril, roosting on the toilet and straining to remove the accumulations of twenty-four hours. Must get more bran and roughage and flaxseed into the system. He scrubs his hands with antibacterial soap, orange and fragrant.

He munches on some garlic crackers, chews down a carrot, and makes himself a turkey roll sandwich with lettuce, tomato and wheat bread. A nectarine for dessert. Good balanced dinner. He mutes the sound on the TV evening news and gets the supered printed text, while listening on his Bose sound system—the one high-end item he owns—to the New York Philharmonic embroider a symphony by Berlioz.

An hour and fifteen minutes later, he changes into gym shorts and cross-trainers, and gets back on the elevator, taking it up to the top floor—number forty-two—which combines a banquet room with the fitness center and indoor swimming pool, and outside, an expansive sundeck. Through the windows, Richard sees some female forms bronzing on the deck in the late-summer sun, coaxing the last coat of pigment before the long, pale winter; he just glances, never lingers. The banquet room is silent, chairs and tables stacked to one side, but in the fitness center, there is the drone and squeak of movable parts, mechanical and human. Richard strides to an open treadmill at far left and steps up. There are five other machines in the row, two occupied, each facing floor-to-ceiling windows. Through the glass, the city's skyscrapers loom like giant rockets.

Richard grips the rubber-sheathed sidebars, alternates extending his legs behind him to stretch the hamstrings and calf muscles, and looks down the row. A hefty guy, about his age, pads along on the middle treadmill, surprisingly light on his feet. Two over from him, at the other end of the row, a woman is moving at a fast but fluid clip. Her body is encased in a gray cotton sports bra and spandex shorts, and she has all the right contours. Red hair as bright as a flare falls onto bare shoulders. Richard feels that ping, the little jolt that tells him this is a woman he desires, who intimidates him. All he can do for now is match her pace.

He drapes his face-towel over the right sidebar, punches up a starter pace on the electronic monitor, and begins walking, quickly goes to a jog, and soon accelerates to a miler's steady swiftness. The soreness disappears from his knee as his speed increases. He doesn't use the Walkman when he works out. His light breathing and the treadmill's hum serve as a sound conditioner and, moreover, he doesn't like sweating into the ear-sets.

The big guy two over steps down after another five minutes, and Richard and the redhead are left to match strides, separated by four vacant treadmills. Visible through a glass wall is the adjoining room, where a weightlifter lets a heavy iron plate fall to the carpeted floor. The thud jars Richard, almost knocking him off his stride. He feels a twinge in the knee, shakes it off, and resumes the pace, glowering toward the offending weight-lifter, who is looking the other way, so it's a safe move by Richard.

The woman is aware of Richard, as any fine-tuned athlete feels the competition without looking at it head-on. Her name is Janet Kroll, and she's been living at the 42s for about a month now, a little less time than Richard. She stays on the treadmill for forty-five minutes, and follows with fifteen brisk minutes of dumbbell and Nautilus work next door. Her shoulders have a small swell of muscle, and her legs are dancer-taut. Richard's discreet glances take it all in, and when the two of them pass on the floor, he notices freckles below her eyes, giving her a vulnerability she lacks from a distance.

2

He completes his typically lengthy workout, an escape hatch from the discomfort he finds in ordinary life. On the elevator drifting downward, Richard towels his face and closes his eyes. With no one else on-board, he feels secure in the space. The elevator descends, a suspended box humming down a barren shaft. Richard feels like he's floating.

The chime and an absence of movement yank him from his repose. The door slides open and, just as he steps off, a tall woman wearing orange hoop earrings steps onto the elevator. She is a mere passing image to Richard, who is already nearing his apartment across the hallway, angling to his left. He withdraws the single key from the back pocket of his shorts and inserts it into the lock. Halfway into the lock.

He wriggles it, jams it, removes it, tries again, gently, like a knife he expects will cut through butter. But this butter is cement; the key will not go. And Richard is lost, a man falling through space, as if he were back in the elevator disengaged from its pulleys and plummeting. It doesn't take much to throw him off-kilter. It's like that unnerving sensation of standing before the mirror and having difficulty recognizing himself, doubting all of existence. Where am I? Who am I? His heart palpitates, as he raises his eyes and looks around and sees the number above the buttonhole on the door: *2307*. His apartment, one floor up. All of them lined up to the sky, floor after floor after floor, but only one that's yours, only one that opens to your special little world.

He is settling back into reality, he feels. The woodpecker pulses retreat from his heart and are replaced by three thumps that promptly exit like a heavy-footed man stomping out the front door. Richard shakes his head and looks back toward the elevator, searching for clues. He's got it. Of course. The tall woman with the orange earrings, out of the corner of his eye. Her floor. On her subsequent way down, a futile stop at the floor just below, twenty-two, which he had pressed when leaving the fitness center on forty-two.

He's taken that post-workout ride almost every day for six weeks now, and this has been the first time it's been interrupted. He's almost always had the elevator to himself for this trip. The languor of that ride. Dreaminess and kinetics. A sense of distance and time elapsed. If the woman gets on at, say, floor thirty-five, Richard checks the panel and stays put.

Clean deductive reasoning. Nice to have a rational explanation for things.

Now he turns to leave the apartment door, and doesn't get a step away before the coarse sound of tearing fabric stops him. It is coming from inside apartment 2307, and is followed by a man's voice saying matter-of-factly: "Don't scream—you won't get hurt."

Richard steps back to the door. There is a shuffling inside, a swishing sound like palms rubbing against one another, then a bang of maybe wood on wood, or metal on wood, then a gasp, a woman's gasp. Then more tearing and the woman's breathless cry. Richard edges even closer to the door and, as the cry becomes a whimper and then a moan, he is concentrating fully, trying to catch every nuance of sound, fighting off the intrusion of his heart which is racing again. He will store these sounds in sequence in his auditory memory. Whatever he is hearing, he will be able to replay as if recorded on a tape. But while he trusts his capability absolutely, he has grown to distrust his state of mind at any given moment. Is he hearing what he thinks he's hearing?

A sharper cry. That bang again, definitely something metallic in it, like gears dropping. Now a blend of noises: a squeaking like bedsprings, a catch in the woman's voice, a rasp. More rasping and, simultaneously, a grunt, a man's grunt, then a muffled but anguished scream. It lasts only a second. Richard stands there, transfixed. He looks down at his feet but they seem to have no purchase; then at his hands, the fingers curled and stiffened. He doesn't feel whole. He feels that he could sift through the door like a wraith. The rasping returns, like a drain trying to clear, then in rapid succession five sounds that are a cross between a fist pulverizing meat and an open-hand smack. Now a thud and—Richard blinks his eyes in consternation—a thump like a ball of wet towels hurled into the dryer, a stack of books plopped on a desk, a body fallen to the floor.

And then someone breathing. A man breathing.

Richard steps back, distraught, and looks nervously around the empty hallway. This is what he has dreamed of and dreaded, a crazy happenstance, a signal from The Stranger's universe of benign indifference. He stands there, muscles coiled to flee, strike, he knows not what. He is caught in no-man's-land. Finally, he moves to the elevator and presses the down button, repeatedly presses it. Sweat that has beaded on his forehead is beginning to fall off in droplets. He wipes his face with his towel, which he then tucks into the waistband of his shorts. A fresh layer of sweat surfaces within seconds. When the elevator arrives, its chime is like an air raid.

On the elevator, a heavyset woman in a tent-like dress takes one look at dripping, disheveled Richard and keeps her distance. He makes his way to the rear, turns, braces himself against a metal rail and sits into the corner.

He is back there, back in the row-house bedroom of cowboys riding bucking broncos across the wallpaper. Through the walls come the muted, disturbing gasps of a young girl. And a man's voice, just a few quiet words. He knows who is speaking and who is gasping, now whimpering. It can be no one else. To his ears, sound permeates these walls as if they were tissue paper. He lies there frozen, not sure of what is going on, but he knows where it's coming from and he knows who it is, and he knows there is something very wrong.

When the elevator door opens, the heavyset woman walks into the lobby, not bothering to look back at Richard, who pauses at the threshold, disoriented. As the door closes, it brushes the back of his damp T-shirt where it bunches at the waist, and he lurches forward.

He approaches the front desk and Frank, who is dawdling on the phone. Richard passes the desk, stops, puts his hands in his pockets, lowers his head, and flexes his knees in a standstill position. Frank watches, as he winds up his phone call.

"You OK, man? You look like you gotta go to the bathroom."

Two young guys with baseball caps over chopped-off haircuts pass with a "yo, Frank" on their way out. Richard tries to stifle his trembling and turns toward Frank, who now looks concerned. Not so much for Richard himself as for the distraction, the problems that might ensue. Frank likes a smooth ship.

"Take it easy, man. What's wrong?"

Richard's instinct is that he must talk to someone. *This time he must.* He steps to the counter. Hesitates. "Who lives in 2307?" He is surprised at the firmness of his voice.

Frank is a bit amused at Richard's uncool style and issues a little smile. "Hold on a second. Just relax and tell me what's goin' on before you start runnin' the place, OK?"

Richard feels the little sting of putdown, a familiar sensation. He must fight through it. "I'm, uh, concerned about something. Can you call up there?"

"Slow down, man."

They look at each other and Frank waits. Richard takes a breath. What did he really hear? Tricks the mind plays . . . Wherever it leads, he must speak up.

"Someone may have been attacked."

Frank leans in with, "What's that mean?"

"I think someone may have been attacked in that apartment . . . It's possible."

Richard is squeezing the countertop ledge with both hands. Frank is no longer smiling, but he's a long way from believing him. "In 2307?"

"Yes."

Frank tries to situate Richard's apartment; he's given him several pieces of mail in the past few weeks. "You're what, twenty-two—. . . ?"

"I got off on the wrong floor."

"OK . . . And?"

"I heard something."

"Like what?"

Richard looks beyond Frank and sees himself reflected in the mirror behind the counter. He could still run away from this, drop it and shrink into the night. "Like a woman being strangled."

Frank deadpans it. "Like a woman being strangled?"

"That's right."

"So you're tellin' me you *heard* this?"

"Yes."

"You sure 'bout that?"

He's damn sure he heard something. "I know what I heard; I can't be a hundred percent sure that something actually happened, you know, that somebody was harmed."

"Well, what exactly did you hear, man? Was there screaming or"—Frank can't resist "choking" himself and making a few strangulated grunts—"or what?"

"There was one scream."

"All right, we got ourselves a scream. A big-time scream?"

"It won't hurt to call up there," says Richard, quietly frantic. "That's all I want."

"Oh, so that's all *you* want." This time, Frank's smile fronts a touch of resentment. You don't have to tell Frank Grant how to do his job. Frank Grant is a self-starter, an in-charge kind of guy. Still, the man's right, he figures, won't hurt to check it out with a quick phone call, put it to rest and demonstrate the power of the front desk all in one efficient move. He picks up the phone and punches in four numbers. Richard rocks nervously on his feet.

"Whadya hear now?" Frank asks, as the line rings.

"Like I said, a scream, and there were whimpers, then kind of a rasping, then a—"

Frank holds up his hand to stop him, and speaks into the phone, "Hello, Doctor Braun?" With that, he arches an eyebrow at Richard, signifying the respectability of doctors as tenants. Frank oversees a mixed roster at the 42s, but he likes to highlight the professional people.

"This is Frank at the front desk. How are you, sir? . . . I know what you mean. Listen, just checking, is everything all right up there? . . . Uh-huh . . . no, no. A neighbor heard somethin', thought there might be a problem, that's all . . . Right. Well, thank you. Sorry for the disturbance."

Frank hangs up the phone and shoots Richard a told-you-so expression. "Everything's cool." But Richard is staring past him in rapt concentration, seeing something awful on the flocked wallpaper that surrounds the mirror. Then he sees his face in the mirror and the old fright shivers him.

"You hear me?" says Frank. "Everything's OK up there. Hunky-dory. You can relax."

Richard looks like he has chills and a fever, like he has just been invaded by flu bugs.

"Hey man, you're startin' to freak me out."

"Braun?"

"That's right, Doctor Braun, Davis Braun. Good guy. Know 'im?"

"Is he married? Who's he live with?"

Frank opens the storage room door behind him. "You takin' a census?"

Richard is back on the elevator and he's headed to the twenty-third floor. The noises he heard—all the tearing and rasping and thudding—are dancing in his ear. He tries to make sense of them. His instincts are guiding him, and in this particular matter, they are powerful. Something falls in your lap and it's your one chance for redemption. Or, he concedes, sorting it out like the psychiatrists who treated him, it could be a matter of wish fulfillment. How often he has lain awake, straining through the earplugs to hear the muted alarm among the disparate noises of the night.

Then, of course, there's the possibility of television, a fake-out, a delusion, but no, there was something very real about this, he thinks, he feels, he must find out.

He congratulates himself on his rationality.

Now Richard is standing in the hallway of the twenty-third floor. Sounds leap out of apartments, keen to his ear: laughter, a toilet flushing, a tea kettle whistling. He walks past the door to 2307, stops and cocks an ear to the wall, stands there breathing rapidly. He tries to slow his breathing so it doesn't distort other sounds, and manages to do so. Still, there is nothing coming from inside 2307. No telltale sounds of panic or improvisation. Nothing at all. He stands there for several minutes, ready to dart away should someone come to the door or someone else leave a nearby apartment.

He walks across the hallway to the elevator, presses the down button and waits. Behind him, an apartment door swings open, and right away he knows that it's 2307, but he won't betray himself, he stares straight ahead at the closed elevator door. Impeccable timing or did the guy see him through the peephole? It will be a guy, of course.

Davis Braun is toting an empty pizza box and a small plastic garbage bag, as he walks out of 2307 and makes his way to the trash room tucked into one side of the elevator alcove. If Richard would look at him, he'd see muscular arms extending from the high sleeves of a pale-green medical smock, sandy-blond hair feathering the forehead, and an expression of relaxed confidence. But Richard is not looking at him. Richard is rooted to the floor, eyes front.

"How ya doin'?" Richard hears, and turns tentatively toward the voice, forces his own voice into the carpet-hushed corridor.

"Good . . . and you?" A monotone.

Braun opens the door to the trash room, holds up the pizza box and smiles. "With this diet, how can I miss?" Richard glances at the evidence. When Braun goes inside the trash room, the door closes behind him, and in a moment Richard hears the creak of the metal trash flap and the whoosh of air rushing up the chute. Braun emerges, unburdened. He seems to be in a hurry.

"I live on that stuff, unfortunately," he says in motion. "Med school doesn't leave much time for cooking."

What about your girlfriend? Richard thinks. Doesn't she cook? *Didn't* she cook?

The elevator chimes.

"Yeah," is all that Richard says, and he steps on. As the elevator door closes, he hears Braun's apartment door slam shut.

So that's him, Richard thinks. Impressive-looking guy. Has a relaxed way about him. Implausible to most people that this fellow is a killer, but he just might be. He just might be.

Back on the twenty-second floor, Richard hears silverware tapping plates, microwaves beeping, snatches of conversation. This time he has the right apartment, and his key opens the door at once. He sits on his garage-sale couch and hunches over the scarred coffee table to scan the Sunday *Inquirer*'s weekly TV booklet, already opened to the evening's schedule. He runs down the listings in the seven to nine p.m. slot, looking for a possible culprit, a television show, or better yet, a movie that he can readily identify. That could be the answer, his fears might be allayed. Or heightened. Yes, TV sounds might have been it, all of it. Or they might have masked or complemented the live deed in real time. A random synchronicity? He knows that murderers can be much more than impulsive; they can be devious, crafty, symbolic. He knows because he has read about them, and he knows because he remembers.

Or simply this: what he heard was all live, all in the flesh.

Or all in his mind.

There it is, right in front of him. A listing that thrills him, one that he has either desired or dreaded, he's not sure.

He hurries into the box-like kitchen and retrieves the Yellow Pages from the lower cupboard next to the refrigerator. He doesn't know when Locust Video closes; a glance at the microwave's digital tells him it's 9:37, give or take four minutes (he didn't reset it exactly on time after a power outage during his first week here). He rifles through the pages, gets the number, punches it in, waits out three rings and hears, "Locust Video is open from ten a.m. to nine-thirty p.m., Monday through Saturday; noon to six p.m. on Sunday. Please visit us for the widest selection of videos in Philadelphia . . ."

3

Frank Grant has worked at the 42s for five years, his first real job after some part-time department store stints. He's top man on the front desk now. He likes being the hub of the operation, the one who deflects emergencies, fetches the fire company, the police, the electric company, the elevator repairman. He sees himself as the man in the spotlight, doling out FedEx packages, greeting and dispatching tenants as their lives crisscross.

Somehow, Frank grew up an intact human being. Life in the projects was a daily battle for survival. The pushers at Wendell Homes on Fairmount Avenue were as prevalent as litter; a break-in was a more regular occurrence than breakfast. It was just Frank and his mother in their little patch of hell, and he made it through thanks to her strength and his, well, his optimism. His mother used to tell him he had a "happy streak." He also had, at a young age, the ability to think for himself. He avoided the traps that ensnared most of the youth at Wendell.

Now he's a young man with aspirations. Two nights a week he takes courses at community college, and he thinks that, someday, maybe he'll go into advertising or public relations. He likes people, figures he can relate to all types, and the 42s is a perfect forum. He's ingratiating to the elderly, hip to the younger crowd. He's fast and efficient and sometimes a bit too impressed by his own energy. He could use a personal and career advisor—a mentor, in loftier circles—though he doesn't realize it. He does have confidence in himself, self-reliance, and that goes a long way. He figures he's clever and quick on his feet, and doesn't hesitate to spar with people. Thinks he has the right touch for that.

When Davis Braun strides through the lobby around eleven o'clock, showered and refreshed and dressed for either a round at the hospital or a late-night gambit, Frank greets him with, "Hey, Doctor Braun, checked out any corpses lately?"

Braun smiles. "Every day at Metro, Frank."

"That's right, I forgot. Didn't mean to cut so close to the, uh, bone."

Braun shuts one eye in mock response to the groaner.

"Listen, sorry for disturbing you earlier," Frank says.

"No sweat. What was it all about, anyway?"

"One of our nuttier inmates thought he heard somethin'."

"Like what?"

"Nothin' serious. Just thought someone mighta been strangled at your place." Frank in his entertainer mode, full steam.

Braun wrinkles his nose, squinting. "Strangled?"

"Yeah, tell me about it." Frank sniggers. "This cat was really shook up. Maybe somethin' you were watchin' on TV, you know, around the time that I called, a little bit before?"

Braun leans an arm on the counter, takes Frank into his confidence. "I didn't want to go into details when you called, understand, but I was kind of busy at the time." He pushes off the counter with a bemused expression. "That's our culprit: I'm gonna have to tell her to keep it down, know what I mean?"

Frank slaps the counter, laughs out loud. "I heard that . . . I dig that kinda stranglehold."

Braun is on his way out, muscular, broad-shouldered, the cut of an athlete. Smooth operator, Frank thinks. That Eleanor girl who lives with him, nice looking lady, no doubt about it. Not a bad move being a doctor, but not Frank's style. Too messy, takes too long to get there, too expensive. He'll do all right, he's got personality, PR man, that's his profile. He looks around the mirrored gleaming lobby, at the vaulted ceiling, the buff-colored couches, the synthetic tree waxy and shining in the corner, the corridor leading to the mailroom and beyond. His territory, he runs the shop. He likes that. But it's just a stepping stone, man. He's goin' somewhere, and along with the ambition, he's a decent human being on top of it. Treats people right. One brush with the law back in Juvy Court days, minor stuff, nobody got hurt, ancient history. Lot of those kids from Wendell are in prison now. Or dead. But he's a solid citizen. Frank's proud of himself.

Richard is sitting cross-legged on his bed, the weak dawn light seeping through the miniblinds onto a small pile of paper clips right at his feet on the pale-blue velour blanket. He interlocks one clip with another, forming an ever-expanding chain as if he were working on a kids' crafts project at summer camp, and as he does this, the sounds are flitting across his brain and he sees the closed door of apartment 2307, that maroon door interrupting the flow of the lime-green walls. But the sounds are not random if he wills them not to be. He can replay them in order, or pluck one out of sequence, like a technician editing a movie soundtrack. He runs the reel over and over again, a grab bag of staccato, his own brand of blood evidence of a crime. Sounds as DNA, as fingerprints.

A crime took place there. In that moment. Maybe.

He empties a second box of paper clips. The skinny wire snake reaches a menacing length before he puts it aside. He removes a new pair of brown shoelaces from a paper clasp and ties and unties knots, slips and grannies and half hitches, his fingers fastidious. He puts the laces aside. He inserts his earplugs and lies back, lies there forever, replays the moment, the sounds, over and over. He falls asleep at some point, but when the morning's screeches and rumbles penetrate the plugs, and his eyelids spring open to the slatted sunlight, he knows he can't have slept more than an hour or so. The paper clips and shoelaces are strewn between folds of the blanket. Richard pushes back the covers and rolls out of his foxhole.

He sits at his desk, affixes a stamp to a plain white envelope and prints a name and address on it: Sheila Braun, The 42s building, 15th and Locust streets, Philadelphia, Pennsylvania 19102. He inks a few squiggly black lines with a razor-point pen to suggest a P.O. cancellation. The postwoman comes every day at three. Nice lady.

Riding the subway, Walkman-protected, Richard squeezes the metal pole as he stands in a crowd and the train rockets through the tube. Stale air flies in and assaults him when the train stops and the doors belch open. He gets off and makes his way across the platform and through a revolving door of iron interlaced bars, then up the stairs to Olney Avenue and the Preston Tower and the elevator to the fifth floor for another big day—this one to be shortened a bit—at Rosen & Wallingford.

In the cork-walled booth, people raise their hands, but today Richard isn't always sure they're coinciding with the audiometer's high-pitched squeals, because those other sounds, unnerving sounds, the thudding and tearing and rasping, have taken over inside his head. He's arranged his schedule so that his appointments are done for the day by two p.m., tells the office manager he's leaving early, and walks past the front desk and Kathy with a "goodnight." With no warning, no groundwork, she pipes up with, "Got a hot date?" This stops Richard cold and he puzzles over her face, searches for clues. Ah, just a young girl firing off an unthinking line. Trying to be cute. Keeping tabs at the receptionist's desk, nothing more.

"No," he says, "just a dentist appointment. You know the drill." He can see that his wit is lost on her; she's already looking away and thinking about some other weighty matter. But Richard is pleased with his performance and aware that, for a moment, his mind has been distracted from the parade of grim sounds that have taken hold of him.

The postwoman has unstrapped her soiled Santa Claus sack and lowered it to the floor, and is inserting pieces of mail into the yawning grid of slots, the shiny facade unhinged like an opened trapdoor. The phony Sheila Braun letter in his hand, Richard watches the postwoman go efficiently about her business. She is all nimble fingers and certain movement.

"Excuse me," he says.

She doesn't miss a beat, keeps plucking envelopes and slanting them into their destinations—not rude, just inexorable. "Yes?"

Richard looks down at his letter and silently reads the name and address, convincing just in case she's watching him. Then he says, "I received a letter by mistake for a Sheila Braun. B, R, A, U, N. No apartment number." He likes the name Sheila, has a second cousin somewhere with that name, remembers they had fun at some family get-together when they were little kids, but hasn't seen her since.

The postwoman finishes distributing her handheld pile and turns his way. In her summer uniform of gray short-sleeve shirt and grayer shorts, she is built like an old-fashioned middle guard, maybe a Yale Bulldog from the 1930s, but her eyes are less fierce than her physique. Richard holds the letter out for her, but she ignores it and dives right into her big bag on the floor and yanks out a computer printout, which promptly unravels like a medieval proclamation. "Lemme see . . . I got a Davis Braun. What's your apartment number?"

"2207."

She flips to another section of the printout. "You Richard Keene?"

"Yes."

"All right, we're lookin' good there . . . I got Davis Braun in twenty-three-oh-seven, along with Eleanor Carson."

"Eleanor Carson?" Richard repeats to firm the name in his mind.

"That's right."

"And no Sheila Braun."

"Nope. You get it yesterday?"

"Yes, that's right."

"That explains it; I wasn't on yesterday." She gives him a knowing smile and points at the letter. "I can take that for you. Probably his sister or somebody visitin'."

"That's OK," Richard says. "I know Davis; I'll just give it to him."

"All right, thanks," she says. "I already done that section."

"You bet," says Richard as he walks away, leaves the mailroom, and exits the building by the rear door. He leans against the brick wall next to the door to the Dumpster room behind the delivery dock, unclips a pen from his shirt pocket, writes the name Eleanor Carson on the Sheila Braun letter, then hustles down the Latimer Street alley past a pair of parking garages to the next block, where the video store should have waiting for him the movie he reserved by phone soon after he arrived at work.

The clerk at the counter at Locust Video has a hacksaw haircut and a small silver earring on his nostril. Call it a "nosing," Richard figures. The other clerk is checking inventory on the stacks behind the counter, and singing as he sorts. Singing too loudly for the venue, but a pretty good voice. Musical theater, priming himself for discovery, Richard figures.

"Richard Keene, I called in . . . *Boston Strangler.*"

"You mean to tell me you're the Boston Strangler," the nose-earring clerk says with a Cockney accent that's not quite the real thing; another actor-type. "Hey, Frank Sinatra, this bloke sez ee's the Boston Strangler."

Sinatra stops his crooning long enough to shout, "Call nine-one-one."

Richard plays along reluctantly. "I'm not that dangerous; anyway, with that accent, aren't you thinking Jack the Ripper?"

Nose-earring looks offended. "Accent? That's not me accent, guv'ner." He breaks into a wide smile of yellow teeth and places the videocassette on the counter. "That's all she comes in." A catch-22: actors need whiter teeth, but must land paying jobs to afford the dentist's bleaching. "Not bad, huh?" he now says in some Northeastern extract, not quite Philadelphian.

"Not bad at all," Richard says, grabbing the video.

Richard sits on his couch and rocks nervously as the VCR clicks and whirs. The soundtrack is distorted, and the film comes up dark and streaked, unwatchable. Richard lets it run for two minutes and sees that there is no improvement. Fast-forwards several times; same thing. He stands, stabs the candy tray on the coffee table and, almost spastically, fires a green sourball across the room. It pings the opposite wall and pinballs to the upright piano he never plays and into the kitchen, where it comes to rest in the open strip between the built-in cupboard and the refrigerator, a space far too narrow for human hand or cleaning implement; graveyard of crumbs, bugs and stray sour-balls.

He's on the phone with Sinatra from Locust Video.

"We have another copy, but it's out, due back tomorrow. Sorry about that, man. I can call our other stores."

"Would you do that?"

"Yeah, I'll let you know if anything turns up."

Richard tries the other two center-city video outlets and a few more a subway ride away. No Boston Strangler. Richard's battered Toyota overheats within minutes and has been awaiting a mechanic's look-see for more than a week as it sits in the 42s garage, so he doesn't bother calling more video stores in outlying areas. He'll have to wait a day. Investigation delayed.

Because that's what he intends to mount this time, he believes: an investigation. No ignoring, no turning away. He is thrilled by the notion that destiny has handed him a chance to redeem himself. The doctors and the time away helped restore some of his bearings, but failed to convince him that he has been flaying himself all these years for no good cause. An eight-year-old is in no position to take charge in such matters, he was told again and again. What can an eight-year-old do, except tell his parents? Which he did.

But the words, the explanations, are useless. He still blames himself for not doing more. His guilt is thick as grime.

Which he tries to run off on the treadmill. Today, like every day. The row is empty. Sudden rain slashes the tall windows of the 42s fitness center, distorting the city's lights speckling the premature, gathering darkness. Richard's knee is throbbing, but he pushes himself harder, trying to run through that, too; physical pain, psychic scars, maybe you can outrun them. Futile, of course, but you keep at it. He notices a new runner stepping up, two treadmills down: the woman with the Olympic stride and the red hair that falls onto her shoulders when it's not tied up, which it is right now. She fits snugly into a pair of short gym shorts, and the tendons just above her knee are like short connective cables as she begins to stride, and her skin is smooth and just a shade lighter than summer tan. He sees her and forgets all about the throbbing in his knee.

Janet Kroll is not aware of Richard's reaction to her. She's not aware of Richard at all. Nor is she aware of the rain pecking and slithering down the tall rectangular windows, or the gray-swathed buildings beyond. She's not even tuned in to the rhythms and pulsing drive of her own body, as her arms pump and her Reeboks pound the rubber tread that spills out below her. Her mind is elsewhere, her thoughts riveted on a young woman who she misses very much, on why she is here in this building and what she wants to see happen, on how she plans to make it happen. On what could go wrong on this dangerous path she has chosen.

After the workout, absent the stimuli of adrenaline and endorphins and Janet Kroll, Richard finds that his knee is sore as hell, and he massages it as he sits on his bed, running shoes and socks tossed onto the carpet. He knows he has an appointment with an MRI machine tomorrow, and though Dr. Natrol has promised him one of the new "open" machines, his anxiety threatens to displace his preoccupation with a certain video and what transpired behind the closed door of apartment 2307. It all builds overnight so that when he reports to work in the morning, his insides are in a vise.

At the ENT shop, Rosen & Wallingford, he gives receptionist Kathy a tight-lipped "morning." As he walks past the photocopy room, someone takes a ream of paper off the shelf and thumps it down on the table, giving Richard a little start, the thumping sound not unlike the one he heard at the threshold of Apartment 2307 thirty-six hours before. Thumps and thuds and groans and cries are very much on his mind, *in* his mind, and he reminds himself that, at the moment of the thump at 2307, the moment he heard it, he didn't *feel* it, didn't feel a shudder in his shoetops, but then, the 42s is a well-constructed building, and the muted sounds may not have come from the very next room but from two rooms away, and the victim may not have been in free fall, may have been half-caught by her murderer as she landed, only part of her anatomy grounded, a thump heard but not felt, a small woman perhaps, not one to shake the walls.

Richard presses two fingers hard against his forehead right above the bridge of his nose to try to quell a headache. A hand at his shoulder startles him. He heard no one approaching, so absorbed was he.

"You all right?"

It is Wendy, the office manager, short blond hair, square frame, creases at the corners of her eyes, her frequent smiles lacking warmth. Checking up, that's all; part of the job description. Richard takes a breath and settles himself down.

"I'm fine."

"You don't look it."

"Just a little headache; I'll be all right." With that, Richard is moving quickly out of Wendy's range. She watches him and shakes her head; he's a strange one, she thinks. Have to be weird to work those little dials all day long.

On his lunch hour, Richard leaves Preston Medical Tower and walks a block to Einstein General, where Radiology's two MRI scanners both have cylinders that are the standard twenty-four inches in diameter.

"Is this it?" he asks the technician, a shambling oaf with corned-beef breath.

"This is it."

"I thought I was to get the big machine."

"This ain't DisneyWorld, babe," says the technician with horsy teeth and a guffaw to match. "This is all we got. Tell you what, though, I got this for you." He hands Richard a pair of foam earplugs. "Just wad it up in your ear there, and you won't hear a thing."

Where did they get this guy? "What would I hear otherwise?" Richard asks.

"Oh, machine makes kind of a knocking noise. Bothers some people."

"It's not that I'm worried about." A double whammy for Richard, who plugs his ears and forces himself to enter the narrow MRI bed, lies on his back as if in a coffin. He looks at his feet and beyond to the tubular nightmare that awaits. Just the anticipation of it is overpowering. His eyes dart about, sweat rushes to his forehead. He tries to close his eyes but can't keep them closed.

This isn't going to work.

He quivers, fights for breath. He doesn't trust anyone to help get him through this, least of all the goofy technician, who is peering down at him like a tourist at an aquarium, asking, "What's the problem?" Richard jerks his torso upward. His face is plum-red and he is gulping air. He has to get himself out of here.

"I can't do this."

"What?"

Richard raises his voice. "I can't go through with this."

"You know, these appointments aren't so easy to come by. Why dontcha at least give it a try?"

Richard rolls out of the contraption to safety. "I'm . . . sorry," he says, slumped and damp.

The technician is both bemused and irritated. "You wanna use the bathroom?"

Richard slinks across the tiled floor and out of the MRI chamber. He'll have to live with a sore knee for a while longer, that's all.

4

Moving smartly about his compact kitchen, Richard doesn't feel much complaint coming from his knee; sure, he can live with the occasional pain. He's lived with a lot more pain than that.

He is tossing a forest of a salad in a large wooden bowl. Strips of tofu and vegetable stir-fry are sizzling in a broad pan above the range's electric coils. Then the doorbell rings and he's surprised, miffed. They're early.

His mother's face fills the spyglass with a funhouse-mirror bulge. When Richard opens the door, she pauses at the threshold and smiles like a TV hostess. "You have company," she says, a lilt in her husky voice. Evelyn is dressed for a night out and, when she enters, a perfumed scent trails her, as does her husband Marty clutching a gift-wrapped box.

"How'd you get up here?" Richard asks his mother.

"We flew . . . the elevator, of course."

"The guy at the desk is supposed to call me," says Richard, always bugged when little things are mishandled.

"Well I guess we looked respectable enough to let through," Evelyn says. "You aren't hiding anyone in the closet, are you?"

When she purses her lips for a kiss, Richard plants a light one on her cheek, then turns to his father.

"Dad."

"Richie."

Marty holds out the box, which is large enough that it requires two hands. "For the birthday boy and his new fancy apartment," says Evelyn, who strides across the living room to the sliding-glass doors that look out onto the city. "Some view from up here . . . very striking, very romantic."

"Potentially," Richard says, propping the gift box against the wall, in no hurry to open it.

Evelyn follows her son into the kitchen. "I know what that means," she says. "Nothing exciting happening, right?"

Richard has pots and dishes to juggle. He wants to put this meal behind him. "Have you been getting out?" his mother asks. He doesn't get out much, has never gotten out much. Of course she knows that.

Evelyn doesn't wait for an answer. "People just don't show up on your doorstep."

"I'm aware of that, Mother." He wields his spatula and the stir-fry spits as it tumbles onto plates. "I've only been here a month."

"There must be lots of nurses and secretaries at the medical center," she says.

"You know women are doctors today, too," he says, setting one plate on the table.

"Doctors want other doctors."

It is an innocent remark—not malicious—but he feels his stomach jump, and then the heat that rises into the throat and, finally, out the top of the head if you're lucky. He could snort steam like some cartoon bull, but he shows no sign of distress, no lid popping. He keeps the boil contained. All he offers is a caustic "thanks" as he places the other two filled plates on the table.

"Well it's true, isn't that right, Marty?"

Marty is taking his turn gazing out the glass doors.

She moves closer to Richard, who is dishing out the salad. "I want your father to get his hearing checked."

"Fine."

"I'm calling Ben to set an appointment for you with Richard," she says to Marty, who finally turns toward her.

"Ben?"

"Doctor Detrick."

"What about him?"

"He has to make a referral."

"My physical's not 'til January."

"Just to get your hearing checked."

"My hearing's fine."

Evelyn rolls her eyes at Richard but he's not paying attention. "Dinner is served," he says.

He pulls a chair out for his mother and nudges it with both hands back toward the table after she has filled it. "What a gentleman," she says. "So tell me, what's this you said the other night on the telephone that you don't like it down here."

"I didn't say I didn't like it," Richard says, sitting down. "It's just a little, uh, crowded, that's all."

"Well, of course, dear, you're in the middle of the city," she says. "That's the whole idea."

"I know that."

"If I lived here, I'd be bankrupt. Every night I'd be at the theater. Or somewhere."

"There's all this construction around," Richard continues, though his audience is not listening. "And they deliver things at all hours—"

"Marty," Evelyn interrupts. "Speaking of center-city, you know we have the Academy Saturday night."

For Marty, the Academy is just another in a series of stops he must make with his wife; he accepts it like cough medicine. At the moment, he is cutting a strip of tofu, wondering what it is, and doesn't even look up at Evelyn, who turns back to Richard and realizes she has been rude, though she can't help it and doesn't really want to. "I'm sorry, dear, you were saying?"

Richard smiles, thin and derisive. "Not much."

He picks at his food, soon stops eating altogether. As Evelyn chatters on, something about her publicity work for some suburban chamber music quartet, Richard braces himself. He wants this to sound matter-of-fact and wants to keep his anxiety in check, but as he prepares to say it, he realizes he can't control such things. His heart is trip-hammering away. He squirts out his words.

To his mother: "Do you ever see Herb Dempsey?"

Her fork slips out of her fingers, and she looks at him with semi-panicked eyes and none of the broader affectation that normally shapes her features; as the emotion heightens, her face contracts further. "God, Richard. Where would I see *him?*"

"I don't know. Anywhere."

Now Evelyn seems annoyed and blood returns to her cheeks. "Well we're not exactly bridge partners. Why do you ask that, all of a sudden?"

Richard pokes the tofu with his fork. "I was thinking about him."

"Why?" She looks at Marty for support, but he is concentrating on his food and either hasn't heard a word or hasn't cared to.

Evelyn firms up. "We're not going through this again." A bid for finality, but the conviction isn't quite there.

Richard looks at her and pauses, forcing her eyes to meet his. "I am," he says.

He explains himself. What he overheard. What he thinks happened. In apartment 2307. They get to hear about it all over again, a brand-new trauma, more than twenty years later.

Marty listens without comment. Evelyn clucks and shakes her head and tells her son that he's out of his mind, that other people's lives are not his responsibility. A familiar response.

"You'll get in trouble, you keep doing this sort of thing," Evelyn warns. "You mark my words."

A very light smile from Richard. "Only if something really happened, though, right?"

"Richard, you're impossible with this, you really are."

"What do you mean?" Marty asks his wife, and her look of exasperation sends him directly back to his knife and fork.

"Anyway," Evelyn says, "what's this got to do with Herb Dempsey?"

Richard looks at her, through her. "Everything."

"He doesn't live here, does he?" She's being sarcastic.

Richard has nothing more to say on the subject for the moment, and they move on to some fatuous conversation about center-city food markets.

"Open your present," Evelyn says, as Richard readies dessert and coffee in the kitchen. "The only kid in the world who could wait to open a present, remember, Marty?"

"Let me give you your dessert and I'll open it," Richard calls in. He knows his father likes heated apple pie with a scoop of vanilla ice cream. Evelyn gets the pie, no scoop. Black coffee for both.

He brings in the goodies, sets them on the table, and attends to his present, tearing off the wrapping paper and crumpling it beyond salvaging so that his mother is not tempted to reuse it. "Read the card first," Evelyn says. Richard plucks a large greeting card out of a red envelope. There's a sketch of a dilapidated house on the front of the card; on the inside, the printed words "the fixins' are great here" and below them in Evelyn's script, "Hope your new life is a whirlwind." Evelyn's eyes are alive with expectation; Richard doesn't know how to react. He knows that whatever is inside the box will not thrill him, and that he will be incapable of pretending that it does. He opens the box and the first thing he sees is an assembly instruction sheet. Slats of wood and metal hinges lurk underneath.

"It's a Lazy Susan," Evelyn says. "Get it? A whirl?" She twirls her wrist, hand and forefinger. "These things are fantastic. Can you put it underneath the counter somewhere?"

"I don't think so."

"Sure you can. Well, if not, then it can go on top."

"Thanks," Richard says. "It's a nice gift." He kisses her cheek, nods to his father. "Thanks, Dad."

Evelyn shakes her head. "Don't get so excited," she says to Richard.

"Leave the boy alone, Evelyn," says Marty, moving to the couch. "What do you expect him to do, jump up and down? He appreciates it."

After dessert and coffee in the living room, their expressions confirm that they've run out of things to talk about. Before long, they're all in the elevator, then stepping across the polished lobby tile, then outside engulfed by the mild September night and the swarm of the city. Richard walks his parents to the adjacent parking garage on Locust.

"What level are we on, Marty?" Evelyn asks.

"Three, I think."

She looks at Richard. "He thinks. Last time in Atlantic City, we got lost at Harrah's."

"Only for a little while," Marty says. "That lot is very confusing."

"They all are when you don't pay attention," Evelyn says and kisses her son on the cheek. "Have some fun, honey bun."

Richard says his goodnights, sees them to the garage elevator. "Want me to go up with you?"

"No, we're fine from here, Son," Marty says.

They disappear as the blackened metal door slides closed. Richard is especially leery of garage elevators. Rickety and unreliable, good chance of spending the night in them if there's a breakdown.

Now that the evening's mission has been completed and they're gone, he feels more regret than relief. Regret that he wasn't nicer, over things he should have said or not said. He feels badly about that.

He moves on to the video store in the next block. Sinatra and Nose-Earring are gone; the girl at the counter has red-purple hair and skin pallor that suggests she's spent all of her twenty years in an attic. She does, however, have Richard's videocassette.

Back inside the 42s, Richard reads the "commercial uses" warning label on the video as he waits for the elevator. He is aware of a woman approaching and stopping near him, an elegant scent that takes hold of him, the woman shapely in her tailored business suit. Janet Kroll, the treadmill queen. It is just the two of them. The elevator arrives and Richard gestures for her to get on first. The gentlemanly thing to do.

Janet presses the button for fifteen. Richard reaches over and presses his twenty-two. As the elevator moves upward, Richard rechecks his selection on the side panel. He looks at Janet with a self-effacing grin.

"Got to make sure. The other day, I got off on the wrong floor coming down from the gym."

Good job, he thinks. Making civilized, relaxed conversation. Still, all he gets for his efforts is a small smile. But that's better than a wrinkled brow and a flash of irritation. A girl with her looks gets plenty of uninvited attention, so her defenses must be well fortified.

"Guess I was half asleep trying to keep up with you," he says. "Coming down from the gym, I mean."

Janet looks at him more closely. "Right, you're the runner."

"No, *you're* the runner."

This fetches a more genuine smile, which vanishes when the

elevator reaches her floor, chimes, stops, and opens.

"Have a nice evening," Richard says to her retreating form.

"You, too," she says over her shoulder.

All right, not too bad, Richard figures. He watches her walk away, as the closing elevator door narrows the frame. Plenty of time to see her at the fitness center. Time to "grow" on her (like mold—his mother's joke). A hint of discernment in her eyes suggests she prefers lean, cardiovascular types to muscleheads. Well, it's worth thinking about it that way. Maybe.

On to other matters. Back in his apartment, Richard has the nervous anticipation of a student about to receive the results of a crucial exam. The answers he seeks are in this video, he's certain, and this copy will work; the chalk-skinned clerk told him they tested it on a VCR right at the store. Richard turns on his TV and inserts the cassette into the VCR, and the film shows up intact. He sits on the edge of the couch, palms on his knees, rocking gently.

He knows the movie from late-night television and remembers the scene in question. Now he needs to assimilate every sound and movement. He fast-forwards and, within a minute, a malignant Tony Curtis is tearing in half what might be an old dress, then he's saying, "Now don't scream—you won't get hurt," then he's tying a naked woman's ankle to a bedpost, unsettled by his own face in the mirror, then he's stabbing a switchblade into the wooden bedpost, then he's tearing more material and tying her other foot. Curtis is disturbing in his concertedness, and the sounds, one after another, jar Richard. Tearing, shuffling, banging, more tearing. The woman gasping, whimpering. *The Boston Strangler*, televised two nights earlier, this very scene, Richard guesses, coinciding with his visit to apartment 2307.

This very scene, he believes, and something more.

Richard rewinds to the start of the scene. On-screen, Tony

Curtis tears the fabric and tells his prey not to scream. A tender ankle tied to a bedpost. The switchblade. Her pleading expression. She gasps, whimpers, moans, finally screams. Richard cringes before the blue-white glow of the screen. When Tony Curtis tries to stifle the woman's scream, she bites his hand. He recoils, then punches her five times in rapid succession; five muffled, smacking thuds and it's over. No more struggle. No more sounds of struggle. He wraps a handkerchief around his bloody hand, retracts his switchblade.

Richard springs from the couch, goes to the VCR, and hits rewind. The scene replays in its entirety, from the first tearing/ripping sounds to the thudding punches and the wrapped hand.

Richard replays it again. Then he rewinds for just two seconds and hits the play button. The woman screams and bites Curtis, and he punches her. Richard hits rewind again; she screams, Curtis punches, five thuds, a handkerchief and the scene's over. Rewind, she screams, he punches. Rewind.

Richard turns off the VCR and the television. He stands there, and he might as well be quaking. Tearing, shuffling, banging, gasping, whimpering, moaning, screaming, thudding. *No rasping.* There was rasping in that apartment; he knows he heard rasping, a different sound, distinct from the others, a palpable distinction. He knows he heard it; it's stored in his auditory memory. And . . . and . . . and he takes a book—a thick hardback biography of Abraham Lincoln he's had since he was five years old—from the shelf above the TV, holds it at eye level with both hands, parallel to the floor, and lets it drop so that it lands flush. When it thumps the carpeted floor, he shivers. It's a different sound, a fuller sound than any movie-doctored punch. He heard it that night, that moment at the closed door of 2307, a thump, a thump of finality, scripted by real life, a falling book, a sack of potatoes, of laundry, a body.

Richard is looking down at the book, motionless. He stands

that way for nearly a minute, sorting out the sounds in his head. What makes you think the thump was a body? he can hear people asking him. It could have been lots of things.

Sure it could have. But the rasping was a human sound. He is sure of that. He heard it, knew what it was, knows still.

Yes, a scene from a movie and something more. A coincident murder, live. Fortuitous or expertly timed. If timed, symbolic or strategic. Or both.

His mind races.

Less than an hour later, he is on the telephone with his mother, stirring up the devil-ghost. It's not the same man, of course; a span of more than twenty years, two different perpetrators. Just keeping tabs on the original.

"You never forget your next-door neighbor," he says.

"Don't start," Evelyn says.

"I never stopped."

"Richard, why do you have to ruin things? Why do you keep torturing yourself?"

"Myself?"

"What's that supposed to mean? Oh, is that it, you're torturing me? Well, congratulations, that's a fine thing to do. I suppose you are; you're exhausting me, that's for sure. Tell me, what were we supposed to do, make a citizen's arrest? Don't you understand? For the last time, for godsake, nothing was ever proved, and . . . and we wanted to keep you out of it."

"And you did."

"Richard, have you been taking your medication?"

"I'm no longer on medication, Mother. The doctors suspended it."

"Are you sure about that?"

"Of course I'm sure."

". . . Richard, it's pointless to keep bringing this up. Isn't that what they told you?"

"You know, when you think about it—"

"Just don't think about it."

"—I guess I should thank you . . . It could've been me, too. He did warn me, in a way."

"Enough, Richard. We did the only thing we could do."

"Nothing."

"Well, what else was there to do?"

"I don't know . . . something."

"You'll put yourself back in the hospital yet, you really will."

"I'm sorry you feel that way."

"So am I, Richard, I really am. You have to ruin a nice evening."

Through the creases in the microblinds Richard sees office-building lights dotting the blackness. Later he will sleep fitfully. The sounds will fill his unconsciousness and unnerve him, prodding him awake, pushing sweat from his pores, clenching his breath.

5

The body. How was it disposed of?

Not so easy from the twenty-third floor.

In sections?

He can't go to the police; they'd laugh him away, he knew that from the start. You heard what? Sure, pal.

Frank. It's Friday morning and Frank might be in an expansive mood. Maybe some more information can be coaxed out of him.

Richard calls in sick. He's got sick days coming, hasn't taken a single one or any vacation days in the year and a half he's been at Rosen & Wallingford. He stays healthy, at least by conventional measures. His announcement surprises Kathy. She'll have to reschedule most of his appointments, and have the doctors do the critical ones. They won't be happy about that.

At the 42s front desk, Frank is organizing several UPS packets of varying sizes, as tenants drift past.

"Morning," says Richard.

Frank looks up and forces a smile. Since Richard is not one to say hello, Frank is suspicious.

"Mister Keene . . . Seen any Boston Stranglers lately?"

A little snake wraps around Richard's stomach and the small of his back. He tries to loosen its grip, parts his lips to say something, but all that comes out is air.

Frank cocks his head at him. "So?"

Richard swallows. "Nothing." Bad idea, trying to enlist Frank's help. He tries to walk away but his body won't move. "Have you seen Eleanor Carson the past couple of days?" he asks, the words remote and fluttering upward toward the high ceiling. Now he steadies his voice. "Eleanor Carson, twenty-three-oh-seven."

Frank looks up from his UPS pile. "Now listen to me, my man. We been through this. I don't want you botherin' those people."

"Have you seen her?"

"Can't you just be cool, man?"

"You haven't, right?"

"You gonna run yourself right outa here, you know that?"

Richard is hardly the bold type, but there is something persistent and sincere in his expression that won't quit. Frank sees it, damn, he sees it.

"You're too much, man," Frank says.

"Where does she work?" asks Richard.

"You know, you need to increase your medication or some-thin'."

"I don't take any medication."

"I'm just sayin' . . ." But now Richard senses a willingness in Frank, a curiosity despite himself. "Just tell me where she works," Richard says, not pleading. "If she's there, that's it; you won't hear another word from me."

Frank thinks about it; it's not a bad deal at that. He's beginning to feel just a touch of respect for this guy's determination. Can't hurt to check, just doing his job, no invasion of privacy. He glares at Richard but sits at the computer terminal and pulls up the file on Eleanor Carson, who shares apartment 2307 with Davis Braun. Her employment information is right there on the screen. Frank smiles to himself, marveling at his efficiency and that of the modern world. He keeps an eye on the screen, reaches for the telephone and presses the ten digits.

"Eleanor Carson, please . . . This is the front desk at the 42s on Locust Street, her apartment building."

Richard looks away, looks down at the tile and scans the scuff marks. The murderous noises have stopped reverberating within his skull. For the moment.

"Yes, Eleanor Carson, please . . . Oh, is that right?" A big, friendly smile forms on Frank's face. "When did she leave? . . . Uh-huh. When will she be back? . . . I see, well, thank you very much . . . No, that's OK, nothing urgent. Bye now."

Frank hangs up and gives Richard the straight story. "She's on vacation, my man. Satisfied?"

Richard is not. "Since when?"

"Tuesday."

Richard's skeptical expression pisses Frank off a bit. "Go there yourself if you don't believe me. Perris and Blumenthal, 21st Street."

Richard believes Frank, but is certain that the employer's information does not tell all. More than anything, he trusts the sounds in his head, returning now, swirling and stabbing.

"Perris and Blumenthal?"

"That's what I said."

"What's that, a law firm?"

"You got that right. She's a paralegal. Now hit the road, my man. Go bother them."

Richard is back in his apartment and on the phone with the firm of Perris and Blumenthal. Eleanor Carson is on vacation, he is told. Her schedule indicates that she'll be back on Monday. The secretary is polite. "I'll reach her then," Richard says. "No hurry."

But there is a hurry. Trails grow cold.

Moments later, he is walking on 15th Street near Spruce,

then past a cavernous excavation dwarfed by a towering crane. This is where the new music center will be built, Richard understands, the new home of the acclaimed Philadelphia Orchestra, whose lush strings have warmed the elegant but antiquated Academy of Music just around the corner for the past century. Richard loves the magisterial sound of classical symphonies, but he prefers to listen to recordings on his Walkman or compact disc player whose volume he can adjust, just as he now turns the volume up a notch inside the Walkman pressed against his ears. A Rachmaninoff concerto. Stirring.

He reverses course and wanders north on 15th Street several blocks to City Hall, the ornate gothic throwback with the soaring tower topped by the great statue of William Penn. Tunneled outdoor pathways spill people into the courtyard, the precise geographic center of Penn's vintage city. Richard disappears through a side door and follows the yellow arrows taped to the floor; they lead him to the elevator that will take him to his destination. He needs time and space to think, and this is an exercise that affords both, a refuge he has visited before. The sign on the wall instructs him to follow the yellow arrows on the floor to reach the "City Hall Tower elevator." He'll take that elevator to the top of the tower, a ride he's taken several times, so he's familiar with the confines of this particular elevator. He'll climb to a place where he can breathe, like a caught fish thrown back in the water. Where he's freed from the shackles that stake him to the ground and the waves of sound that envelop him, all the oppressive blare and clang and caterwaul of the street-level depths.

Funny, heights don't bother him at all; in fact, quite the opposite, they're exhilarating, a release from the tight suffocating spaces that frame so much of his life.

The sun is bouncing off of Cindy Dempsey's cheeks as she sits on the edge of the schoolyard sandbox on the brightest morning possible in a world that keeps flowing back, like a mountain stream, into memory and consciousness. Richard is near her, sitting on the green wooden ledge, and as they speak to each other in low tones, kept private from the other kids chattering and moving about, they shovel sand with their hands and let it run back into the pile. Beyond them is the broad expanse of schoolyard, its sloping pebbled asphalt stretching toward the L-shaped, yellow-brick school building and the surrounding chain-link fencing. A bounded universe.

A few paces to one side of the sandbox, boys and girls on metal swings arc toward the sky, the boys more reckless in their flight. To the other side, monkey bars rise from a patch of dirt like tangled scaffolding or the skeleton of a kids' clubhouse. The older boys assault the apparatus with muscular grips and thrusts, moving smartly from level to level. The younger ones are more tentative in their movements, assuring themselves of stability before climbing or descending. One of the older ones, a kid who lives on Richard's block, hollers in the direction of the sandbox, "Hey Keene, you scared to come up here?" Cindy glares up at the boy, then looks at Richard, who is sifting sand. "Come on, Keene," yells the boy on the monkey bars. "The sandbox is for babies."

"He should talk," Cindy says, under her breath. "The biggest baby of all."

Richard smiles at her, rises in deliberate fashion, and walks to the base of the monkey bars. There are four kids aloft, the one boy at the top and smirking. "Whoa, look out, here he comes." Whereupon Richard Keene—the strange boy on the block, the boy with supernatural hearing, the freaky kid who makes oddball expressions—scales the monkey bars in rapid fluid progression, a perfect over-and-under maneuvering, an expert alternating of hand grips synchronized with upward knee and the purchase of feet, and within seconds, he is at the top, forcing the other to share that domain. The bigger boy is none too pleased. "Shit, that's not bad," he says, but he's irked that his goony neighbor has shown him up a bit and takes a swipe at Richard's ankles, trying to upend him, but in the process he loses his balance, and is falling, his head bouncing off one of the bars, and only a desperate convulsive hug saves him, his arms wrapping cold blackened steel. Richard treads across the top, as surefooted as a high-wire walker. "You OK?" he asks, looking down at his clinging detractor. Rattled and embarrassed, the kid steps down all the way and stalks out of the area into the dizzy scampering of the schoolyard, a hundred little games, a thousand moving parts. Richard straddles the highest quadrant on the monkey bars and surveys the scene. His limbs feel as light as paper, dragonfly wings. He looks down at Cindy and her expression tells him that he need not hurry back down, that he has triumphed and she wants to watch him at that vantage point for awhile.

The windowed elevator rises through City Hall tower's gizzard so that Richard sees the spooky infrastructure crisscrossing in the shadows. It is a nonfunctional tower—the municipal offices housed in the broad blocky wing below—save for the large yellow clock facings high up at each exposure, beacons for the grounded populace.

When the elevator reaches the top, more than five hundred feet above the cluttered courtyard, the door opens and Richard steps onto a circular walkway just below the base of the looming statue of city founder Penn, a towering bronze likeness that seems a giant blackbird commanding its roost. One huge hand is outstretched in a vanished gesture of civility; join us, the massive figure suggests. Brotherly Love.

Wind whips through open window space, as Richard looks miles to the south and sees two planes inching across opposite trajectories. He feels great up here, the wind racing through his sinuses, the view untrammeled. Like he could fly.

Soon enough, though, the insidious sounds seep back. Death

sounds. Even here, he cannot escape them.

He needs a plan, and that plan must include other people. He can't do this alone. Surely there are others who will join him, who have a connection to this matter, a stake in it, information, insight.

He walks around the observatory once more, tilts his chin to the max to look up at William Penn. The founder is mute, invariant. But if he could speak, Richard is convinced, he'd speak about patterns, about the importance of people connecting, of community. This is, after all, his city, his commonwealth, his creation; the great municipal grid that fans out below is his very concept, sprung from his drawing board. Yes, if Penn could speak, he'd tell him to reach out to people. Maybe he'll find someone special.

A half hour dissolves in the wind and Richard leaves this perch, takes the elevator down, and walks out of City Hall past Market to Chestnut and Walnut and then Locust. The day has slipped away from him and the twilight is coming on with a sky enlivened by floating blue-black clouds. The 42s seems to sway beneath them, as Richard gazes skyward, then lowers his head and walks through the sliding glass door.

He has a plan.

In his apartment he retrieves a clipboard and a thin cardboard shirt box from an undisturbed corner of a shelf in the bedroom closet. He fastens a sheet of copy paper to the clipboard, and wraps the white box in plain brown wrapping paper, seals it with mailing tape, writes a name and address on it with a Magic Marker, the pungent smell of the thick ink leaping up his nose.

The elevator takes him up one floor, and once off it, he doesn't go left to 2307, but angles to his right to the first apartment across the hall: 2305. This may seem a bit on the silly side, it may prove utterly fruitless, he concedes, but he wants a look at the next-door neighbor. A "delivery" can bring a face-to-face.

He presses the doorbell and waits, his heart is thumping. He keeps waiting. He considers another ring, but then from inside, a woman's voice, small and sweet: "Yes?"

"Uh . . . delivery." He hasn't said it with much authority. He imagines she envisions a nobody, some skinny guy with an oversize Adam's apple. A delivery boy.

A few seconds pass; she must be eyeing him through the peephole. Finally, the door opens a crack, restrained by the chain latch. Indeed, a small, sweet-looking, young woman peers at him through the opening. He smiles at her.

"How come they didn't buzz me at the desk?" she asks. "That's what they always do."

Well, they didn't buzz when his parents came last night, Richard reminds himself. "I don't know," he says, wondering about what he has initiated, about how this is going to play out. "He just sent me up. Are you Eleanor Carson?"

"One door over," she says, keeping the door latched.

Richard looks at the paper on his clipboard, puzzled. "Really? I have twenty-three-oh-five. That's what this is, right?"

"Yes."

"But you're not Eleanor Carson."

"Sorry, Ellie's next door."

Richard looks at the clipboard again, at the box itself, then back at the young woman, mid-twenties, he guesses, with short brown styled hair and, he can tell through the narrow opening, a slim figure in her jeans and sleeveless cotton T-shirt. "I'm the one who's sorry," he says. "For bothering you, that is."

She looks at the box, can't quite make out the writing on it. "Since when are you guys coming to the door?"

"What do you mean?"

"We always pick up at the desk."

"Don't know. Maybe because this one needs a signature."

"We always sign at the desk. Where are you from?"

"From . . . ?"

"What delivery service?"

"Oh, uh, Airborne Express."

"Where's your uniform?"

His planned answer is that it's being dry-cleaned, but now that strikes him as unbelievable, and as he ponders this, the young woman steps back with a sudden "I'm calling Frank" and shuts the door.

Richard almost presses his lips to the door as he speaks rapidly in low, urgent tones: "Look, I'm not with Airborne, but I'm not a stalker or anything. My name is Richard Keene and I live here in apartment 2207, just one floor below, and I guess . . ." He slows down. "I'd just like to talk to you . . . It's important, at least to me." He has heard his voice echoing off the walls, and cringes at its pleading tone.

A moment, and the door opens, still latched.

"What's the name of this building?" she asks.

"Huh?"

She waits. "They call it the 42s," he says.

"What's the street address?"

"1526 Locust."

"What's the name of the guy at the front desk?"

"Frank."

"I already gave you that, I'm afraid. What's the backup's name?"

"Mike."

She sizes him up, can't stop a little smile from breaking through. "You're a little weird, aren't you?"

"Yes."

"You'll have to tell me what's in the box." She points at it.

Richard looks at the box like it's something that has just

materialized in his hands. He looks up at her. "Nothing."

She removes the latch, opens the door a bit farther, and laughs. "Very inventive, Richard Keene. That's the best pickup routine I've seen in a long while. But is it intended for me or Eleanor?"

"Eleanor—I mean—"

"Can't help you; she's already got a boyfriend."

"Davis Braun?"

"You know him?"

"Sort of."

"You know that's pretty tough competition, then."

"It's not that," Richard says. "I think she's in trouble."

"Trouble?"

"That's right."

Her eyes open just a bit wider. "Really?"

"Yes . . . really."

"What sort of trouble?"

Richard says it earnestly. "The worst kind."

6

He always heard things that no one else could. Hot water straining the pipes before the awful wail in the walls. Trucks shifting gears on a highway miles away. Unseen animals rustling in the far-off brush, tiny throat gurgles preceding a cough. When he anticipated things and told people, it made him seem clairvoyant.

The sensory gift left him continually distracted, and this hurt his performance at school, where teachers labeled him a daydreamer and his grades suffered. Kids in the neighborhood thought him strange, his odd expressions and the way he tuned out in the middle of a conversation; from an early age, he was excluded from their street games. He grew up a loner.

Except for the little girl next door. Cindy Dempsey was a year younger, but with an intelligence and a sensitivity far beyond her age. She and Richard seemed to have an almost telepathic way of communicating. When he'd hear something in the distance and cock his head like a cat getting a neck scratching, she'd try to guess what it was and often did. He loved her for that; she was his refuge in an oppressive world. His mother treated him like secondhand furniture; his father was kindly but detached. But Cindy was crazy about him. They'd play Chinese checkers on the patio for hours, fingertipping the marbles into place as they fastened their eyes on one another, Cindy breaking the spell with a shake of her head, or Richard with some observation that would make her laugh, a laugh like a cascade of coins.

"You're a strange boy, Richard Keene," she'd say to him like a sophisticated young woman, and it was the very strangeness that she found endearing. She felt an urge to be at his side. She would help this strange boy whose eyes shrank in fear or shone with excitement, depending on the stimulus that had taken hold.

The kitchen is on the right in apartment 2305, the bedroom area to the left. Like a matching bookend to the "07" apartments. The young woman in the bluejeans offers Richard something to drink, but he isn't interested. He just wants to talk to someone about things that are obsessing him, and she could be that someone, a grown-up version, maybe, of Cindy Dempsey.

"Lori Calder."

She is extending her hand toward a puzzled Richard, who takes it and releases it. Puzzled because she seems so polite. And like she cares.

"How do you do," he replies stiffly. ". . . Uh, Richard Keene."

"I know."

Richard looks blankly at her, then shrugs and smiles self-consciously, as he realizes he has already given her his name.

"Let me ask you, Richard Keene, why didn't you just knock on my door and tell me what it is you want to tell me without the charade?"

"I don't know. Maybe I had to see you first, you know, before I made up my mind."

"What makes you think Ellie's in trouble?" she asks.

Richard gathers himself. "Do you know her well?"

"Not that well, but we're friendly."

"When was the last time you saw her?"

"I don't know. Few days, I guess."

"Can you remember exactly?"

Lori thinks about it. "Tuesday . . . Tuesday afternoon . . . She said she was taking a little vacation or something. We bumped into each other at the elevator. So what's up, what is it?"

Richard thinks this over. She never made it to that vacation. "What time of day did you see her?"

"Oh, uh, five-thirty, six o'clock. Yeah, I remember, I was back from work, waiting to get on the elevator. She got off."

"Did she say where she was going? For her vacation?"

"No, she was in a big hurry."

"Davis Braun wasn't with her?"

"No. And he's still around, he's fine, I saw him yesterday. Will you tell me what this is all about?"

Richard senses that she's getting a little annoyed at him, but he wants to exploit that tension further, in the interest of serving both his information gathering and what he hopes may be some sexual chemistry between the two of them. Extraordinary circumstances triggering a charged relationship. It's a distraction, he realizes, but he can't deny his attraction. "Would she take a vacation by herself?" he asks.

"Well I can't speak for Ellie, but it's been known to happen," Lori says, idly stroking a slender forearm. "Maybe they needed a break from each other."

"Maybe."

"Or she had something special to do, like a working vacation. Why don't you ask Davis directly?"

Richard doesn't like her familiar use of Braun's first name, a comfort level there. But so what? She's the next-door neighbor; she knows them both, is on friendly terms with both. "You know him well?"

"A little better than her; I see him around more."

Richard doesn't like that, he can't deny it. Funny, he just met this girl, but already he feels a need for her and, at the same time, a desire to protect her. She's just the type he wants. Sweet and slight, but with a certain brightness about her, a sharpness of features and speech. The conspiratorial nature of his intent is a kind of aphrodisiac. He wonders if there is a similar effect on her. Doubts it.

"Look," she says, "you're probably making a big production out of something that's nothing. What's your connection to El-lie?"

He searches for the right way to phrase it, to keep her interested in him, keep her from thinking him a nut. "Random," is all that he says.

"What do you mean?"

"Well, not exactly. I was supposed to contact her about something, uh, work-related"—he is fumbling—"and we never—"

"Oh I get it," Lori interrupts with a look that says she's found him out. "Work-related, huh?"

"Yes."

"What do you do, anyway?" she asks.

The question reaches him a beat late, as if on a delayed broadcast transmission. There are so many other contending sounds and thoughts inside his skull. "Sorry . . . I'm a medical technician." Sorry about that, too.

"And not a private detective?"

He takes her smile as a message: maybe they are getting along, on the same wavelength. Personally. Definite progress.

"No, not a private detective."

"You're doing a pretty good impersonation."

"I'm just trying—"

"Are you gonna tell me what's going on, or keep me in suspense all night? You really think something's happened to her?"

"I do."

"And you're suspicious of Davis, aren't you?"

"I am."

"Looks like two can play this game—I'm pretty good, huh? . . . Why? What makes you think something's happened?"

He must explain himself, or leave her alone and . . . leave her.

"I can't stop it," he says.

"Can't stop what?"

He looks at the ceiling, back at her. He is very close to choking up, forcing out a tear, and he doesn't know how much is genuine and how much is self-induced. For effect. For her benefit.

"Stop what?" she repeats.

"What I hear," he says.

The townhouses on Spruce Street seem to sag a bit, their redstone steps and walls and doorways defenseless against the hard new light, like a rouged woman of a certain age trying to dial back the years with a splash of color. It is Saturday morning, and Richard, as is his custom, is alone on the sidewalk. The 42s looms a block behind him, and in motion, he studies it as it towers over the flat roofs of the townhouses. On the corner of 16th Street, a red-brick telephone company building is sealed tight as a bank vault, and in the next block, Coggins Elementary School is an old square pile fronted by a dimpled asphalt yard enclosed by spear-like, wrought-iron fencing above a concrete retaining wall. Two thick, gray-barked, freckled oak trees rise from dirt flats in the asphalt and spread generous branches toward swings and monkey bars in one corner of the schoolyard.

He has left the Walkman in the apartment and is facing the world with naked ear. He hears the creaking of swings long before the little girl comes into view. Then he stops to watch her. She's arching skyward, then dropping to earth so that her small sneakers brush the ruts in the dirt, then she heightens the backswing by leaning forward, gripping the hanging chains, a human pendulum in full abandon. Richard is watching her but he sees another little girl on swings, the creaking with each reversal, this other little girl's wanton flight, her little body precarious in the seat, dauntless, a clinging confidence, no screaming like other girls but a look of relaxation, incongruous for one so young and in such a vertiginous state. Cindy, Cindy, swinging up into the clouds, floating there and disappearing, vaporized and eternal. Cindy, taken up by the sky.

There can never be a goodbye, a letting go. Never can be one.

He told Lori the full story yesterday—not about Cindy, nothing about Cindy, but about what he had heard three days earlier, what he hears still, his suspicions. No, more than suspicions, convictions now. The proof is in his head, auditory DNA. Exhibit number one is the movie tape, and there are more to come. He is on the case and he will not get off it, because the sounds will not let him. The sounds have a life of their own. They are the bitter pills of his past, and the parasites of his future. Sounds with a permanent shelf life.

Lori wasn't quick to embrace his theory. She didn't accept it at all, as a matter of fact, but she'll come around, she'll help him, he senses. She'll be the inside track. Next-door neighbor. He's the outside man, the orchestrator, the prosecutor. Second chances rarely come so recognizable. This time, he'll have help.

His plan is beginning to take shape. The world is your prison only if you allow it to be. Passivity does nothing for the soul. The Stranger had no soul, that was his problem. Action, as a direction, is critical; it is the only path to freedom, it is the way to celebrate yourself, as Whitman urged. Deep inside, Richard feels he understands that and must not squander the insight.

The weekend is two gray days drifting toward dark blank nights. Richard walks on Locust Street to 18th Street and across to Rittenhouse Square, where the leaves have not yet begun to fall and the pigeons chase peanut shells as if they were gold nuggets. It is a patch of tranquility in the urban landscape, a welcome interruption to the ceaseless surge of intersecting cars and footwalkers. The movement here is unstructured, carefree; plump pigeons, young mothers wheeling baby carriages, strollers taking in the scenery, bodies lolling on blankets and beach towels. Cisterns perch on pedestals, balustrades rim a central plaza. Richard eyes the square's adornments, its statuary. He greets his sculpted friends: the graceful young woman clutching a duck to her side, the fierce lion crushing an open-mouthed serpent, the giant frog ready to spring, the two Grecian youths hoisting a sundial toward the heavens. A nineteenth-century guardhouse keeps watch at the confluence of two diagonal pathways that run from one corner of the square to the other.

Richard works his way past benches and across lawns onto the elevated plaza, where college students are trying to digest philosophy and psychology texts. Just outside the square bounded by ramparts of stone, a bus belches black fumes that carpet Walnut Street before dispersing, the sooty smell overpowering the stale scent of marijuana sneaking onto the periphery. On the patios of tony restaurants facing the square from across 18th, patrons eat gourmet omelettes and chatter with intensity. From afar, Richard watches solicitous waiters and hears them recite the day's specials, hears them as clearly as do the customers seated right at the table. He'd like to order a big breakfast, a pile of eggs and French toast with syrup, but he's mindful of his cholesterol count, he's been fine-tuning his ratio of HDL to overall. He doesn't want to stray a point beyond the AMA's recommended levels, knows that thin guys, too, can have such problems.

He circles the square and decides to head back, walks past the Curtis Institute, where something symphonic pours out of a third-floor window, and student-musicians huddle and smoke greedily on the side steps. If only all the sounds of the city could be symphonies. Two blocks down, a jazzy-looking Cadillac parked in front of Marco's Bistro is commanding some attention. People pause to watch on the sidewalk, as a photographer fires off a series of shots of a mini-skirted woman posing by the hood ornament. When the flurry is complete, she scans the small crowd, looks right past Richard to a middle-aged man with graying temples and a golf-course tan, commandeers him with a toss of her raven mane and a flash of teeth. They disappear into the Caddy, her legs settling in nicely as the door closes. The man's in the driver's seat, but they're not doing any traveling. She brandishes brochures and a booklet, some other papers. She's ticking off the attributes of the spiffy new model. Richard can hear her pitch through the rolled-up windows. He feels better; she's just a salesgirl, a decoration, her middle-aged quarry a better prospect for the Caddy.

He continues on his way. Monday morning can't come fast enough. Back in his apartment, he reads the Sunday paper, at least part of it. He skips Review & Opinion, which is full of dull commentary by executive directors of this organization and that, reads every word in Arts & Leisure, which includes reviews of a couple of books he'll reserve at the library. The Sunday Magazine has a piece about an image painted on a brick wall of an old center-city building adjacent to a parking lot where an architectural treasure of a church once stood; the image is that of the vanished church itself, as if it were still standing and reflected in the brick wall that the artist has endowed with the qualities of a mirror.

After reading nearly sixty pages of a dense biography of Theodore Roosevelt—a man of action if there ever was one—Richard gets through the night by settling in front of the television, a History Channel special about the American Revolution, then another look at *The Boston Strangler,* the entire movie this time, the strangulation scene three times for final confirmation. It's all there; he'll return the videocassette tomorrow. He could keep it a week but doesn't need to view it anymore. It's all in his head, and his ears.

Not much sleep and tomorrow does come. Monday morning. Richard calls in, makes his voice sound weak.

"Kathy, I can't make it in today."

"Again?"

He issues a convincing cough. "Sorry, I'm still in bad shape. You know I'm off tomorrow, right? I figure I'll stay in and knock this thing out of my system . . . How's today's schedule?"

"You've got a lot of appointments."

"Can Jeff handle?" What's the difference, a monkey could handle it. He thinks of Jeff, the work-study student from Temple, eager, energetic, great career opportunity. Comes in Mondays.

"I guess he'll have to," Kathy says. "Maybe we'll reschedule some of them. I'll tell the docs . . . Better take some extra chicken soup."

Kathy trying to sound grown up. Well, it's better than sounding like a high school girl.

Richard slips on a pair of chinos over a thin short-sleeve shirt and hits the street. It's a crisper morning, and the rising fumes of the city smell smoky-sharp. Then the subway trains rumble beneath Broad Street and the updraft shoots mustiness through the grates. Richard passes Philadelphia's venerable Union League, a dark-hued eye-popper in the modern city, its twin serpentine staircases and portico brown as battlefield mud. A bronze Union soldier at right-shoulder arms guards the gates. Richard salutes him.

In the next block, the cut-stone squares of the Land Title Building are cool and gray on the shady side of the street. Office workers on a cigarette break huddle like lepers near the main door. The lobby clock marks the hours with gold Roman numerals, which Richard concentrates on as the elevator door closes.

The law firm of Perris & Blumenthal occupies half of the eighth floor. Richard opens the walnut double doors and approaches the receptionist seated behind a sweeping counter. She has the icy blond look of corporate grooming.

"Richard Keene. I have an appointment with Eleanor Carson." He is trying to project an air of quiet confidence.

"Thank you, Mister Keene." Her voice is more human than her looks. She presses a button among the phalanx on her telephone. "Richard Keene to see Eleanor . . . She's not?" She repeats Richard's name. "OK," she says and hangs up.

"She's not here yet. Are you certain your appointment was scheduled for this morning?" She speaks with precision and wears a tailored business suit, and Richard wonders why she's not smart enough to do better than receptionist, why she lacks the brains to match her voice and looks.

"Absolutely," he says. "She told me she was returning from vacation, and to come in at eleven."

"Perris and Blumenthal." The receptionist fields another call, sends it to its destination, and returns to Richard, who is feigning disappointment and a touch of anxiety, impressions he doesn't have to work too hard to make.

"She is due back today," the receptionist says—no nameplate, Richard notices; high turnover in this job—"but there's no record of your appointment."

"She probably didn't put it in the book," Richard says. "It's a special case."

"Can we reschedule, or would you like to speak with her first?"

"I'm afraid I can't reschedule."

"Perris and Blumenthal."

Richard whispers, "I'll call," turns and walks out of Perris & Blumenthal, certain that Eleanor is not coming back to work there or anywhere else, sure about it, though he'll call later in the day to check, a routine procedural move, the mark of a pro.

So at 1:30, he calls Perris & Blumenthal, and is told that paralegal Eleanor Carson has not yet returned from vacation. At the end of the day, another call, same result. What he sees that night as he sits on the edge of his bed has nothing to do with Eleanor Carson. Nothing . . . and everything.

A red-and-white ambulance and a black-and-white police car at curbside in a row-house neighborhood, paramedics wheeling a gurney slowly down a shared walkway, an opaque white sheet covering a small body on the gurney. At the foot of the walkway, two policemen stand before Herb Dempsey, as morning light slants across their cheeks. One of the officers is big and blocky, the other dark-complected, smaller and trim. Dempsey is unshaven, hair uncombed, clothes hurried on. Neighbors watch from their stoops, keeping their distance, a chilly hush settling over the street. Dempsey is talking to the police, talking in low tones, a word or syllable here and there shrill in the cool morning air, but Richard, standing frozen on his patio, can hear most of it, can hear what other neighbors can't. "I heard something," Dempsey is saying, arms extended, palms upturned as if in supplication or bewilderment, "but it was like in a dream or something, know what I mean?" His expression swings from shock to anger. "It's not possible," he says. "It's just not possible." The gurney passes them and reaches the sidewalk, but Dempsey is not looking at it, he's looking only at the police, even as they turn to watch the gurney being collapsed and loaded into the back of the ambulance. "We

75

*can't find any signs of forced entry, Mister Dempsey," Richard hears
the smaller cop say. An instant later, Richard can hear, coming from
inside the Dempsey house, a woman's sobbing seep through the rain-
stained bricks. The early morning rotates and spins into space, out of
focus. When the ambulance and police car pull away, Dempsey walks
back toward his front door, looking at no one until he sees Richard
standing there, a lone little boy fixing him with unyielding eyes.
Dempsey reaches the top of his stoop and yanks open the screen door.
Richard does not waver, and Dempsey, as he grips the screen-door
handle with his left hand, draws his right to his lips and presses
lightly with two fingers, and Richard hears the little hiss escaping
between them, the "sssh" like a snake's rustle.*

Richard sees it and hears it, as he sits on the edge of his bed
and the city's sounds swirling outside his window provide a
backbeat. He is frustrated that he must wait, that he cannot
move more quickly in this matter, but the deed is done and the
evidence cold, so he understands that his task is to mount a
meticulous investigation and convince the police to follow
through. It's the only feasible option.

He must recruit a partner, a sidekick. Lori. He feels good
about her. More than good, excited.

He calls her, her number's in the book.

"You said you'd keep an open mind," Richard says.

"I know I did, but I need . . . I need something more."

Still the sweetness in her voice. He feels emboldened. "Lori,
you have to believe me. And I'm not asking you to—"

"Richard, you know I don't think you're some kook. I just
think that the mind plays tricks on us sometimes, and maybe—"

"I'm just asking you to keep your ears open, that's all. In a
very natural way, you see him, you talk to him—"

"You know, I'm not exactly a professional at this sort of thing,
Richard. Suppose he is guilty—did you ever think of this?—and

he picks up something in my voice or something like that. Where does that leave me?"

"He's too smart to do anything really crazy. You just keep your distance afterward, stay away from him."

"He's right next door, remember?"

"Of course, what I'm saying is—"

"Richard, this is getting ridiculous. You've got me making Davis into a homicidal maniac."

"No, Lori, he did that all himself."

"Richard, don't you realize it's dangerous to be so sure of yourself?"

"Is Eleanor from Philadelphia?"

"What? You mean originally?"

"Yes."

"I don't know . . . no . . . I think she's from Washington or somewhere."

"She was due back from vacation today. Have you seen her?"

"Well, I haven't gone looking for her. I could go two weeks and not see her. That's the way it works in the big city, Richard. How do you know she was supposed to be back today?"

"They told me down at Perris and Blumenthal. That's the firm she works for. In the Land Title Building at Broad and Chestnut."

"She's a lawyer?"

"Almost. A paralegal. I went down there this morning. Then I called in the afternoon. Twice. End of the day, she hadn't come back. They were expecting her."

"Really?"

"Really."

"Well, so she's late getting back. For all you know, she might be in her apartment right now."

"Let's call and find out."

"You call."

"All right, but you listen in."

"At your apartment?"

"No, I won't call from here. Anyway, I want to see you, Lori. I want to explain to you what I heard."

"You already did, yesterday."

"No, I mean in real detail. Then you'll understand. Have you ever seen the movie *The Boston Strangler*?"

"Oh sure, I love movies like that. A regular chick flick."

Richard is sorry he's mentioned it on the phone. "Never mind, I'll explain it when I see you."

Lori exits the 42s by the rear door and walks on alley-like Latimer Street to 16th, then to Locust and across. The life-size statue of an urban gent clutching a spread umbrella is about a quarter of the way down the block, and there next to the black-bronze, in the flesh, is Richard Keene.

"This cloak-and-dagger stuff makes me feel pretty foolish," Lori says.

"Thanks for coming," says Richard. "It's right up here."

They walk on Locust. Richard dissects for her every sound he heard in that moment, separating the Strangler sounds from those he believes were happening live. His description is controlled and precise.

"I believe you believe it," says Lori. "But that doesn't mean that's what happened. It doesn't mean a murder was committed."

Richard touches her elbow and they stop at a red light. "That's why I want to see how the facts add up," he says. "That's why I need help. Things have a way of getting ignored in the 'big city.' "

The light is green and Lori has a little smile for him. In the next block is a pub with fist-thick sandwiches and beer and billiards and a vestibule with a public phone, a vanishing breed.

There's one right outside the 42s, but obviously to be avoided for this particular mission. Richard inserts a quarter and dials. Davis Braun is in the book. Nothing to hide 'til now.

"You know," Lori says, "if he has done what you say, you ought to watch out for yourself, Richard, running around, digging things up. Know what I mean?"

Richard smiles. "I think I do."

"Not that I believe you, understand."

Davis Braun's voice comes through, familiar to Richard after one exposure. ". . . Please leave a message . . ." Richard holds the receiver out to Lori. "Nobody home," he says.

They walk slowly back toward the 42s. Misty rain drifts down from the invisible sky, streaking the bronze umbrella-bearer.

"I have something else to tell you," Richard says. Lori blinks away the light rain. "A long time ago, I heard a little girl being murdered." They pause at the corner of 16th and Locust, Richard wary, the front entrance of the 42s coming into view.

"And I did nothing."

Now that Lori knows the whole story, she'll come around. Sleep evades him as usual. The next day will be a legitimate day off at work, scheduled in advance, one due him for the many Saturday mornings he has put in. Richard knows what he will do. He will track his man.

7

She looks at her face in the bathroom mirror, that altered face, angular cheeks, eyebrows thinned, hair color changed. It still surprises her when she meets it in the mirror, though she becomes more accustomed to it every day. The cheeks and her body seem natural because they've slimmed gradually, but the brows and hair still startle. Especially the hair. All that red hair.

She's always preferred understated makeup and that hasn't changed. Indeed, her new look calls for low-key cosmetics: moisturizer for supple skin, a few touches to thicken the eyelashes, some deft strokes from the lip-liner, a spritz of perfume behind the ears and on the wrist. The pumps fit just right over her nylons, and her business suit tapers smartly to the waist. Janet Kroll is still surprised by what she sees in the mirror, but that doesn't mean she dislikes it. To the contrary.

When she gets on the elevator, her expensive scent wakes up a couple of riders. She faces front, clutching a small briefcase. When the door reopens, eyes follow her as she strides through the lobby; at the front desk, Frank gives her his best smile.

"Morning, Frank," she says, in motion.

"Yes ma'am," he says.

The day has come up muggy, a lapse into summer's stickiness. Janet has some things on her mind as she walks to the 42s parking garage. She thinks she has a buyer for the three-bedroom condo at The Philadelphian, and she could use the commission. Finances have tightened since she moved into the city a month ago. And anxieties have expanded, even as she maintains a cool exterior. Yet something has hardened inside of her, a resolve that has changed the shape of her life. Yes, she has some things on her mind. Making a living is one of them, but it's well down the list.

Davis Braun is aftershave-smooth in a powder-blue tennis jacket, as he walks through the lobby and greets Frank on the way out. "Hey there, Doctor Braun," Frank says, looking up from a stack of flats.

Outside, the morning is creased by glaring shafts of sunlight that hug the sides of gray-brown buildings, and dagger street and sidewalk. Braun joins the flow of pedestrians; he's casual and refreshed among the frenetic and the disenfranchised. Were he to glance back at the entrance of the 42s, he'd see Richard emerging from the shadows, tentative at first, then determined in pursuit. Richard's Walkman is sending a Grieg piano concerto into his earspace.

Braun walks to 20th Street and then several blocks north past Market and John F. Kennedy Boulevard all the way to tree-lined Benjamin Franklin Parkway, Philadelphia's version of the Champs-Elysées in Paris. He passes the Rodin Museum fronted by the sculptor's black-bronze *Thinker* hunched and brooding, all muscular tenacity and weary contemplation. It's a long, leisurely walk, but Braun's size and natural athleticism propel him at a swift clip. His follower stays in step, well behind and always separated by at least a few people.

When Richard reaches *The Thinker,* he wants to spend time appraising the iconic statue, this grounded cousin of William Penn, who looks down from his aerie at the end of the Parkway. But this is not the time to linger; Richard has communed with *The Thinker* before, he'll do so again.

Braun walks up 22nd and reaches a police station. It is a

two-story brick-and-glass building, long and lean with a flat roof, a 1950s structure that originally housed insurance offices. A narrow parking lot horseshoes the building, squad cars angled between white-painted slats on the asphalt. Braun opens the glass double-doors and goes inside.

Richard is watching him from across Callowhill Street, standing there with his hands in his pockets, partially shielded by a streetlight pylon. He moves forward as if he'll cross the street, checks himself, ambles over to a vendor's pushcart at the corner, gets a cup of coffee.

The day is gathering itself, a warm busy hum replacing the jagged spurts of early morning. Richard paces the sidewalk and sips his coffee, drifts into the adjacent supermarket parking lot, returns to his sidewalk stakeout—not a suspicious-looking guy, just another city character taking in the air. He loiters there for twenty minutes or so, until Braun reappears at the police station front door. Richard tosses his cup into a tall metal trash can and waits for Braun to chart a new direction. Now Braun is on the move, and Richard parallels him down one block, then another, maintaining a comfortable distance between them, moving inconspicuously among the scattered pedestrians. Retracing the trip. Callowhill to 20th, back across the Parkway, the Boulevard, Market, Chestnut, to Walnut and down to 16th to a 1930s neoclassical building and a First Federal branch. Richard follows his man in to the main banking floor, where ribbed columns rise to a vaulted ceiling and the day's brightness comes through tall arched windows.

Braun is standing in the teller line restrained and guided by thick ropy cordons like in a vintage movie theater. A security guard watches over things, prodding stragglers away from incoming traffic, routing newcomers to their destinations. Richard plants himself next to a display carrel well off the line and fingers several brochures, while keeping an eye on Braun. The slotted brochures are benign pieces of modern marketing fluff: IRAs, cash management services, CDs, premium checking, all explained and extolled in neat, bite-sized, meaningless chunks of prose. Richard's heartbeat hops around its chamber, as he shuffles the brochures and angles himself in such a way that the carrel hides him from Braun's view. When a "next" calls Braun to a teller window, Richard strains to hear the exchange. Scattered voices, and heels scuffling and tocking the marble floor interfere with the transmission, the sounds magnified in the cavernous space. "I'd like to—," Braun is saying, some of his words swallowed in echo. He slides something as small as a check or a deposit slip toward the teller, a young guy in a white shirt and red tie. "—form of ID," the teller requests. "Sure," Braun says and removes his wallet from his pants' back pocket. He retrieves a small card from the wallet and hands it to the teller, who inspects it and makes a notation before handing it back. "Thanks."

Simple enough. The teller counts out some cash, making sure no bills are stuck together, and hands to Braun, who has completed his business at the window. When he turns to leave, Richard rotates round the carrel to stay out of sight. Braun walks through the revolving door and into a flood of sunshine. Richard holds back a few seconds, then follows him through the door whose glass is laced with towel smears and sponge strokes laid bare in the sun.

He considers the possibilities. An innocent transaction. No. Braun has just forged a check and cashed it, or phonied up a withdrawal slip. The dead girl's signature.

No, he wouldn't be that stupid.

Yes. Super confidence, or maybe even a taunt.

It's easy to lag behind Braun, keep the separation comfortable, others flitting in and out of the breach. Richard kind of enjoys this cloak-and-dagger stuff, as Lori put it, though he wants to be all cloak and no dagger.

They're back in the 1500 block of Locust and Braun walks inside the 42s. He moves like an athlete, a taut gracefulness confirming muscles and command, and as Richard watches him with envy rather than fear or distaste, he realizes that Braun's stride has been unperturbed throughout the jaunt, that he has neither hurried nor shown uncertainty, but has simply strolled about the city, a morning constitutional. No guilty tics. But no urgency to reach the police station, either. He hardly seems distressed.

Richard walks past the 42s entrance to the phone kiosk, flips up the attached phone book, gets the police station number from the blue pages, drops in a quarter. A man passes, munching on something that leaves a greasy fragrance. Cars dash by, to Richard's ear rumbling like tanks, now that he's removed the Walkman.

"Fairmount Station."

Richard lowers his voice a register. "Yeah, I was just in. Davis Braun, wearing a blue jacket. I forgot to tell the officer something. Can you connect me?" He bites his thumb cuticle.

"Who'd you talk to?"

"Uh . . . sorry, I can't re—"

"Never mind, I got it here. Hold on."

Subway sounds rise through vents and, above ground, the grinding gears of a big delivery truck signal that it yearns for the open road. Richard cups a hand to one ear, the receiver to the other. Now that he's experimented a couple of times with leaving the Walkman at home when venturing out, he's decided that he's got to have it with him to fend off the din of the city. Experiment over.

"Missing Persons, Sgt. Oliver." Gruff but not off-putting.

Richard smothers his mouth with his hand and nearly shouts through it. "This is Davis Braun; I was just there."

"Yes sir."

Richard bobs his head as he speaks, a little gesture of self-affirmation. "Did I give you Eleanor Carson's work number?"

"We've got it, Mister Braun."

"Just wanted to be sure. Thank you." Richard hangs up the phone. Breathes.

Inside, Frank is speaking with Mrs. Levitan, an ancient woman barely taller than the counter. She is expecting something from her granddaughter, a photo album of events surrounding the birth of her first great-grandchild. The granddaughter lives in Minneapolis, where her husband was transferred by Honeywell. It's really something how these young people move around these days, she tells Frank. She wants him to keep an eye out for the parcel. "You'll know as soon as it arrives, Mrs. Levitan," he says with a smile enhanced by the Crest whitening strips he's been using for the past two weeks. Appearances are key, Frank believes, his shining teeth cousin to the sheen of the lobby floor and the gleaming mirrors. Once a week, the service comes in to wax the floor and sparkle the mirrors, but Frank doesn't mind grabbing some Windex for a touchup in between. He treats the place like his living room.

So when Richard walks in, Frank sees a mess in the making. He thrives on problem-solving—a lost package, a stubborn lock—but some messes make you crazy because there's no way to clean them up; they stink or stain forever. Life is that way, he knows that. The best way to deal with messes is to avoid them, or somehow catch them before they spread all over the carpet. Often, you can do neither.

"She's missing."

This is what Richard says, as Frank tries to hide in the *Daily News* sports section. The Flyers and Sixers are starting camp. He doesn't look up.

"Did you hear me? Eleanor Carson. She's missing."

"I'm too busy today, Keene."

Richard sees that Frank is busy only with the sports section at the moment, but smart remarks are not his thing, though he can think of them as quickly as the next guy.

"She never returned to work."

"Uh-huh. So she took a longer vacation. So what?"

"They were expecting her back."

"Maybe you should go to work there, straighten them out."

"Davis Braun was just at the police station."

Frank looks up from the paper. Richard is looking right at him, eyes quiet but dead earnest. "He filed a Missing Persons Report . . . Interesting, huh?"

"Somebody's gonna smack your ass, you keep this up."

"Think about it," Richard says, his hands gripping the counter, squeezing home the point. "His girlfriend's due back and he reports to the police that she's missing. That takes care of the extended vacation idea, Frank."

"Maybe they broke up, how do you know?" Frank tugs at his collar, scrunches his eyes. "You're prying into people's lives, Keene. It's none of your business. And you're getting on my nerves now, big-time." He flips the newspaper onto the desk behind him, and the tabloid pages separate and swim across the flat hard surface. "I've got a building to run here."

Frank turns away but immediately turns back with enlighten-ment in his eyes. "Anyway, if he's taking it to the police, he's concerned she's late and all that. Doesn't sound like someone who killed her, now, does it?"

Richard doesn't smile, doesn't fidget, doesn't even change the inflection of his voice. "Sounds like it to me."

Frank slices the air with a dismissive backhand. "C'mon, Keene. Gimmee a break."

A FedEx delivery man arrives with a big box clutched to his

armpit, releasing Frank from Richard, who walks to the elevators. Frank signs for the package, watches Richard's retreating form, puffs his lips into a snicker. That's right, he likes things neat and orderly, under control. Hates things that mess you up, turn a clean gig into a pain in the ass.

But he keeps his eyes open to all things, doesn't ignore the reality that life does get very messy at times. He knows that too well. He knows all about bad behavior.

What if the skinny sucker is onto something?

8

Through the tall windows, the weathered gray buildings mass, the modern Liberty Place towers flickering cobalt blue back at the sun, the venerable Bellevue Hotel and its rooftop restaurant, antique City Hall, the statue of William Penn diminished by distance to a little boy's toy soldier that can be grasped and manipulated. Richard pounds his threadbare cross-trainers on the treadmill and shuts his eyes against the glare of the skyline, the soaring buildings seared onto his retina, shimmering silhouettes. He holds on to the sidebars to maintain balance, as the constant thumping takes its toll. A big toe aches, the right knee serves notice that it might buckle. He feels a rivulet of sweat crawling down one shoulder blade and onto his flat chest and ribs. He keeps his mouth closed and breathes through his nose, even at this accelerated pace.

Running is the release that enables him to cope. It settles his nerves even as it drains his energy, then mysteriously refills his inner reservoir for the next cycle.

Through his earphones, percussion punctuates a looping melody from a local university jazz station, a major part of Richard's musical territory staked out between the vapors of easy listening and rock's ugly blast. He runs with the music, scurries around it or strides to its beat, double-time with the sax, a syncopated skipping with the drums. Despite the unsteadiness of his knee.

When the clangor of a banging Nautilus stack explodes the

reverie, Richard opens his eyes and shoots a look toward the adjacent room, where a gorilla in a mud-brown T-shirt and matching pants has just risen from the bench and wears an aggressive, self-satisfied expression as if he has just quaffed a mug of his favorite brew or popped somebody in the chops. Richard is quick to look away and not catch his attention. He steers clear of confrontation, and certainly does not want to tangle with some dumb thug over an irritating noise. His thoughts careen to Braun, who, in his estimation, is neither dumb nor a classical thug.

Afterward, the Walkman stuffed in the pocket of his gym shorts, Richard towels his face as he waits for the elevator. When it arrives and the door slides open, Janet Kroll is there, poured into spandex. Richard gets that little kick inside, that jump-start, even before she's in full view. Their paths keep crossing. Something about this girl. A stunner, yes, yet her eyes suggest both reticence and intelligence. It's not an automatic that she's after a hard-ass Hercules. Not nearly. He would like to build a bit on their meeting at the lobby elevator. See if she can find a way to be interested in him. "Hi," he says, as she steps out of the elevator and their eyes meet unavoidably.

"Hi," she says with a smile, which might be a recognition of their minimal familiarity, or be merely politeness. Richard remembers faces and names after the briefest of encounters, and hates it when the recognition is not reciprocated. In this case, they haven't yet exchanged names.

She seems pretty smart, though, and the smile is a reference point, he concludes. He gets on the elevator and reaches down to rub his sore knee before pressing number twenty-two.

Got to get her name.

While Richard is running on the treadmill at the 42s fitness center, Davis Braun is pumping iron at the Downtown Athletic

Club two blocks away. His thousand-dollar-a-year membership affords him a much wider and slicker array of equipment and women. With beachboy locks feathering his forehead, wide-set blue eyes, and well-muscled arms and shoulders, Braun tends to get noticed among the young professional females (and some of the males) at the Downtown, and the fact that he's a future surgeon doesn't hurt his chances. He's well aware of this. He knows that it's a myth, this psychobabble about women being drawn to the mind rather than the body, one of the Mars–Venus tenets. Right.

Fact is, he's got both qualities working for him: rugged and sensitive, tough and tender. And to showcase it all, he's cool on approach, articulate but off-the-cuff, very much at ease with himself. In short, rather irresistible. Got to be honest about it.

But he's no pillaging Hun. He *likes* women, and they understand that. Makes him doubly irresistible. He should be the one to write the book. Of course, it all goes nowhere unless you have the looks to begin with.

He and Eleanor have an Open Relationship. Which means that, in between their nights in bed, he squires and squeezes a batch of lovelies while she remains loyal to him because she's too uptight to do otherwise. Beautiful, smart, inhibited Eleanor Carson. They each have free miles to use, but he's been the only one to take advantage. Still, he doesn't lie, makes no apologies, and treats her right when he's with her. Like a lady and a lover. That's how he sees it.

The Downtown A.C. is on the top two floors of a 1920s building that once was a department store, and now houses attorneys, accountants, insurers, and consultants of various stripes in the converted offices below. The strength training/ cardiovascular area encompasses the entire top floor with no partitions, a hangar-like space with steel beams crisscrossing the ceiling and huge arched windows at either end. Braun moves through the cycle of stations, isolating and challenging all of his muscle groups. Delts, trapezius, biceps, triceps, chest, abs, quads, calves. He wants the symmetrical look—not like a lot of the iron-pumpers who build massive arms larger than their legs, which look atrophied by comparison. Those jokers are not athletes, but engorged lummoxes as inert as the barbells they heft. Some of these dummies even use illegal juice to further inflate their muscles. That'll work out just fine in a decade or so, when their testicles shrink to the size of walnuts. Braun is an athlete; he swims, bikes, plays tennis, would never touch a steroid. In terms of social/sex appeal, he's the complete package, with an inner cockiness that projects confidence to the world.

Braun is yanking opposing pulleys downward from shoulder to waist when he sees a blonde bunny three stations down using the incline chest press with the undoubted aim of increasing her bust size. She has a tight little body and a hard look that functions as repellent for men that bug her. As she finishes a set, a candle-white guy, a bit flaccid and with a severe part in his hair and a three o'clock shadow, settles in next to her, smiles pleasantly, and says, "Back to the torture chamber." Instead of ignoring him, which would be bad enough, the bunny fires off a "what?" of such annoyance that it's clear she doesn't desire a clarification, not only wants to be left alone but craves casualties in the process.

The poor guy lurches into his workout so he can justify his reddening face. Braun does an extra set on the pulleys and waits for the bunny to come into his zone. There's no need for that kind of snapping; she gives women a bad name. But she is a sexy little thing, no question. Soon enough, she's a machine away from him, on the "lats" rig, interesting because girls usually avoid it. She catches sight of Braun, and he can tell right away that now she has a different impulse, the kind of urge she elicits in others come to visit her, something bothersome but pleasure-inducing, an itch to be scratched on her underarm perfectly waxed and lightly tanned. He hovers, stretches; she finishes and looks at him.

"Did you want to get on here?" she asks.

The voice is neighborhood-Philadelphia, a clatter of diphthongs and mangled soft palate. Braun is a Milwaukee native and he's managed to homogenize the dips and swells of his indigenous midwestern twang; he can be either amused or disgusted by the torturous Philly sound. He does like female speech to be as cool and smooth as a lake at dawn, with a few suggestive colors in the flow. Auto mechanic speech out of a pretty face is like bad breath shot through perfumed jaws. As they say in the East, fugettabodit.

But he gives her a conquering little smile and a polite "no, no, it's all yours . . . thanks," and walks away, no interest shown, leaving her petulant enough to blister through a second set, her scorecard evened on the day.

It is exactly one week—168 hours—since the deed, since a fiercely random moment handed Richard a chance for redemption. So he believes.

He is in Lori Calder's apartment for a report. His stark tale about Cindy Dempsey last night was the clincher. She seemed to believe him, to feel for him, and reluctantly agreed to find a way to approach Braun and then "keep her ears open." She didn't promise anything, but that was good enough for Richard. A day later, she has some information, and so he has walked up one flight and checked the hallway before hurrying to her door, though Braun, she told him, was scheduled to work at the hospital this evening. Richard now regards her as his field agent, a slim petite girl with short coifed hair and a sweet smile, something special about her. She can't weigh much more than a hundred pounds. They sit a comfortable distance apart on her plump hazel-colored sofa, the slit vertical blinds partitioning Philly's nighttime skyline.

"Why would he do that if he killed her?"

"It's the smart move," Richard answers. He is speaking softly. "It draws suspicion away from him. She never came home and he reports it. He's doing what he should be doing as a faithful, concerned boyfriend. Right?"

Lori has the kind of face that could never turn ugly-angry, Richard thinks, but right now its sweetness has evaporated and it has the abrasive edges of a piqued curiosity.

"Could be . . . or it could be he really is a faithful, concerned boyfriend."

Richard stares at a piece of sculpture on the coffee table, a naked couple enmeshed in a full-body cling and kiss. Greek classicism. "Is this a miniature?" he asks.

"I think so."

"Michelangelo? Rodin?"

"I don't know. I think so." She seems distracted, upset.

"So . . ." He doesn't want to press her. "What'd he say?"

The question helps Lori regain her focus. She looks directly at Richard. "Just that she hasn't called and he's worried."

"Uh huh." Richard nods, processing the information, no surprises in that. "Anything else?"

"That's it."

"That's it?"

"I didn't want to be obvious."

"I understand . . . And he seemed perfectly sincere?"

Lori fingers her ear and a small jade earring. "Yes. He did. As far as I could tell. Remember, Richard, I don't know him all that well."

"But you're a perceptive person."

Her eyes open a tiny bit wider and the corners of her mouth

suggest a smile. "You don't know *me* all that well."

"True."

"Maybe *you're* the one who's perceptive."

"Maybe." Richard wants to appear in command, but as he feels himself drawn closer to Lori, the familiar nervous self-doubts fill up inside of him. Stay with the task at hand. "You'll return the coffee maker tomorrow?"

A little more of her smile. "Of course. Don't want him thinking I'm a caffeine freak." Her straight teeth show no gaps, good genes, and a dentist's hand.

"I don't want you doing or saying anything you're uncomfortable with," Richard says, "but . . ."

"Yes?"

"Can you find out where she went?"

"He could say anything."

Richard jabs a forefinger and shakes his head. "No, he'll play everything straight. The police, a neighbor's inquiry. Consistent. Get it?"

When she stretches her arms behind her head and massages the back of her neck, the sleeves of her T-shirt climb up her arms to her shoulders, an erotic stimulus to Richard. But instead of running for cover as he usually does, convinced that the impulse is a false lead, instead of succumbing to self-doubt, he reaches for her, touches her left arm as she lowers it, lets his hand rest there.

His touch startles her but not sufficiently that she draws back in any way; there is no threat. She looks at him and his face is all vulnerability. "Do you believe me?" he asks.

Her body language says maybe. "Of course I do. Like I said, I believe that *you* believe."

Richard looks away, taken down a peg. Lori is quick to re-assure.

"Richard, you can't expect me to believe in all of this the way that you do. The fact that you're here, that I'm doing what I'm doing is your answer . . . I still think that, when you get through all this, you'll see that nothing's happened. Things only happen when we're not looking for them, I'm convinced of that."

"I wasn't looking for this. You're right, and that's the whole point."

He furrows his hands through his hair. He's about to step onto shaky terrain, minefield territory. "Do you have a boyfriend, Lori?" Follows instantaneously with, "I'm sorry, I . . ."

"No, that's OK . . ."

It's so sweet a smile, the mouth curling slightly, no teeth showing, most of it in the eyes. It takes him over, as she says, "No, I don't have a boyfriend," and as he wonders where this wonderland rabbit-hole might deposit him, he knows he has no choice but to yield to its gravity.

9

"I see you're among the living."

It's Kathy's greeting to Richard as he enters the reception area of Rosen & Wallingford after a jangled, Wednesday morning subway ride. He'd like to think he's improving his ability to cope with the noise and the confinement, but admits to himself that progress has been non-existent of late.

He's been absent from work and Kathy could not resist trying to act sophisticated, though, of course, she missed the mark. Why can't she just be a pleasant, unassuming twenty-year-old?

He'll show her the face of true maturity. "Good morning, Kathy. How are you?"

His voice sounds genuine and she is puzzled, uncertain how to react. Finally, she says, "OK, I guess."

"That's good . . . I guess," and he smiles at her, not too big, just right. Her skin has cleared up and she has a certain softness about her that she chooses to de-emphasize. Her decision; maybe she'll reverse it someday. At any rate, he's past her and into the corridor, heading toward the hearing-testing room, his work station.

He's leaving early today for another bout with an MRI, this time at a different hospital, so his appointments are scheduled to conclude at three o'clock. The first customer of the day is Mrs. Kohler, a not-young woman who makes an arduous effort to transport her bulk into the booth, as if she were grappling with a hot-water heater. She smells like she's been sweating under her flower-print dress, and her eighteenth-century perfume is insufficient to neutralize the human scent.

"Have you been having any problems hearing, Mrs. Kohler?"

"I don't think so; doctor wants to check it anyway. I had a sinus infection; I think that's the problem."

"What kind of problem?"

"I've been a little dizzy"—she holds her hands to her temples—"and my head still feels like it's filled up with something, you know what I mean?"

Richard nods with a "hmh," and says, "Well let's see how the machinery's working inside those ears," as he rigs the audiometer for duty. "This will produce several faint, high-pitched sounds with no particular rhythm. Each time you hear a sound, I want you to raise your right hand. OK?"

"Yes."

"Are you right-handed?"

"Yes."

"Good. I always forget to ask that."

He has coaxed a smile from her pinched face. He leads her into the cork-walled booth and helps her fit the earphones comfortably over her dyed-brown hair, then leaves and sits back down at the audiometer, adjusts the volume and frequency dials. He looks at her through the glass, a nod of reassurance, then looks away so as not to prompt or distract her. She is motionless in her seat, eyes saucering behind thick glasses.

He raises a squeal on the audiometer and she raises her hand.

He hears a woman whimpering, crying, crying out. Then a rasping from the throat. Fabric tearing. A thump. A chorus of death. Death on film, death in the apartment on the twenty-third floor, paying him a visit, swelling inside his head, unbidden, a riot in his head, the cycle repeating, the order changing, the sounds stinging him like thorns. Richard's thumb and forefinger move on their own and the audiometer's volume dial does a half-revolution. He hears nothing but the sounds of death. He shakes his head to chase the intruders but they recycle and amp up. He sees a fallen body in a twenty-third-floor apartment, a woman's body. He sees a little girl on swings, in a sandbox, at a Chinese checkers board, sheeted on a gurney. He sees a riotous kaleidoscope in his head, each sound pulsing a color, searing red and frozen blue, brown like the mud of an engorged river, and it's all spinning madly, careening, and . . . his eye catches Mrs. Kohler through the glass, her mouth contorted in agony, hands clawing her earphones now askew and stuck in her piled-up hair.

The sounds in his head vanish and their absence shatters his equilibrium. The tester becomes the dizzy patient. He reels in his seat, his mouth agape, his fingers glued to the dial, the unearthly frequencies shooting through poor Mrs. Kohler whom he knows he must save before it is too late, for he sees her throes in the booth, can hear—faintly, but he above all people can hear it—her shrieking in the soundproof booth, and he wills himself out of his paralysis, sees the scorpion pincers of his right thumb and forefinger on the dial, and immediately spins the volume to zero.

Mrs. Kohler slumps, defeated or worse, her heaviness settling to an undeniable center of gravity. All but unconscious, she slides out of the chair, a mass of collapse, hits the floor like a sack of flour, and damn if the thump of her doesn't give Richard a start and spin him right back into the other unreality. A body fallen to the floor. The twenty-third floor.

He rises shakily and stands right by his chair, as if stepping too far away would leave him untethered and discharged into space. He is sweating like the high school harrier he was, a full-body sweat after a cross country race, sweat in the socks even. He would run those distance races on the plateau, with the autumn clouds racing overhead and a river of wind streaming past his ears, its sibilance inaudible to the other runners but a tunnel of sound to him, escorting him through the loneliness, masking the clangor of his heart and lungs.

Mrs. Kohler is examined and tested and peered at and pronounced fit for departure, hearing and all inner organs intact. Dr. Wallingford himself does the workup, then asks Wendy for an immediate report. Not on Mrs. Kohler's condition, but on R&W's legal exposure.

Wendy Klein is the office manager cum human resources person for this busy practice of doctors, nurses, technicians and secretaries, twenty-two employees in all. As her hands join in a prayerful pose and she leans forward on one of the two-seat sofas in her office, her blond bangs seem to dig into her forehead, a row of scythes.

"What is it, Richard? Something's wrong here."

He sits opposite on the imitation-leather sofa jammed against a squat, flimsy end table supporting a bulbous lamp. "I'm . . . sorry," he says, which is true enough and about all he can say. Now he props an elbow on a knee and presses a thumb onto the bony ridge between his eyebrows.

"You realize this thing could become a lawsuit," Wendy says.

"She's all right, isn't she? She seemed to be all right afterward." Richard has dropped his hand and looked up in alarm.

"I think so, but that won't necessarily stop her. She has a pretty good case for trauma."

Richard sits back wearily. "I don't know what happened," he says. "I must have blanked . . ."

"Well at least you're not blaming the equipment," says Wendy, rising and circling behind her desk. "But this is a high-profile practice, Richard. You understand that."

He's beginning to.

"You've been missing work. That hasn't happened before. What is it, Richard?"

He spiders his fingertips against each other. "I guess I've had some things on my mind."

Wendy's smile suggests that's an understatement. "The doctors don't know right now whether you should get a second chance. They don't know whether they can afford to give you one."

Richard drops his hands and just sits there, something washing through him from his forehead to the pit of his stomach, something tingling yet calming, a portent of change, desired change. He hears some movement and talk wafting down the hallway, a patient leaving with her husband perhaps; he's trying to buoy her with "not too bad, huh?" and she's sounding frail, vulnerable. Yes, it's time he left this insular world of mechanical sounds and pulses channeled to the human ear, thinned at high frequencies and piercing the invisible air. Time to work somewhere else, a place of visual stimulation perhaps, an art gallery, a museum . . .

"It's a difficult situation, Richard. You've been a fine employee until now."

He nods his head three times slowly.

"Take the rest of the day off," she says. "We'll have to figure this out."

He rises and moves trance-like to the door, opens it and waits.

"I'll let you know," she says.

He's halfway through the threshold. "You already have."

The ultra-sensitivity to sounds has been there as long as he can remember. It was one thing to spook parents and classmates with his ability to hear things they could not, quite another to cringe in literal pain with an airplane's sonic blast passing overhead, a clap of thunder on an awful humid night, or just ordinary household sounds: a rapping hammer, a telephone ringing out of the stillness (now living on his own, finally, he has set his telephones on "low pulse"), even a thick hardcover slammed shut after a satisfying read.

Marty and Evelyn had his hearing tested when he was only six years old, years before the schools typically began such tests. Richard scored off the charts, picking up sounds beyond the canine range, but neither the technician nor the doctor could explain the gift (curse?) or remediate its painful effects. Some people simply have exceptional hearing, went the explanation, like others have exceptional eyesight or speed or strength or intelligence or artistic ability. The inexplicable landscape of the brain. His auditory apparatus seemed normal enough, the eardrum, the cochlear canal and all of its tiny appendages. They asked if he suffered from intense headaches, migraines, which typically heightened the sensitivity to sound. No, he didn't. His condition was not quite dismissed as something he'd grow out of, but the doctors believed that his acuity would "level off" as he aged, and offered the sobering assessment that it might be "something he'd have to live with." What they really believed was that they had a neurotic little kid on their hands.

With no relief from the medical community, and little sympathy on the homefront, Richard dealt with his gift/affliction on his own terms. Which meant, to a great extent, withdrawing into his own world, solo excursions and daily perambulations, alone in a crowd because of what he heard in its midst and beyond, clamping ponderous earphones to the side of his head for an untrammeled session with the stereo, damming up his ears with cotton or plugs when things got too bad, but that could make it worse, trapping his pulsating inner machinery, all its beats and flutters dancing in his ear. No wonder he made funny expressions and people found him strange, confused his wonderment with imbecility, his agitation with hostility. He *was* strange, possessor of an unharnessed power, one without apparent utility.

Then when the Walkman came along, for Richard it was penicillin, the Salk vaccine, and Prozac all in one. He could go anywhere, anytime, snuff out much of the unwanted soundtrack in his vicinity and substitute his favored smooth jazz sounds or classical strains . . . and be socially acceptable. It was a miracle invention, the Walkman. Funny, this most commercial of products becoming a godsend for Richard Keene.

Except in dreams. They had a language and a soundtrack all their own, and there was no Walkman to parry them. The dreams came like streamers hurled by the wind, some rippling past him at high speed, others clinging like crepe and winding about his neck, strangling him. Not every night, but often, and always the same feeling if not the same setting: a little boy trapped in sheets and blankets, or drowning just under the surface of the water, or stuck to the tracks and facing the headlong rush of a train. A little boy with no release. No mistaking the identity of this little boy.

He had an undistinguished record in high school and then more of the same in two years of community college. He had trouble concentrating, paying attention in class. He liked music because it soothed him, and took piano lessons, learned a few guitar chords. But he felt he wasn't a talented enough musician to pursue a career, and so he drifted from job to job, saving a few dollars while continuing to live at home, now a nicer home in the suburbs, one with uncramped bedrooms and no bucking broncos on the walls. He tutored at the local high school, made tuna fish hoagies at a deli in a strip center, made 11.4 calls per hour for a telemarketing firm, trained with an insurance company to be an auto claims adjustor but the sight of a wreck began to unnerve him, even a battered fender was disturbing.

They moved him to the billing department and there he labored in white-shirted anonymity among the computer-generated invoices, becoming adept at on-screen navigation and mindless processing. He tried to strike a truce with life and with the past, earning wages, handling chores at home, avoiding crowds and noise and unpleasantries. But the past would not be filed away. It returned with increased ferocity, like a hurricane gathering strength from tropical waters. Sounds of horror, and a little boy immured beneath blankets. There was no leashing the past, it was a timeless monster. Still, he tried to slip by it, stay a step ahead. Until the full-length mirror hanging on the back of his bedroom door drew him back one night as if by magnetism, the awful reflected reality he had avoided for years. And he looked himself up and down, and stared at his face, his eyes. The dormant dread flared, an unhinged soul. Who am I . . . what am I . . . why this face and form . . . what if there were no people, no world, no universe, nothing? And the edges of his vision blurred red and he thought his forehead was vibrating and a stranger stared back at him from the mirror.

Marty and Evelyn rushed into his room when they heard the screaming. A neighbor taking an evening stroll froze on the sidewalk in front of the house. Richard heard nothing. When his parents thrust the bedroom door open, banging the mirror into his nose, he backpedaled to his bed and got under the covers. There he lay awake all night, fully clothed.

His next bedroom was one without mirrors.

The idea of being an audiometric technician hit him the day he came home from the hospital, and he was proud and rather relieved that he was thinking in such pragmatic terms. He knew his special auditory capability was no real asset in this regard; technology did all the work. But the psychological appeal for him was to confront the demon on its home field, an auditory proving ground. And he could offer a certain empathy or counsel to those suffering auditory discomfort or deficit. He got the job at Rosen & Wallingford, did well at it, even mustered the energy and courage—with the psychiatrist's support and his parents' financial assistance—to finally leave home and get his own place.

And now that job is gone.

Wendy calls him at one o'clock. Two weeks' severance is already in the mail.

But when Richard takes the call, he is not thinking about Rosen & Wallingford at all. He is thinking about the case.

Now he can concentrate on the case. Full-time.

Eight days since the murder. No doubt in his mind there was a murder. The evidence, so far, would satisfy only him; it is time to move to the second stage and ferret out the pieces of the mosaic. For the first time, he begins to ponder motive. A lovers' quarrel turned violent turned deadly, or something more sinister, something planned? Of course it was planned, premeditated, as they say. That the sounds were masked by the movie scene was no coincidence, but the result of meticulous timing. No, he will not be thrown off the trail, not this time. The matter of motive. It's not his concern, really; he's not the prosecutor. But he is curious, naturally, and suggesting a plausible motive may help prod the police. For he will have to enlist the police eventually, he knows that.

He wonders if there's a financial motive. Braun and the transaction at the bank. Legit?

He wonders what became of the body.

What became of the body?

An intriguing question. What do you do in a highrise? Bodies do spoil after eight days. Before eight days. But medical residents have resources.

He needs more from Lori, he's relying on her, she's his

confederate. Maybe more than that. When she told him that, no, she didn't have a boyfriend, she seemed to be opening a door. They looked at each other in silence for as long as it takes to hold a normal breath. Then back to business.

Business has brought them together. Right now, Richard has some other business: a four p.m. appointment for another go at an MRI, this one at a site closer to home and, as ordered, in an "open" machine. His knee remains sore and buckles at high speeds on the treadmill. Something's wrong somewhere.

He walks down to Metropolitan Hospital on Ninth Street, checks in at Diagnostics, and sits in the waiting room with a dozen other patients and a bunch of dog-eared magazines. He wonders if this is the hospital where Braun is doing his residency. After twenty minutes of reading two paragraphs of an old *Newsweek* article and eavesdropping on snatches of conversation throughout the room, he hears his name called, and a plump pleasant nurse leads him to the interior mystical chambers. He follows her into the scan room and the MRI apparatus, which reminds him of cold storage, cryogenics, but without the frozen steam. Then he thinks of mailing tubes dropped down the postal chute at the building that housed his old job at the insurance company, the kind of tubes you send winging from your car window to the drive-in teller at the bank, suburban-style. Evelyn used to send him on such errands.

The MRI doesn't look any bigger. He takes it calmly.

"I had some trouble the last time I went for an MRI," he says.

"Really?"

"Yes."

She looks at him and tries to move from pleasant to compassionate, but makes it only halfway. "You get uncomfortable?"

"Yes . . . very. This looks like the same kind of unit I had at Einstein. I was supposed to get the 'open' type."

"We're supposed to be getting one in very soon," she says, "but it hasn't arrived yet, I'm sorry. I know, we're getting more requests for that these days . . . Would you like to try? We can do some things so that you don't feel like a sardine."

Richard casts a wary eye at the tube.

"We have these glasses that enable you to see behind you and into the room as you're lying down so you don't feel like you're trapped in there," she says and hands him a pair. "Then we can pump in some soothing music to relax you. And I'll give you a buzzer to hold in your hand. If at any time you feel panicked, just squeeze it and we'll hear it in the control room where the technician is receiving your scan on the computer. That's right over there." She points to a glass-enclosed booth, where an attractive young woman waves from behind a computer screen. "How's that sound?"

So the tables are turned; he's the one under observation, while a detached technician is at the controls. Turnabout is fair play. Richard figures he has to give it a try. "OK."

"Oh you'll be fine, you'll see."

But as soon as he climbs in and lies on his back, he begins sweating and shuts his eyes. "Try the glasses," the nurse says, and he fits them on, no optical lens, but twin mirrors reflecting the room behind him, wavy, mildly distorted. She gives him a headset to place over his skull and onto his ears, then clamps some sort of coil around his knee. "That landmarks the area we want to focus on," he hears her say through the headset and the surf-like music already filtering in. He goes with it, tries to visualize a scene that might soothe him, the seashore, a big blue restful sky feathered with wisps of cloud, a broad beach stirred by ocean breezes, and the ocean itself stretching in great sunlit ribbons toward the endless horizon.

She slaps the plastic buzzer in his hand. "Give me a ring if you need to," and she's gone. He doesn't like the mirrored glasses, so he closes his eyes again and he's at Playtown Park in the Philly suburbs, and Cindy is next to him in the two-seat compartment as the kids' Ferris wheel loops skyward in a lazy arc, the open compartments dangling, the ground retreating beneath them; amazing how heights relax him, while small spaces terrify. Evelyn and Marty watch from below, and Cindy's mother is there, but not Herb Dempsey; he's nowhere in sight. Cindy and Richard sit side by side, and when they reach the apex of the wheel, the motion torques their bodies so that their arms press against one another, and they look at each other and smile. He can feel her arm. It is a magic moment, but now it's gone in a blink because Richard can't hold onto it, can't keep his eyes shut as he slides into the doom of the narrow tube.

He looks up, above the glasses, and the metal is right on him, as if it would crush down through his nose. The apparatus is humming and spitting ominous knocking noises, the magnetic fields dancing, and Richard hears them cut right through the tepid music in his headset. Now additional sounds, the cycle of murder sounds, join them like an orchestral duo, and he can hear it all distinctly, a world-class conductor who hears every note in the recesses of the stage. He has to urinate. He rolls his shoulders and the glasses slip across the bridge of his nose. He begins to realize that, once again, he's not going to make it, despite all the accessories. He must get out. He thumbs the buzzer. Hears nothing, figures it doesn't make noise but triggers an emergency light or shows up on the computer screen in the control booth. Nothing's happening. Presses it again, like a button on a pinball machine. Waits for rescue, time suspended.

He is pounding a fist against the side and roof of the cylinder, the cold metal, short incessant blows, for that is all the space allows. He pounds as hard and as fast as he can, and as the seconds tick off and he remains trapped, he shouts in a voice not quite his own, and the shouting becomes screaming, the effort spraying mucus and saliva onto the metal as if it has begun to rain. He tears off the mirrored glasses and the headset, the futile music continuing to trickle out. When the nurse reaches him and fetches the tube from its tunnel, his face is a contorted mask, the mouth a stroke victim's rictus, and his right hand, still clenched into a fist, is bloodied at the knuckles.

"Oh my god," she says, "oh my god, I'm so sorry, what happened to the buzzer? Did you press the buzzer?"

As if oxygen has just now reached his brain, Richard bolts up like a reflexed cadaver and spurts out of the contraption. "You're bleeding," the nurse tells him, and he looks down at his bloody hand, aware of its condition for the first time.

10

The hell with it, Richard thinks, as he walks up Locust Street back toward his apartment house, his right hand bandaged. If they can't figure out what's wrong with the knee without a damn MRI, then he'll just live with it, that's all. What'd they do before MRIs? If the regular X ray doesn't get it, the hell with it.

He's got the Walkman set to an FM oldies station that's playing Motown, songs that impress him with their energy and musicality; he wasn't around in the heyday, but realizes why this music had such an impact. A man passes by wearing enough cologne to counteract the fumes emanating from the garbage truck loading up in the alley at mid-block between 11th and 12th. Martha Reeves and the Vandellas sing their hit "Nowhere to Run," the driving beat quickening Richard's walk.

Back at the 42s, Richard walks past the entrance and into the building's parking garage, which takes up the first nine floors. He has his '88 Toyota parked at G-5, level G, space 5, he remembers, secure in the knowledge that he has the vital information written down on a scrap of paper in his wallet, a necessary step since sometimes the car may sit there for weeks if in need of repair, its current status, and locating a parked automobile when you have forgotten its precise location can be a maddening experience in a facility like this, replete with pillars and transverse ramps and levels that replicate each other right down to the puddles.

He approaches the shed, where Jay presides at the crossroads of incoming and outgoing traffic. Jay is an ever-smiling Indonesian man, wiry with warm brown eyes and an omnipresent blue baseball cap. Richard likes him. In fact, he likes him more than anyone else he has met in center-city. Jay's a smart guy. He's about halfway there with the English language, and is taking night courses toward a degree at Temple University. Richard admires that.

Since Richard doesn't use the car that often, and hasn't at all in the last two weeks, he doesn't see a great deal of Jay, but they've developed a rapport based on just a few meetings. For one thing, they know each other's name. Richard is one of the few 42s tenants who addresses Jay by first name. They speak about more than just the monthly parking fee.

"What happened to hand?" Jay sees the bandage wrapped around both sets of Richard's knuckles as if protecting his right hand before it slips into a boxing glove.

Richard glances at the hand. "Ahh, little accident. Put it through a window. I should get my eyesight checked, huh?"

Jay looks concerned. "Everything OK?"

"Thanks, everything's fine. Jay, let me ask you something; you might be able to help me."

Jay nods and his eyes tell that he'd be happy to help Richard, and he trusts that Richard would not put him at risk in doing so.

"There's a woman who lives here by the name of Eleanor Carson," Richard continues. "Is she a monthly?" He points to the smooth, copper-colored cement at his feet, meaning does she park here at the garage.

Jay broadens his smile. "Mister Richard," he says. "Is she pretty?" He reaches out and brushes Richard's sleeve, a friendly gesture.

Richard returns the smile, but turns serious again. "I don't know, I've never seen her, at least I don't think I have."

Jay looks puzzled by Richard's inquiry. He pays strict attention to rules and regulations, but he's inclined to help his friend. Sensing uneasiness, Richard gives Jay an earnest "it's important," and Jay grabs the register on a shelf in the shed. "How spell?"

Richard spells her last name.

Jay's got it, and he struggles with the first name. "El . . ."

"Eleanor."

"Here she is. Volvo. You need license plate?"

Richard smiles, wishes for a moment he were a state trooper so he could run the plate, but what would that get him anyway? "No thanks, not now. What about Davis Braun?"

Jay has tapped out a four-digit number on a keypad next to a mini-computer screen. "Her car's still here."

"Really?"

Jay points at the little screen. "It tells me who's here and who's not."

"I didn't know that," says Richard, recalling that the magnetic strip on his seldom-used passcard raises the turnpike both ways. "What about Davis Braun, Jay? Does he have a car here? B . . . r . . . a . . . u . . . n."

"I know that guy," says Jay. "Nice guy. He went out this morning. Not back yet." Leafs backward through some register pages, looks up. "A . . . c . . . u . . . r . . . a."

"Acura."

"Yeah, Acura."

"That's Mister Braun's car, huh?"

"Yes, that's his."

"Thanks, Jay."

"You're welcome," Jay answers, and his grin is not simpleminded but shows pride in his work and once again suggests that he trusts Richard, who says to him, "I'll explain this another time," and gives him an appreciative tap on the shoulder.

"Silver Spring, huh?"

Richard and Lori are sitting on the sofa in Lori's apartment, closer to each other than the last time. Lori wears shorts and sits in a yoga position, folded legs pressing calf muscles into prominence. She winced when she saw his hand and heard about his MRI escapade. Richard liked that, figures she's concerned. For real.

"That's what he said," Lori reports. "She was going back to visit her father for a few days."

"Of course she never arrived."

"He didn't say that."

"He made sure to call there when she didn't return, and the phone records reflect that." Richard is building his case with hypotheticals that he is sure have happened, climbing into the criminal's mind. As he explains, he looks directly into Lori's alert brown eyes. "By the way, her car is still in the garage; I checked with Jay."

"Who's Jay?"

"The guy at the shed, you know, when you drive in."

"How's he know?"

"It's on computer."

"So, maybe she took a cab to the train station."

A small smile from Richard. "None of the dispatchers will have it in their logs."

Lori holds out her arms, palms up. "So? Maybe their records aren't so good." Her eyes open wider. "Or maybe he drove her to the station."

"He wouldn't do that, and he won't say that, too many things to connect," says Richard. "Did Frank see them walk out? Did Jay see them come in, and then Braun return by himself? Nah, he won't say he drove her. And, of course, he didn't drive her."

"There'd be a credit card payment for the tickets."

"Amtrak?"

"Yup."

"She paid cash."

"Eleanor wouldn't pay cash."

"I thought you didn't know her that well."

"Just an impression, call it woman's intuition."

"What I'm saying is that he suggests to the police that she paid cash. She didn't pay anything—she never got to the station." Richard rocks on the sofa, inhabiting a murderer's mind, breaking it down cleanly for Lori. "See, she really *was* taking a vacation. Just like she told you."

"OK."

"And the law firm had her scheduled for one."

"So you're saying he killed her before she could leave, and he planned to do that all along."

"Exactly."

Lori shifts her folded legs on the couch cushion. "But why? Why would he kill her? You need a motive, Sherlock."

There's some chemistry here, Richard is thinking, but he doesn't want this dissolving into a parlor game; the stakes are too high. "You knew them. Any ideas?"

Lori unfolds her legs and stands. Richard takes her in. She's slim, but there's a nice curve to the legs, at the waist, and at the shoulders. "They're like an All-American couple," she says.

"Appearances can be deceiving," Richard says.

"I never heard any shouting, you know, through the walls. Not just that night, but any night."

"Slow burn."

"Never a mark on her face when I saw her."

"Uh-huh."

She sits down again and clasps Richard's hand with both of hers. "I still think you're wrong about him. Doesn't it occur to you that you could be wrong?"

"Do you know her father's first name?"

She lets go of him and sits back. "No."

Richard nods; he didn't expect that she did. "I'll find it. Silver Spring, Maryland, right?"

"Unless he was lying."

"No, why should he? She left for vacation. He reported her missing. That's all he knows."

Lori closes her eyes. "All right, Richard, tell me this. How did he get rid of the body?"

"What do you think?"

"I *don't* think. This is your show."

"He's a medical student, isn't he?"

"Yes."

"Maybe he's creative."

Sunlight at dusk is a golden hue that clings to the Thermopane of the tall buildings and bathes the streets below. Richard walks past the shops on Walnut Street, turning his head to glimpse his reflection in the windows. At the novelty store Accents, a little snow globe on display catches his attention. It is a winter scene, a young girl and boy outfitted for the weather, the snow just waiting to be shaken through the miniature, aqueous wonderland. And now he's looking beyond the scene and the store and into a dimension that exists only for him, and there's Cindy in her bright red scarf with matching earmuffs, she and Richard planted on a sturdy sled tugged down snow-banked Airdale Road by affable Marty, who grips a healthy length of rope attached to the sled's iron grill. The two kids can't be more than five years old, little people on a glorious ride down the middle of the street, snow packed densely on the road surface, polar hillsides plowed against cars sitting silent on a Saturday morning. The agreeably cold air stings their apple cheeks, as they shield their eyes from the sun flaring off of Marty's shoulders as he trudges forward. Cindy's blond hair is like silk, strands playing about the earmuffs. Up and down the street Marty pulls them, two round trips, corner to corner, sweet-tempered Marty at the reins. When they pass in front of their row houses, Richard is the only one to see Herb Dempsey hovering behind his storm door, glowering into the morning. Marty is concentrating on the roadway, and Cindy is purposely looking toward the opposite side of the street.

With a shudder, Richard turns away from the store window and resumes his march down Walnut Street to Rittenhouse Square and through it. A few people are slumped on benches; a young woman totes a creamy shopping bag with black handle-straps, fresh from a fashion excursion. The library across the street from the west side of the square is open until nine o'clock tonight. Through the turnstile and just past the reference desk is the shelf full of yellow telephone directories. In the Maryland section, Richard finds a book marked "Bethesda, Chevy Chase and Silver Spring." Lots of Carsons in there. He finds a dime in his pocket and photocopies the page, the directory's bulk raising the lid like a bridge opening, the machine's oppressive light forcing him to look away. He takes a tiny pencil from a jar at the librarian's desk and jots down the Silver Spring prefix.

He jogs home to test his knee and experiences no discomfort. Mike is at the front desk, a lummox but pleasant enough. Richard's in a hurry and he conveys this to Mike with a raised open hand and a quick "hi Mike," as he lopes toward the elevator.

His apartment is backlit by the city's fluorescence. The tensor lamp on the bedroom desk is a spotlight. He has eleven Carsons to contact in Silver Spring. Or fewer.

The digital clock says eight-sixteen. Primetime for evening phone work.

"Mrs. Carson?"

"Yes?"

"Do you have a daughter named Eleanor?"

"No I don't. Who is this?"

"Sorry to bother you. I have the wrong number."

The forefinger and thumb of his bandaged hand pinching a pen, he lines out "Albert Carson." City lights peek through the open slats of the miniblinds to mingle with the desk lamp's harshness.

"Is this the Carson residence?"

"Yes it is." Another woman, about the right age, so she sounds.

"I'm trying to reach Eleanor Carson."

"There's no Eleanor Carson here."

"Do you have a daughter Eleanor?"

"No, I do not."

"Sorry to bother you."

Next two calls, voice messages. They sound too young, but you can't be sure, nor do you know what combination of people may live in the household. He decides not to leave messages this time around.

Fifth call, a man, contentious at the sound of a strange voice. "Yeah?"

Richard tries a different approach, just for the hell of it. "Mister Carson, my name's Richard Keene. I'm a neighbor of your daughter Eleanor in Philadelphia."

"Well, she's not here."

"She's not?"

"That's what I said."

"I'm sorry, I was told she was visiting you."

"You were told wrong."

"I see. Uh, we live in the same building; I have some important information for her."

"Who the hell are you?"

"Just a neighbor, a friend. Actually, she told me she was coming down to visit you."

Carson eases his tone a bit. "Yeah, she was, but she never showed up."

"Really? She never . . . did she call or—"

"Listen, buddy, tell me what it is you want and if she gets here, I'll tell her, OK? Or better yet, tell her boyfriend, you know him?"

"I do."

"Good, get the message to him. OK." Hangs up.

Richard holds the phone to his ear for a few seconds and listens to the dial tone. "Daddy's little girl," he says to himself.

Cars slash by on Kennedy Boulevard, their beams like broadsides into the night. Richard waits at the light for the pedestrian icon to flash at 20th Street canyoned below broad, towering apartment buildings where soft silent night-lighting watches over mezzanine-level shops. He has overruled himself and left the Walkman at home, is taking the city's best shot by night. He moves quickly on the sidewalk, hugging the buildings' granite bases, skirting shadows, veering streetside for a better vantage point when alleys interrupt the pathway, just in case someone or something is lurking. At The Brasserie, a self-consciously hip hangout that boasts the town's widest selection of brews, a couple sits at a two-seat circular table just inside the window, the girl twirling a swizzle stick in her drink and looking up with adoring eyes, the guy with a sleepy-smug expression.

Down by the Parkway, activity picks up. Red-jacketed parking valets at the Four Seasons Hotel scurry to collect sedans, as a fountain spurts over the gray raised-brick driveway that aprons the entrance. With the traffic light, Richard jogs across the Parkway, its numerous lanes and broad medial strips. He's retracing his steps from the previous day. The time has come for phase two.

117

From the outside, the police station looks like an ordinary office with a few people working late, several windows lit. The desk sergeant sends Richard back to see Sgt. Oliver, who handles Missing Persons most of the time, including tonight's shift. Richard wears imitation-Reebok sneakers that pad along the tiled corridor. Oliver's office is deserted except for the sergeant himself, a big man with a hoagie roll girdling his midsection and pushing his belt buckle south. His hound-dog eyes and cheeks betray a weariness that makes it difficult to assess whether he'll tilt toward friendly or nasty when pressed. Richard faces him on the other side of the half-door. Oliver has him by a good five inches.

"Can I help you?" Oliver asks. He notices Richard's bandaged hand.

Richard, his arms crossed at parade rest, knows the name and the clipped voice after yesterday's brief telephone conversation at the outdoor kiosk. Same man working both shifts. Good omen. "Missing Persons, right?"

"That's right. What can I do for you?"

"Uh, you have a missing person reported yesterday named Eleanor Carson."

Oliver is looking dead at Richard with flannel-gray eyes that you expect to be watery but aren't. "Uh-huh," he says.

"I have some information that might help."

"Who are you?"

"My name is Richard Keene. I'm a neighbor of Miss Carson's."

"Neighbor?"

"We live in the same building . . . one floor apart."

Sgt. Oliver scratches his considerable ear, checks a loose-leaf folder stuffed with papers. "The 42s, right?"

"Yes."

"OK, Mister Keene, whadiyou have?"

"She was supposed to be on vacation visiting her father in Maryland, but he says she wasn't there at all."

"We know that, we've already talked to him."

Richard has figured as much, has counted on Braun to supply all information excluding the fact that he committed murder. He nods at Oliver, one investigator acknowledging another.

"How'd you find this out?" Oliver asks.

"I called Mister Carson."

A smile from Oliver. "You investigatin' the case, son?"

Richard reflexively stares at his shoetops. "Better let the police handle it," Oliver says. "You a good friend of Ms. Carson's?"

Richard looks up. "I think you should broaden your investigation." Matter-of-fact, no dramatics.

Oliver sees intensity in Richard's eyes, but is not receptive to recommendations from sources other than his superiors, and at this stage of his career, only occasionally from them. He's had enough dead ends in MP and other assorted beats to stock a medieval maze. From the mayor down to kindergartners, everybody likes to tell the police how to do their job.

Oliver leans into the opening, his weariness slouching toward irritation. "What would you suggest, young man?"

He's being patronized—Richard feels it—but it's not the neck-burn variety, just business. Accordingly, he has nothing smart-alecky in his voice when he answers, "Investigate her boyfriend."

Oliver starts to close the door's top half, as he says, "Thanks for the tip," but Richard stops him with an earnest, "Sgt. Oliver, I know who did it. She was murdered and I know who did it." Oliver angles his bulk back into full view. "Say again?"

"Eleanor Carson was murdered, Sergeant, or at least somebody was, yesterday a week ago in apartment 2307 at the 42s building at 15th and Locust."

Richard's faint trembling subsides. Something he had to spill out. The peace, of course, will not last long.

"What happened to your hand?" Oliver asks him.

"Banged it against some metal," Richard says, with no hesitation. "Nothing to do with this."

"Glad to hear that," Oliver says wryly. He feels something for this guy standing before him. Not a whole lot yet, but something. Thirty years as a cop on the street, a metric ton of slop and ghastliness, and he's almost been hardened to the point where human discomfort is of no account. But he still thinks in terms of results. Maybe what he has here is the discomfort of confessing to an odious crime. "Tell me about it," he says to his potential confessor, and thuds open the bottom half of the door with the heel of his large hand. Richard follows him inside the office and sits down at a gray metal desk whose rubberized top lips the sides.

He tells his story as precisely as he can, which is to say, he has command of all details and doesn't leave a single one out. About the Eleanor Carson case, that is, nothing about Cindy Dempsey. This isn't the time to go into that. Oliver takes notes and tape-records Richard's testimony, including his delineation of all of the sounds and their sequence. It is an amazing story, to be sure, unique in Oliver's personal annals and one he has never heard about elsewhere. This business of sorting out subtle sounds, the real ones interspersed with the movie soundtrack. He cannot be sure if Richard is a genius of sorts, a jilted suitor, or a neurotic nutcase, a guy who's—yeah, right—seen too many movies. Keep an open mind, his training tells him. He tells Richard he'll be following up on the bank visit, that he'll know if anything irregular has occurred. Routine.

"By the way, where's the body?" Oliver asks.

Richard looks at him, not knowing whether to smile or look serious. "I don't know," he says. "But I'll find out."

Oliver's wide face relaxes into a tired smile, a career's worth of having seen just about everything. Just about. "Keep me posted."

After three decades on the Philadelphia Police force, Robert J. Oliver has been marking time until a year-end retirement, a pension, a party, sayonara, and exit to a cabin near a lake in the Pocono Mountains. Freeze your ass off in the winter, but fishing and true-blue skies when the weather warms. Nice way to play out the string.

He's a respected cop after all this time, though he's a husk of the man who walked beats, caught his share of bad guys, and helped innovate community policing in Philadelphia neighborhoods. An offensive guard on his high school football team several centuries ago, he was an indomitable foot soldier who created daylight for flashy ballcarriers to run through, and his style remained the same when he put on the blue uniform. He thinks Philly top cop Frank Rizzo went too far, poured fuel on racial fires, though he liked the man's toughness, leadership, charisma. New York import John Timoney hit all the right notes, a capable lower-key leader. Different time.

Oliver worked the long hard hours, but always sought balance between his job and his personal life. His easiest assignment was to love his wife. He was also crazy about his kids. Well, at least his daughter.

Balance, Sgt. Robert Oliver learned, is a state of mind and of reality that can easily become imbalance.

He has let his body go, let it get soft and bulgy, no use trying to get back in shape, no one on his ear to do so. He's fired on people, hit some, never killed anyone, not in thirty-two years. Took a couple in the body, sheathed by a protective vest, no damage. Closing out the show on a desk, tracking the missing, those who run away or wind up in a river or are never heard from again or come home after a seventy-two-hour washout.

Kids on a bus to nowhere, vanished housewives and college students, guys fleeing their lives, perplexing, absurd, sometimes downright silly, sometimes very very ugly.

He's a widower, his wife claimed by cancer. It's been five years.

His daughter is dead.

Three years ago, she was twenty-three, the convertible on the losing end of a collision with a tree trunk anchored to a hillside on a wicked country curve thick with 20 m.p.h. signs, her boyfriend at the wheel going three times that fast, no drinking, just indescribable arrogance and stupidity. Death instantaneous for both of them.

Playing out the string. Can't ride to the rescue anymore for somebody else's misfortune. His own is too strong.

This Richard fellow, this Richard Kane, whatever it is, Richard Keene . . . something about this guy. He's got a helluva concoction here, but doesn't come across as out of it or self-important. A strong personal connection to the case, but not panicky or full of "why don't you do something?" So, he told him he'd call the missing girl's boyfriend back and maybe send the police out for a look-see.

Of course, if the kid's nuts, then he's nuts, and nothing Oliver does will help him. Such things, like most things, are out of his hands.

Richard moves furtively through the night and back home to the 42s. His investigation is indeed entering a new phase, branching out. He needs to show what might have become of the body, as a prelude to determining what did become of the body. It's up to him to develop the hypothesis; nobody else is working on one.

Time has passed, eight days to be exact, more than enough time in which to dispose of a body when no eyes are on you and no one's pressing to know of the missing person's where-abouts.

Braun's a med student, has access to special resources. Sure. He sneaks the body into the morgue, then on to the crematorium before anyone knows who she is, knows what's happening.

No, impossible, too many people in the process. Too much chance for discovery.

He just dumps it in the river. Crude, but effective. A possibility.

Whatever the final destination, there's the challenge of removing the body from the highrise. Twenty-three floors up.

When Richard opens the sliding-glass door and steps onto his balcony, the city's night sounds hit him like a dam break. The building directly across Locust is fourteen or fifteen stories high, he guesses, and its rooftop compressor below him hisses into the night. He hooks his hands around the top of the metal railing, leans forward and stares between buildings through to Walnut Street, a block north, now glazed by drizzle. A rude car horn seems to leap up the curtain of mist and smack him in the face.

He looks left toward an office building and squints to pick up any movement in the dim light behind the immovable windows, something as pedestrian as a cleaning cart being pushed between cubicles, or as prurient as a coupling on top of a desk. All he sees, though, are shadows and barriers and the still-life of computers and swivel chairs.

In the twenty-second-floor hallway, the lights mounted to the wall buzz like hives of hornets. Richard stands before the elevators, hands on hips as if daring the closed doors to spring open and toss him answers. He moves to the end of the hallway and opens the door to the fire tower. Wire grids the thick glass of the little square window at eye-level. Inside, Richard stands on the landing and peers over the railing, downward at the alternately angled flights of stairs that continue beyond his span of vision. It is a long way down to lug a body. But a body in, say, a tall rectangular box (for a pedestal lamp? a barbell?) could ride smartly down the elevator, then be carted on wheels or even carried by a strong fellow like Braun to a waiting car in the parking garage. A one-man job.

Or a body sectioned in two could make the trip in a pair of large suitcases. Gruesome, the stuff of tabloid front pages and Hitchcock movies, but possible. Feasible is another question, the noise of sawing off body parts, the mess, the time and effort, the potential for discovery. But that lamp box. Sure, maybe. Then the next problem becomes disposal, disposal that precludes discovery.

Richard returns to the elevators and sees the door to the trash room tucked into an alcove. He enters and shuts the door gently behind him. A mild scent of spoil and cinders climbs through his nose and plops onto his tongue. Flattened cardboard and stacked newspapers adorn the wall opposite a fleet of battleship-gray circuit-breaker boxes and a tangle of cable lines. A metal flap fronts the trash chute embedded in the wall. Richard tugs it open and looks into the blackness, the garbage scent rising from the depths. He lets go of the flap and it snaps shut. He stands there, staring at it, then opens it again. He's jammed some fat trash bags down there, he knows that much.

He sniffs the air, opens the flap again, halfway, lets it spring shut.

He's back in his apartment, at the kitchen phone, calling Lori. Tucked under the cabinetry, the soft counter lighting gives the room a relaxed glow, the soothing light Richard always associates with a kitchen at nighttime.

"Hello?" He loves the sound of her voice.

"Lori, it's Richard."

"Hi, how's your hand?"

"Fine, it's OK. Listen, how about he brought her down in some kind of tall cardboard box, like for curtain rods or something?"

"And then?"

Richard smiles to himself. They're thinking alike.

"Good question . . . And then he dumps it somewhere."

"Where?"

"I don't know, in the river or something," Richard says, just making conversation now.

"Hmmm . . . awkward. Lugging that thing around. And the chance of getting found out. He'd be smarter than that, wouldn't he? How 'bout slice and dice?"

Richard cringes in fun as if she were in the room with him. "Lori, please."

"Sorry."

"Maybe, though . . . surgical instruments . . ."

"Or a good hacksaw."

"You're murder, Lori." Maybe she's just playing, but maybe it's more than that.

"He doesn't seem like the type," she says.

"What type?"

"A hacker."

"You don't always get what you expect."

"True, life's full of surprises."

"Exactly."

There's a charged silence between them, delicious to Richard.

"So, inspector?" she asks.

"Well, whole or not, he needs a way to ship it out of there."

"Airborne Express?"

He can't help but laugh. "Very funny . . . How about this: down the trash chute."

"The trash chute? Come on, too skinny."

"I don't think so; it looks wide enough to me for, say, a slender woman. You could fit down there, God forbid. Down the chute, into the Dumpster, and off to the landfill. No one's the wiser."

"Wrapped in something."

"Nice and tight. Right down into the pile. Stays overnight or he makes the drop early the next morning timed for pickup. The whole thing orchestrated with that timing in mind."

"Richard . . ."

"Yuh?"

"This is getting scary." She doesn't sound like she's kidding now.

"It was scarier for Eleanor Carson."

Richard's in the elevator and his senses are on high alert, every fiber taut and pointing him toward the center of this matter. He can feel how attracted he is to Lori, and another part of his brain worries that this will impede his work. He can't let that happen, must harness his feelings.

He approaches Frank, working a double shift this day, just standing there, watching Richard step off the elevator and walk toward him. Frank sees the bandaged hand and shakes his head. "Here comes trouble," he says, but the words are rimmed with something close to affection at this point.

Richard is direct, but with none of the uptight mannerisms of earlier go-rounds, his voice relaxed. "Frank, you know this building pretty well?"

"Been here six years."

"Structurally?"

Frank settles in; the 42s is his joint. "Well, I'm no engineer, but try me."

"When you drop something down the trash chute, does it go all the way down?" Richard's forefinger leads his right arm down from shoulder-level to mid-thigh to underscore his question.

"Straight to the Dumpster."

"In one shot?"

"One shot."

"That's what I thought, from no matter where you are."

"No matter where. Same thing, every floor."

"Straight down." Richard reprises his arm motion.

"Straight down." Frank enjoys being the answer man.

"Thanks, Frank."

"Anytime, my man. You think you got somethin' stuck in there?"

"No."

"Good . . . Hey, what happened to your hand?"

"Ah, nothin'."

"You takin' on Mike Tyson or somethin'?"

"Not yet," Richard says, and chuckles at his retort, not because it's witty but because he feels good about engaging in such mindless banter, being one of the guys. As Richard heads back to the elevator, Frank shakes his head in amusement. Just as he's about to press the button, Richard whirls on his heels like a marching soldier doing an about-face and, indeed, marches back to Frank.

"You didn't by any chance see Davis Braun carrying out anything large and bulky in the past week?"

Frank folds his arms, thin short-sleeves hiking up past the knot of muscle just above the elbow. "You gotta ruin things, don't you?"

"Can't help it."

"You mean like a body or somethin'? No, he didn't parade nothin' past me."

Frank turns away and doesn't catch Richard's expression that stops just short of a smile. "Good," Richard says, and Frank doesn't quite know what to make of that.

11

Richard figures that Frank knows his business but, just the same, he must test the assertion about the trash chute. He opens the bifold door to his bedroom closet and pulls down from the painted-white metal shelf a plastic shopping bag embossed with the words "Worthington's Sporting Goods," the shop on Chestnut where he picked up some socks and gym shorts a couple of weeks back. In the kitchen he dumps his trash can's contents into the Worthington's bag, empty tuna and sardine cans and moldering banana peels and crumpled tissues cascading from the plastic liner to a new home. Then he pulls the bag's drawstring tight and knots it, carries the bag out of his apartment and into the trash room, where he promptly drops it down the chute. He hustles to the elevator, takes it to the lobby and as he approaches the front desk, calls out, "Frank, can you let me in the Dumpster room for a second?"

"What now, Keene?"

"Just checking on something."

"It's locked after hours."

"I know that. That's why I'm asking you to open it."

"What for?"

"I want to make sure you know the chute as well as you think you do."

A worried look in Frank's eyes. "What'd you drop down there, a mattress?"

"C'mon, let's have a look."

Frank gives in and follows him through the mail area and the rear door outside onto the loading platform; keys open the door to the Dumpster room. "You know you can't get back in this way."

"I know." Richard steps past Frank and looks back at him. "You don't have to hang around, I'll be fine."

"Knock yourself out," Frank says and closes the door.

The overhead lights stay on all the time. The huge green Dumpster sits below the chute mouth, or, to be accurate, the chute's rectal opening. Richard's a stickler for accuracy.

He strides to the Dumpster, steps onto a low ledge, reaches upward until his elbows clear the top, and hoists his torso up and over for a look-see. As he does this, several trash bags slide through the chute and onto the Dumpster's asymmetrical pile, at the center of which a volcano-shaped mound of refuse has formed.

Something else is coming down the chute with the whoosh of trailing air and gathering speed. Richard can hear it way up high as it free-falls, and as it draws closer and the rush of its descent whistles through the cylinder . . .

He is careening down the waterslide, its sturdy plastic lubricated by a constant flow of chlorinated pool water propelled onto the surface by tiny jets at the base of the curved sidings. As he zooms downward, he likes to focus on a single object: the clock mounted to the clubhouse facade on the other side of the pool is his usual target. He watches that clock all the way down, its hands unmoving within the couple of seconds it takes for him to hit the water. There is something tantalizing about courting the combined danger of height and speed, leaving caution behind, not even following the course with your eyes, secure in the safety promised by an adult world of structure and equipment. Nowhere on earth does he feel safer than on the waterslide, which deposits him in the boundless pool waters that ripple and chunk toward the shore of clubhouse and horizon. And now it is her turn, and he waits in the shallow water, moving back a few feet to allow her landing room. She is sitting at the very top of the slide, where it levels into a seat just above the last rung of the ladder behind it. Other girls scream when they slide down, and their arms and legs fly out with abandon as the bottom drops out from under them, but Cindy pilots her ride, controls the descent, enjoys it but doesn't give in to it. She is a young athlete in a young girl's one-piece bathing suit, navy blue and molded to her smooth sun-carameled skin. She slaloms down the slide on outstretched ski-legs and enters the water with the clean minimal splash of an Olympic diver and, in that moment, as in many others, Richard is proud of her and feels something of the love he might have for a sister if he had a sister, but something beyond that, too, something he can't quite locate, since he is only eight years old after all, and . . .

A shopping-size paper bag plops into the Dumpster, contents spilling out: a jar of spaghetti sauce laced with red remnants not headed for the calmer climes of recycling, a disfigured TV dinner carton, scattered large fruit pits someone kept from a clash with the garbage disposal.

So many ways to dispose of things.

The Worthington's bag is sitting there, sandwiched between a bundle of newspapers and a bulging oil-colored Hefty jumbo. Richard nods to himself and eases off of the Dumpster.

The next step will be to test a body-equivalency down the Dumpster. And then give the results to the police. It's not an automatic, but they just might pay attention.

While Richard is sparring with the MRI machine in the late afternoon, Lori Calder is pruning some verbiage from proposed credit-card solicitation copy, as she sits at her desk in her First Federal Bancorp office on the seventh floor of Two Liberty

Center, a dark monolith that has joined the ranks of towers dwarfing Philly's former skyline apex, the statue of William Penn on top of City Hall. Penn still looks proud and unperturbed, but no longer so grand, as he holds his perch amid the steel-glass forest.

Lori is the designated writer on a five-person crew that develops marketing campaigns for which the department vice-president takes credit when they go well, and from which he distances himself when they bomb. She's the only person within thirty cubicles who knows an adverb from an adjective; the others crunch numbers, remedy computer program glitches, or devise "systems" flow charts with lots of boxes and arrows and jargon. Department VP Dan Stubbleman is an erratic manager and a clunky writer who appreciates Lori's fluid prose and trim little body. Though she has no plans to have him sample the latter, she's not averse to wearing short skirts, well aware that sweet-and-sexy is a potent combo in the corporate world, as it is just about anywhere. And someone who can write a complete sentence as well? Suffice it to say she has a bright future at First Federal.

It's been only five years since she graduated from Villanova University, where she was the brainiest girl on the cheerleading squad, moving adeptly from splits-on-the-hardwood at Philadelphia's creaky Palestra or 'Nova's fieldhouse to shunting Bunsen burner flames in chemistry lab and writing mature essays on Romantic Poetry and twentieth-century fiction in English Lit classes. She didn't, however, have specific career goals, and her Bachelor's Degree in American Studies wasn't a passport to any specific destination. When First Federal offered her a job after an interview on campus, she liked the salary and the center-city location. Living blocks away from theaters and concert halls is her idea of a lifestyle, as is dancing with attitude in late-night clubs like the Boiler Room on Second Street or Destiny on

Columbus Boulevard down near the Delaware River. There she can transform herself if only for a few hours, put on the cutaway tank top and the leather mini, and do some serious undulating, grind hips with guys who may not frequent Barnes & Noble, but look pretty damn good in their hardcovers. Lori digs life, likes to explore the facets of her personality.

As the afternoon at First Federal veers toward the witching hour, Lori blue-pencils the hard copy she's been handed by Stubbleman, the prose that she originally crafted manhandled by his mangled syntax and unfortunate word choices. Choosing the right word to appear in print is like taking a good shot in basketball, thinks Lori, a former high school point guard. Most people don't perceive nuance or seek originality; they just regurgitate TV-speak or sports lingo or the excruciating phraseology of formal reports.

Still, Stubbleman is smart enough to relax his ego and entrust her with the final draft even after he has dumped his bricks onto the page. When he can't find his way through a tortured explanation, he spits out in the margins, "Something like that," leaving the substance of that "something," of course, to Lori. She feels his pain, the galoot. Sure she does.

"Here are the present-value calculations," says Steve Bettinger, breezing into her tidy little office and dropping a sheaf of papers onto her desk.

"Thanks, Bettinger."

"Anytime, Calder. How's the writing coming?"

"The usual. I write and he rewrites. Or tries to."

"Tell 'im to get bent."

"I'll try to remember that phrase come review time."

"Absolutely."

Bettinger is a young guy with a slight build and a well-cultivated mustache. He likes to act as casual as humanly possible, which is a plus to Lori, but he also tries to be clever all the time, and he's never clever, so that's a minus. Not that she's considering him romantically—he's not her type, plus he's married—but as co-workers, they have a fair amount of interaction, and Lori likes things to crackle, to sing.

"Check those PV figures," Bettinger says, moving to Lori's side of the desk and pointing at his stack. "This thing could make us a mint."

"Always looks good on paper," Lori says, clucking her tongue like a schoolgirl. "Anyway, *we* don't make the mint."

"I'm a company man; what goes around comes around." He's on the move again, making an exit. "Don't forget to get my name in there, sweets. Compiled by Bettinger, two T's."

"Got it," Lori says, waving him off. Not a bad sort, this Bettinger, but nothing dynamic there, either. A numbers cruncher saddled with a family at a relatively young age.

She stands and stretches, up and down on her tiptoes to give her calves a little work, and moves to the window. In the distance, the Parkway shoots straight to the Art Museum, and a ribbon of Schuylkill River curls past upraised train tracks that bank and wind toward the yawning blackness of the 30th Street Station underpass.

While Lori is massaging her boss's First Federal Charge Card Department written proposal, Janet Kroll is at Felice for a cut and some color. She's diligent about masking her natural brunette with an autumn-leaves red—not to satisfy some personal indulgence but to be sure, just to be sure. That, along with the eyebrow thinning and the pounds she's shed, making her figure model-curvy rather than plumply voluptuous. Just to be sure she's not recognized, even though it's a long shot she would be, even with no modifications.

Felice himself does her hair in his walk-up salon on Locust near the Square. Janet likes him; he's a handsome guy, fortyish,

Mediterranean, with sensitive eyes and the sweetest temperament she's ever encountered in a man. His wife, also a sweetie, interior-decorated the shop, and handles the books along with the manes of the few male customers; they like her to do the honors on a shampoo and cut.

As Janet approaches the redstone steps, she sees through the tall window facing Locust Street that Felice has just finished with his two o'clock, a woman with hollowed cheeks and coarse bruise-colored hair that Felice has just smoothed and lightened back to presentability.

"Hi, Phil," Janet says, entering.

"Hello, beautiful."

"Thanks, Felice," his refurbished customer says, eyeing Janet and looking around for a clock that can be pushed back thirty years.

"You very welcome," he says, opening the door and giving her a wide berth. "You look very nice . . . absolutely."

"Thanks, honey," she says, stepping down. "See you in a month."

Felice closes the door and turns to Janet with a smile that lights up his face and the room. "Here she is," he says. "My stunner." And with her svelter figure, now prominent cheekbones and perfectly framed hazel eyes, Janet is magazine-cover material. "Honey, look who's here," Phil calls to his wife, who pokes her head out of the rear-office doorway.

"Hiya, Janet," she says.

"Hi, Chris."

Janet settles into the cushioned black leather and cocks an eye at Felice.

"So?" he asks.

"How about some blond highlights, Phil, what do you think?"

He appraises her in the mirror, knits his brows and nods. "I like it." He steps toward the mirror and plucks an expensive-looking bottle off the counter. "I've got some new foil." He offers it to her like a Christmas gift. "The best . . . from France."

"Foil me, baby." Janet winks at him and Felice laughs.

"You hear this, Christina?" he hollers toward the back.

"I'm keeping close tabs," she says, slightly nasal, out of view.

Janet looks straight ahead at her image in the mirror, as Felice fastens the sheet around her neck. Not bad, she thinks, not bad at all. She was always pretty, wholesome, kind of hearty-sexy, but now the features are classical and the body contours sculpted. She's been training for months, the last several weeks at the 42s. The new red hair rivets the eye; spike it with some blond and voila . . . overpowering. Janet Kroll, erstwhile girl next door.

Her ex-husband would pop his eyes.

She finds that she likes this aroma of intrigue, the element of danger. But she won't let it overwhelm her or seduce her. She's too smart for that. She is at risk, and is not about to lose sight of what she's after.

Sex as weaponry is a new dynamic for her. Her prime asset was always her brains, which are considerable. Karen was the one with the personality and the sly sexiness, the little sister with the rebellious streak, big sister Janet stable and straight A's and always battling a tendency to chubbiness. Karen the one with the boys flocking, Karen the one embracing hip fashions, then bad-girl duds. Two very different girls from the same suburban upbringing of ease but not opulence, a doting father and a mother who was loving but a little tougher, a backyard patio and paramecium-shaped swimming pool, holiday barbecues, exchange visits with cousins. Karen was no dummy, but a cerebral match for her sister only in math, a terrific facility with numbers, one she would utilize in her job as a casino blackjack dealer, a job that her parents despised.

Felice works fast, expertly. "I think you rather like this, no?"

he says to Janet as they both appraise her now blond-streaked red hair in the mirror. He's cut it shorter, and it hangs straight and moist, shower-emerged.

"Very cool," Christina says, escaping her ledger in the backroom and walking to her husband's side behind Janet. "Very cool," she repeats, and Janet is taken with what she sees in the mirror, her furtive smile a reflex confirming that this further altered appearance offers even greater protection, and that aesthetically, it is quite welcome.

It's not external noise that robs Richard of his sleep this night, but the clatter inside his head, the churning anticipation of what he must do the next day and the day after that, and continue to do without letup until things are set right.

He dozes off just as the sun is coming up, and catches an hour or so before the morning racket and his own internals jar him awake. A half hour later, the sun is burning off the haze cloaking the skyscrapers, as he searches his short stack of business cards pinched by a rubber band. There it is, Terry Runnels, General Motors, all the way out there in some suburb of Detroit. Terry Runnels, an engineer now, always a whiz in math, a high school and then a college classmate, a guy who, unlike Richard, transferred to a four-year college and completed his bachelor's degree.

Terry Runnels, the man to call for a crash-test dummy.

Richard waits an hour to call because Michigan is on Central Time.

He is building a case piece by piece, constructing a plausible scenario for the police to act on, one that he envisions will lead to a court order to dig up a landfill somewhere and produce a body. He will demonstrate how the crime could have been committed, how it was committed; the *why* will follow.

137

He is sure of himself, sure of what happened, sure of who did it and what he did afterward. He feels the certainty deep inside, in what some may call his soul.

Meanwhile, since he's newly jobless, between revelations, between breaks in the case, he needs to kill hours and, in the afternoon, is back on the treadmill, sweating, running at an unbearable clip, every once in awhile wincing from the pain in his knee. He can run through the pain, it's always been his way. Pain in the joints or of the psyche, no different. Just run through it. Somewhere, sometime, he sees himself coming out the other end, to a place where soothing light drapes the landscape and the very air is a balm. The pain evaporates and the world relaxes as if it has just rid itself of a muscle cramp.

His day goes by in daydreams.

He finds himself holding a half-gallon jug of filtered water, as he stands in line at the Wawa convenience mart two doors from the 42s parking garage. One man in line wears unbuckled galoshes and a green army jacket suited for temperatures about forty degrees colder. Young women, early twenties, ask for cigarettes, cartons of them. The register clerk is flabby-cheeked and congenial, dispensing death.

Richard totes his water back toward the 42s and, as he draws to within fifty feet, he sees a couple emerge from the entrance alcove, two people who are immediately familiar to him but not as a pairing; he has not seen them together before. The woman has a great shape in her form-fitting cocktail dress and sharp arresting features topped by chin-length red hair now with blond highlights like streaks of gold dust. The man is broad and athletic, an easy gait in his powder-blue sportcoat and charcoal slacks, lots of blond hair falling naturally onto his forehead.

Janet Kroll and Davis Braun are obviously out for the evening and looking quite pleased with each other, sufficiently absorbed not to notice Richard, who angles past them and into the building, keeping some distance and averting his face. Inside, he steps quickly to the front desk.

"Frank, can you watch this for me?" Richard holds up the transparent jug of water. "I forgot something; I'll be back in a minute."

Frank gives him a half-lidded look and a mocking tone. "Why sure, my man. That's all part of our 24-hour service here at the 42s."

Richard's not dense, he knows the score here, he'll take what he can get. He's winning Frank over gradually, he thinks. "Thanks," he says simply and is already in motion, headed back out the door. Right away, he's got Janet and Braun in his sights; they're at the end of the block, crossing 16th Street. He follows on the other side of Locust, the sidewalk busy with two-way traffic. The Couple of the Evening—they are a helluva couple, Richard concedes—cross at 17th and continue two more blocks to Potcheen's and its row of outdoor tables dressed in linen. Janet and Braun step under the canopy and sit at a table; Richard stays to the other side of the street and keeps walking.

They are holding hands across the table.

"A surgeon," Braun says.

"Why?"

"The responsibility. A surgeon holds your life in his hands, delves right into your center, your inner workings. I'm talking organ surgery, of course."

"Open heart?"

"Yes . . . lungs, thorax, a vascular surgeon."

She feels the veiny strength of his hand, the sinewy web between thumb and forefinger. "You have the hands for it."

He smiles and gives her hand a little squeeze. "I think I have the temperament for it. You have to be cool under fire . . . fierce concentration."

"Which you have?"

"I think I do."

"You're probably being modest."

"No, not really."

Janet takes a sip of Chablis. "Money's not bad either, huh?"

When Braun smiles a small smile, there's a flash of white teeth. Handsome guy, she can't help but realize. "You're in real estate," he says, "so I know you don't think money's a bad thing."

"That's certainly true, but I only make it when I produce."

"It's the same, to varying degrees, in any profession."

"You're right, of course. Except real estate's a bigger pain in the ass than most."

Braun laughs, and this time the teeth are bared between his creased cheeks. He likes this Janet, a dynamite-looking, ballsy woman with a nice sweet side, too; more direct and confident than Eleanor. He's always had the open relationship with Ellie; live-in but not exclusive. So no guilt here.

They dine on seafood—scallops for her, crabcakes for him—lubricated by the white wine. When their waitress arrives with their check in a leather billfold, Janet reaches for it first.

"I get the commission on that Society Hill townhouse this week," she says. "And you're not a surgeon yet."

Wow, this is some girl, Braun thinks. "You planning to spoil me?"

Janet slips her American Express card behind the billfold's soft-plastic flap. "That's my prerogative."

"Just checking about that trip to the bank, Sergeant. He didn't by any chance cash a check endorsed by her, did he?"

Richard's back in his apartment and on the phone after a one-hour stakeout of Janet and Braun during which he walked around Rittenhouse Square several times until they paid their tab, left Potcheen's and walked to the Sameric at 19th and Chestnut to take in a movie, his guess the romantic comedy with Sandra Bullock. On the other end of the line, Sgt. Oliver got on with a gruff flatness, but now is forthcoming.

"As a matter of fact, that's correct," says Oliver, pulling another night shift, a note of surprise in his voice. "We picked that up right away. Braun says Miss Carson post-dated a check so he could get the funds in her absence. You guessed that, huh Keene?"

"Yes."

"Well don't get excited, they'd done it before."

"She didn't disappear before."

"Neither did her money."

"What do you mean?"

"She just closed her account."

"By mail?" Richard is rocking in his chair, nodding to himself, going with it, anticipating something like this.

"In person."

He stops rocking. "In person?" Now he wants the rest of the story. "OK, so she's back in town, huh? Case solved."

"Not exactly. Braun hasn't seen her. Neither has her employer."

Of course they haven't. "But the bank ID'd her?"

"Not quite, but the signature can."

"It's a phony."

"We're having it checked."

"Well, did his description match Miss Carson?"

"The teller can't really remember what she looked like."

Richard's adding things up, then—"Wait a minute, don't security cameras record every transaction these days?"

"When they're working?"

"You mean . . . ?"

"You got it, they were on the blink."

141

Richard looks at his reflection in a narrow rectangle of darkened bedroom window, the bottom of the blinds bunched a foot above the sill. "Great. Isn't that a little suspicious, Sergeant? The teller could be in on it."

Oliver's sniffer hasn't dried up; he doesn't need a pathfinder. "Let's hold the conspiracy theories for the time being, OK, Keene? It's not out of the ordinary for a store clerk or a bank teller not to be able to positively identify a customer. Could be someone he's only seen that one time, nothing special about the transaction."

"She closed her account—isn't that pretty involved?" Richard asks.

"Not necessarily. Can be a routine matter."

"Nothing special happened that he remembers?"

Oliver likes Keene's doggedness. Or the guy could be a murderer playing with him. Either way, he's had enough for now. "We know how to question people in these kinds of circumstances, Keene. We can do our job without your oversight, all right?"

"All right."

Oliver hangs with him on the phone, sensing across the line this boy's need for help, a silent cry. Help for what? It's Oliver who keeps the conversation going. "You know that super-hearing of yours?"

Richard sounds faraway. "It's a curse."

That kind of talk makes Oliver uneasy; he doesn't want this kid to be a nut. "But you're pretty sure of it, aren't you? I mean, you trust it."

"Yes."

"All right, that's important. That's a big part of being a witness. If you don't trust yourself, how can we?"

"True."

"Good, we're in agreement."

Richard wants to tell him things. "When I hear what no one else does, I feel like I've been given a weapon but I don't know how to use it. What can I do with it, except what I'm doing right now? When I scale the heights, you see, when I get way up high and out in the open, like, nothing bothers me, I'm fearless. More than that, I'm *free*. When I hear things, I'm scared and . . . I'm trapped by it."

Oliver blows air through his lips, forcing them open, his cheeks puffing out. "What are you, a mountain climber or something?"

"No, not exactly. Bridges, towers, wherever I can get away."

Oliver isn't sure what the hell Richard is talking about, but he can't bring himself to dismiss this young man, feels the need for a small concession. "You know what, son?" He's giving the kid the benefit of the doubt, and his voice relaxes enough so that Richard picks up the change in tone. "Your instincts are good. I did expect that teller to make a positive ID."

That snaps Richard back to business. "He does say it was a woman who made the transaction?"

"That's right, there's no question about that."

"At least he remembers that much, huh, Sergeant?"

Richard has Silver Spring on the line.

"I didn't want to bother you again, Mister Carson, but maybe you can help. The police are investigating a check endorsed by your daughter over to Davis Braun, and—"

"Are you with the police?"

"No sir, I'm not."

"Then what business is it of yours?"

"Let me get this straight, sir, it doesn't bother you that—"

"What bothers me is *my* business."

"I think Braun had the check forged."

"Then the police'll find that out."

"Don't you care about your daughter, Mister Carson?"

The voice turns from agitated to ugly. "You got nerve, kid, I'll give you that . . . Look"—with that single word, Carson suddenly sounds like he's no longer angry, like he wants Richard to understand—"none of this is any big surprise. See, she's been known to disappear from time to time, short stretches, clear her head. I don't know, she's a free spirit or somethin', get it? If you know her, you know what I mean."

Richard swallows, squares his shoulders and delivers the line with the calm certitude of a coroner. "I think your daughter's dead."

"Really?" Now a mocking tone flares in Carson. "And why do you think that?"

"Because I heard her getting murdered."

"You are a sick puppy, you know that? What the hell's the matter with you?"

"I'm sorry you feel that—"

"You pissed off about Ellie or somethin'? What's with you?"

"Ask yourself this, Mister Carson: Why would I bother you about it?"

"How do I know? 'Cause you're a nut." Richard hears the receiver bang down, a harsh cracking noise followed by the unsettling void of a dial tone.

Spanning the Delaware River between Philadelphia's waterfront Penn's Landing and long-blighted Camden, New Jersey, the Benjamin Franklin Bridge is anchored on great granite piles sunken in the riverbanks like medieval castles with submerged drawbridges. Above the bridge deck, thick cable lines soar toward steel towers painted a gas-flame blue and, on outboard sidings, high-speed trains usher commuters back and forth across the river. Old, faded structures hard by the bridge are dwarfed by the skyward sweep; an aged church steeple once toppled onto the roadway, denting the macadam and displacing a congregation.

Davis Braun is tooling his Acura on the Ben Franklin, headed back from Jersey into Philadelphia, Janet Kroll by his side. Moments ago, they were strolling on the Camden waterfront, where the lit-up State Aquarium etched its reflections on the black creases of the Delaware River, and the late-night breeze off the water both soothed and stirred. The sky sported a honeydew moon. It was a quick trip, a romantic whim, an evening capper after the movie.

Now Braun looks at her and their smiles are the mellow suggestion of comfort with each other, as good a fit and as sensual as the leather contours beneath them. When he interrupts the mood by plucking his cell phone out of the console between the bucket seats and punching in the Verizon message retrieval number, Janet feels a little kick inside herself, a reminder of why she's here. "Sorry," he says. "Just checking messages . . . expecting something." He's only five or ten minutes from home, but likes to get a jump on his messages, prepare himself mentally for the proper response to important ones. He's already getting offers to join hospitals, surgical practices when he completes his residency next year. He would not mind returning to the hospital near Cape May, New Jersey, where he worked last year under the reciprocal agreement with Metro. He likes the seashore.

He's thinking about such things, but is not surprised when he hears Dan Carson's voice, the second message. He's not surprised, either, that Carson sounds upset. "Call me right away," Carson's message commands.

Janet does not at all seem put off by Braun's distractions. She could be daydreaming, as she gazes through the side window. Across the bridge, the city's lights look like a swarm of fireflies. "Well, doctor, any emergencies?" she asks, looking back at him when he clicks off the phone.

"No, nothing much," he says.

The bridge dumps them onto Sixth Street, and Braun heads south from Vine to Walnut, past Independence National Park and the steepled hall where the ghosts of Founding Fathers are said to shuffle their quill pens by night. It's an unbroken string of green lights on Walnut to the left turn on 15th and the right on Locust. Braun pulls into the garage at the 42s. As he inserts his card and the crossbar lifts, he points friendly-like toward the little shed and Jay, who returns his gesture with a smile as always. Braun and Acura scale six levels before finding a space. He gets out and opens the passenger-side door for Janet, a gentleman. The garage elevator takes them back down to ground level. Next door at the 42s, another elevator and an updraft to the 15th floor and Janet's apartment, where a long kiss at the door, against the door, ends their evening by acclamation, early starts in the morning for both. "Thanks for a lovely evening," she says, their lips parted but not by much. "Thanks for picking up the tab," he says, just loud enough to be heard, even in the echo-rich hallway. They break and smile and kiss again lightly, and she opens her door, backs into the apartment.

Then he's back in the elevator and seven floors higher and keying open the door to his apartment. He goes right to the telephone, listens to the messages again, Carson's the only important one. Braun wants to be helpful, but what can he say? He makes the call.

"What the hell's he talking about?" Carson asks. "Where's he get all this?"

"I don't know, Mister Carson, I don't even know him."

"This business with a forged check and *he heard her getting murdered?* What's with this guy?"

"Mental case, I guess. Maybe he has a thing for Ellie."

"That's what I was thinkin'."

"I'll tell you what, Mister Carson, I'm gonna introduce myself to this lunatic."

"Yeah, have the police get after *him*."

"Right."

"Anything new on your end?"

"No, sir, I wish there were. I'd call you right away. I just don't get it."

Carson issues a phlegmy cough and tries to clear his throat in its wake, but is only partly successful. "Look," he says finally, with no "excuse me" for the throaty interruption. "We've never met, kid, but you sound OK to me. I've seen Eleanor with some real beauts. Appreciate anything you can do here. She doesn't talk much to me."

"You bet."

Braun hangs up and shakes his head, thinking about what Ellie's told him of her father, how he was never around when she was growing up, how he tuned her out even when he was around; thinking also, in fairness, that she's not always the best communicator on the planet when it comes to personal matters, that she saves such skills for her legal research briefs.

And now Davis Braun turns his thoughts to Richard Keene, to this weird runt of a guy who came from nowhere and is being rather disruptive.

The phone number is unlisted, but he maneuvers Mike at the front desk into giving it to him. Mike realizes that the way it should be handled is to call Keene, tell him Braun wants to speak with him, and give him Braun's phone number (with Braun's permission). But why not give Braun Keene's number directly and save time, what can it hurt?

"Hello." The voice is deeper, more resonant than Richard remembers from their first encounter or the voice mail greeting.

"This is Davis Braun. You want to tell me what this is all about?"

"Excuse me?" He's wondering how the hell Braun got his number.

"Ellie Carson . . . and me . . . Do you pry into everybody's social life around here, or just mine? What's with you?"

Richard clenches the phone so that his knuckles bulge, turning the ridge's wrinkles into onion skin. He all but tastes the fear that swells inside of him, fear of a schoolyard bully, a Herb Dempsey, a belligerent father, though his own father was always gentle and semi-invisible, his mother the bully of the household. Now Braun is speaking in a voice that is light and airy and burnished with a kind of preppy ease, Richard thinks, beachboy mild rising all the way from the shoetops of loafers with no socks. "You want to give her father a heart attack, for chrissake? He's an old man." Then the beachboy turns irritable. "What's the matter with you? . . . You're the guy who eavesdropped on me that time, right? *Right?* Reported some silliness to the front desk? Johnny on the fuckin' spot?"

Richard doesn't realize how hard he is pressing the phone against his ear, which is turning crimson, matching the streak of color that enlivens the dish towel draped over a plastic rack magnetized to the refrigerator.

"You've got one hell of an imagination, buddy," says Braun. "But now you've become a major pain in the ass, understand that? This has got to stop."

Richard gently hangs up the receiver, and when Braun hears the click, he slams his phone into its wall console. He's out the door and moving swiftly to the fire-tower stairwell at the end of the corridor. One floor down and over to 2207; he got that from Mike, too. Directly underneath his own pad. His knuckles rap the door sharply, then the side of his fist thuds into the sturdy shellacked wood.

From inside, Richard's tame "yes?"

Braun positions himself right in front of the eyelet. "Let's talk."

"We have nothing to talk about." Richard sounds like a man who has just come out of anesthesia.

"I think we have."

"Go ahead, then."

"Face to face."

Richard finds some courage, comes alive. "What are you so worried about all of a sudden?"

"You really need help, buddy, you know that?" No suaveness, now, in Braun's voice.

Just as quickly, Richard feels the fear again. "Leave me alone, or I'm calling the police."

Braun laughs into the door, so strong that saliva droplets fly into the lacquer. "Police?!" More spit tracings on the *p* of police. "I understand you're keeping them busy these days."

A door opens down the hallway, and Braun decides to cut the interview short. It's late and he doesn't want to wake up the building, not that his voice has been all that loud. But this Richard guy really has him upset. It's not like him to lose control, even just a little. He steps back and away from the door, shakes his head, walks away. On the other side of that door, Richard is frozen, his eyes darting about like in REM sleep. His upper body trembles and, to stop it, he rams a shoulder into the door, then slides his torso downward until he's sitting on the floor, back wedged at an angle between the door and the wall, knees up, arms folded on top of them, co-cooned, paralyzed.

He closes his eyes and forces himself to imagine a scene that will transport him from this nerve-wracking discomfort, from the fear and shame of the moment, to a place of utter relaxation and sublime confidence and a belief that this world of natural wonders and infinite complexity is not only hospitable, but a great engine of hope and joy, and he finds himself, at first,

waist-high in the Atlantic Ocean on a summer afternoon at the Jersey shoreline, and the water is running up his little-boy thighs and underneath the oversize swim trunks to the white webbing, and the sun-heated water is warm as it irrigates him, and he dives under a wave and bobs to the surface of a curtain of level water, blue-green and white-flecked and shifting sideways with the wacky current, and as he stands, he can feel the undertow on his shins and feet, and he respects it but doesn't fear it; it's a force of nature commanding and inexorable, but if heeded, a sweet coexistence results, the warm thrilling feeling of riding the power, living with the earth's elements, and being part of an impossibly vast and detailed tapestry of rise and fall, search and rescue. The lifeguards on their stands behind him are part of that tableau, rowboats ready on the hard sand. Help, when needed, is on the way.

And then he's no longer in the ocean, no longer wet and sloshing about, but getting a foothold on limestone steps hardened and flaked by the centuries. The steps are narrow and the ascent is steep, but he climbs without hesitation, no railing to grip, just a wide-open canvas of sky above and whitewashed ruins below, sheared-off foundations and crumbling facades, greenery filling the breach. Up he goes toward the summit of the ancient temple, others tentative and angling their bodies and pausing to sit on skinny steps, but not him, he's marching upward on this Mayan pyramid like a prince about to offer a religious sacrifice, as if he has made this trip a hundred times, not this first time as a college student intrigued by ancient exotic cultures, by any society not his own. The stairway is like a 150-foot ladder angled against the side of a house, so steeply is it pitched. He mounts these stairs, unfazed, summoned by a higher order. The fantastical headdresses of the Indian priests and the corpses of people buried within lodge in his mind's eye. People buried with their finery and jewelry, servants with their utensils, all for use in the next world. And the sacrifices, the gored animals, the bark spattered with human blood. But all of that shrinks to a footnote, for when he reaches the peak and takes a panoramic survey of the world around him, a thrill ripples up his arms and across his shoulders to the base of his neck. Here he is unshackled, stoked by the rarefied air, free free free . . .

And now the landscape greens further into farm country below, and he's at the top of the observation tower at Gettysburg Battlefield, the arena of death spread below him, stilled and tagged for modern consumption. The Round Tops, the swath where Pickett charged, where Chamberlain held the line, where they all fell in their deathly hot uniforms, snap-blast of rifles and concussive splintering of musket balls, searing pain and shock and, finally, muggy oblivion. Richard has it all in his sights, the high school history text revisualized, and from up here at the top of the tower, the shrine is quieted by the twin tranquilizers of time and distance, and he is at peace with the world.

12

Cassie Oliver was the kind of daughter who thrilled fathers, tomboy-tough as a little girl, pretty and athletic in high school, good grades, and good enough on the basketball court to get a partial scholarship to St. Joseph's University, where she played varsity for four years, a playmaker who ran the offense like the kids' treehouse club she invented in her own backyard. Her father did the carpentry work for that organization, installing a plywood retreat amid the thick trunk and its main arteries; Cassie captained the membership, including kid brother Bobby, Robert Jr. Her leadership gifts were such that both boys and girls had allegiance to her. She steered expeditions to the movies and the 7-Eleven, organized street ballgames that developed into full-fledged leagues with teams from different blocks, led pretzel sales and car washes, set up lemonade stands and trained younger kids to take over the summertime business when she reached the ripe age of eleven. Cassie's Cavalry, her father called the treehouse band of seven: three boys and four girls including his two children. She was a throwback, a character out of Mark Twain. Indeed, with her creativity, beguiling smile and occasional pugnacious streak, it seemed that she had sprung from the pages of a storybook.

But the mature Cassie Oliver was very real and, above all, a woman of character. When her mother got sick, she cared for her with the skill and commitment of a full-time nurse. Aside from chemo sessions, there was to be no hospital for Libby Oliver until the very end, when the cancer shut down her organs, one by one.

Her father thinks, all the time, about both Cassie Olivers, the little indomitable girl and the young woman of strength and promise. The twenty-three-year-old whose boyfriend disregarded a curving roadway and yellow caution signs, and plowed his convertible and the two of them into a tree as unyielding as a brick wall, crumpling the car, crushing Cassie between the bucket seat and the glove compartment, ensuring in the electric blur of an instant that her insides would never have to submit to the wasting visited on her mother.

Sgt. Robert Oliver has lost them all, including the son who, in his eyes, never measured up, now a stranger living on the other coast, almost as dead to him as the cherished daughter and her mother. Oliver's hatred for Cassie's boyfriend—her murderer, he called him—finally lessened many months after the accident. The kid, after all, was dead, too; did himself in. But Oliver's enduring hatred is for a father's helplessness, a feeling so sickening, so infuriating, that only by anesthetizing it with emotional numbness can he prevent it from descending into self-pity or some kind of incommensurable fury. And so his instincts to help people have dulled into a clockpuncher's en-nui. He musters enough energy and clarity to follow rules and see a task through, but without the dedication, the extra juice that once made all the difference. "Burnout" is the modern terminology, and Oliver figures he's earned it. Missing Persons detail.

Once in a great while, a case prods him into action beyond the paperwork. An individual with a certain conviction, a persistence, will reach him in a place that's pretty quiet these days.

Maybe this Richard Keene. If he's not a crazy or a murderer himself. Oliver has checked him out—not so much as a traffic ticket. That's a good sign, but the six months in a mental hospital is not. Every unraveling starts somewhere.

Something about this case. The father's attitude. And that bank account. The young lady, Eleanor, could simply be avoiding this Davis Braun fellow. Unhappy situation, doesn't want to see him. Doesn't want to see the father either, the guy's no prize, that's for sure. So she disappears on them. She takes some time on her own, then returns to get her money and leave town. She'll send for her things later. Braun's a tough read. Seems like a guy who's got it all, so the cynical view is that he's a killer. If he is, he's sure as hell not a dummy who would rig this bank thing for a few dollars and hand over a motive on a silver platter. Unless that's the height of arrogance.

Oliver figures he probably doesn't have enough yet for a search warrant on Braun, but he can legitimately have Burnside and Alvarez make an inquiry. They're a pair, those two. Burnside on the downside, Alvarez as eager as a racehorse at the gate. Good balance, skills and temperaments.

Come to think of it, maybe, with the right judge, there is enough for that warrant.

After an hour in semi-fetal position and an escape of the mind, Richard has roused himself and is fighting back. He's on the line with Lori, telling her about his run-in with Braun, asking her if she has anything else to report about her next-door neighbor.

"No," she says. "Haven't seen him."

"Good. Don't even think of getting anything more from him, Lori; he's too dangerous. You've done enough." He tells her that he plans to drop a dummy down the trash chute as a demo to build the evidence. "Will you witness it?" he asks her.

"Sure, why not."

"Thanks, Lori, that helps. Makes it look stronger to the

police. Like I'm not a raving lunatic. Know what I mean?"

"Sure, I'm well acquainted with raving lunatics."

"I'm serious."

"I know. You can count on me. Just wait 'til I get home from work."

"Of course. I should get it tomorrow morning. It'll come in sections. I'll have it put together by noon. When will you be home from work?"

"About four-thirty."

"I'll call you."

"OK . . . I can't believe he came after you that way. It seems so out of character."

This annoys Richard, as if she doesn't quite believe him. "Lori, I told you, guys like this can be very deceptive."

"Richard, listen, if he's guilty—"

"I don't think it's a matter of 'if' anymore."

"If he's guilty, he's just trying to intimidate you. There's no way he's gonna pull something in a highrise with a thousand people around."

"You mean like he did with Eleanor?"

Nothing on the other end of the line, then, "All right, Richard. I get the message."

"Listen, Lori, one other thing. He's seeing another woman."

"Really? That's fast. I haven't seen anyone around."

"She lives in the building."

"How do you know?"

"I know her; I've seen her a lot at the gym."

"Wow . . . How do you know they're, uh—?"

"They're out tonight, I saw them leave the building. Dinner and drinks at Potcheen's. A movie afterward. Didn't look like a first date."

"You're too much, Richard." There's admiration in her voice. "You followed them?"

"Of course."

"Maybe they're old friends."

"It was too, uh, cozy for that."

"Hmnh . . . What's she look like?"

"Red hair. Attractive, athletic."

"Sounds like you mean kind of sexy, Richard."

". . . Yes."

"What's her name?"

"I don't know."

"You don't know her so well, huh?"

"Not really."

"This is major, Richard . . . Oh my God, she could be—"

"Yes she could."

Richard looks at the angry scabbed knuckles on his right hand now shorn of its bandage. He sees dark bruising red-turning-purple-brown on a woman's neck. "Yes she could," he repeats.

He must speak with this girl. Warn her. Save her.

First, he must find out her name. Several bump-intos at the fitness center and the elevators, and no exchange of names. He's not much of an operator. No kidding.

Frank. No, Mike's down there now. Try him.

That's how Braun got his number. Probably.

At least get her name from Mike. If he knows it, the dunce. Actually, he's pretty good with names, especially the women. Richard's picked up that much at the front desk.

The elevator pops his ears and fills them with a harsh whir. It feels like it's rushing downward more quickly than usual, almost like it's falling uncontrolled.

Mike is talking with a sixtyish man who looks like he has time to kill and this is his best alternative. Their conversation pauses as Richard approaches.

"Hey, Mike, you know that pretty woman with the red hair, lives on fifteen?"

"Yeah, yeah, the redhead . . . wow." Mike's tight jaw forces out a crooked smile. "She's way outa your league, pal."

"Don't I know it," Richard says, thrilled inside that he's getting so smooth at this game. "Can't blame me for trying, though, right?"

Mike's conversation partner nods and blinks his bloodshot eyes.

"What's her name?" Richard continues. "I've talked to her lots of times at the gym, and never got it."

"If it's that redhead on fifteen, it's Janet Kroll you're talkin' about," Mike says without hesitation. "You made a special trip down just to ask me that?"

"Yeah, it's been on my mind, that's all. Thanks, Mike."

"You know where her apartment is, but don't know her name?"

"Oh, I just saw her get off the elevator there one time. Thanks again." He walks back toward the elevators and Mike says, "Good luck, pal, you'll need it." Richard picks up a throaty snicker from Mike's buddy.

"Will you let me sleep?" Lori says into the phone, but there's no anger in her voice.

"It's Janet Kroll," says Richard, glancing at the digital in his bedroom: 12:14. "The girl out with Braun . . . Janet Kroll . . . That's her name. Know her?"

"Nope."

Janet Kroll is lying in bed, thinking about her appointments tomorrow. She still does have to earn a living. She's showing a couple of new listings in Society Hill, one a two-bedroom in the Towers with a river view, the other an Olde City brick townhouse with a private courtyard. She's been told that she's too nice, too principled, to really make it in real estate, but she's hardworking and well organized, and she's done all right for herself since the divorce two years ago.

Someday maybe she'll have her own agency. Or get into the commercial market. Or switch vocations, go into public relations, corporate marketing, who knows? She's still young enough.

Or maybe get married again. To the right guy, of course. A guy with some of Davis Braun's characteristics.

But only some of them.

He can't find in the phonebook a J. Kroll or J. Krole or any other possible surname spelling he conceives. He didn't want to arouse Mike's suspicions any further by asking for a spelling or the apartment number. Of course, he doesn't know it, but Janet is too new at her current address to have a listing in the directory.

He'll seek her out tomorrow. And hope she's in no jeopardy tonight.

It's past midnight. He needs a place where he can think clearly, figure things out.

Funny how the mind rules, how phobias flourish, yet people have the capacity to find comfort in danger. Far from intimidating him, the heights have always beckoned Richard, given him a feeling of security that he lacks on terra firma. He should have been a construction worker tightwalking his way across the suspended beams of skyscraper scaffolds.

Tonight, he knows where he wants to go. Up there, with the night wind ripping across the sky and the dark swirling about him like syrup, he can sort it all out.

Or, it's a simple matter, an available option, end it all, dive out of the straitjacket and into the floating sirens of the air.

He doesn't plan to do that, not at all. Coward's way out. He has a mission to fulfill. People are depending on him.

Still, nice to know there's a way out. The ultimate release. If the noise in his head becomes too great.

He's never been up there, but he's dreamed of it. Now's the time.

The Ben Franklin Bridge stretches into the night. Smoky-blue lights necklace the giant, cabled suspension arms that sweep up to steel towers on either side. Below and on the Philadelphia side of the river, Interstate 95 bathes in bright yellow light as it races below a concrete overpass. The highway lighting is like artificial sunshine in some laboratory, creating a mini-world at extreme variance with the majestic, somber span that arches into the dark sky and traverses water so black it's invisible. Cars sprint across bridge and highway, conveyor lines at right angles and different altitudes.

There's a coolness at the riverfront, as Richard walks through the parking lot of the Hyatt Regency, a converted office building more pedestrian than regal. He has walked here from the 42s, a half-hour walk at a brisk clip. No complaint from the knee. The hotel parking lot seems to slant down toward the river, threatening to slide all the cars, massed hive-like, into the depths. Richard notices a BMW and a Chrysler Sebring under a light stanchion. For a fragile moment, he wonders where his car is parked and whether he checked the lock (something he ordinarily does three, four times when he parks it), then he realizes that he walked here, that the dingy gray Toyota is out of commission and sitting in the 42s garage.

Richard leaves the Hyatt property and walks along the waterfront, past abandoned docks and pilings, past rancid soggy shores, until he reaches the very foot of the bridge where cars careen off of Vine Street and jockey for lanes curving upward past the massive stone anchorages that loom like medieval castles above ground, and root beneath it like submerged quarries. He steps over a guard rail and onto a skinny shoulder that turns into wider pavement as the bridge climbs. But before that transition, meant to usher normal walkers safely away from speeding vehicles, Richard mounts the left-hand suspension beam and begins to take the skyward gradient, steadying himself on the restraining cables that send a barely perceptible vibration up the nerve endings in his arm. It is a treacherous task, this ascent, without attaching pulleys and clamps that painters and bridge inspectors use, but Richard is fearless in this element, and there is something exceptional about his balance, another undetected piece of sensory prowess linked invariably, he once concluded, to his middle ear, those organs tuned beyond a concertmaster's highest standards. Perhaps an autopsy would reveal some structural oddity, he muses, as he grips and climbs, but no, no one will look for that. They'll just bury the clues, those subtle perhaps microscopic indicators embedded in living tissue, ganglia and the like, send the exquisite wiring into the loamy earth where it will disintegrate into a puff of chalk dust.

The air is heavy, picking up moisture from the river and lifting it up the span, as Richard trudges higher. The city, fanning out below him and joining him on high with its eruptions of buildings (the yellow clock-face of City Hall a beacon, bronze William Penn now Richard's comrade-in-air from a distance), seems to be watching him skywalk, as oblivious motorists stream underfoot. Richard feels safe here, removed from harm and the clutter and cacophony of the grounded life. Free of elevators and subways and congested streets. All those insidious earthbound noises, the beguiling and the stomach-churning, now diffuse and regather into a giant cochlear seashell, a muted roar like the ocean's, white noise in the great outdoors. Braun can't get to him here. Even the past with its relentless grasp is at arm's length. Unencumbered and unfazed, he climbs toward the top.

From this vantage point, the past can be laid out and studied bare like specimens. Richard sees with eyes teared by the wind. Still, they are floodlights that turn the black curtain of sky into a pull-down movie screen, or a gauzy veil behind which shadows play out their dramas. He can see even beyond the mustache-like strips of white-gray cloud that float on the pitch canvas, and it is there that Cindy exists, in this infinite theater of the mind, and it is from behind the cloud wisps that she emerges, radiant as an angel, a hand extended in play, an invitation. Richard is now at the top, the very top of the steel tower, and the cars move like ladybugs beneath him, and the wind embraces him like a dance partner, and the air is a thousand impulses that stretch in one huge loop, like the bridge's suspension arms, toward Cindy, who grows larger and brighter against the curvature of the sky. And in that instant of safe harbor, that seductive offer of release, Richard glances away from Cindy, spreads his arms on the railing like a boardwalk stroller taking a pause, and looks down at the constellation of lights; it's as if the stars were shot down to earth. He could stay up here forever. Well, maybe not forever, but for a long long time. A week, a month, a year. If he had a little, open-air biosphere to take care of his needs.

But that thought is a distraction because there is an invitation at hand, Cindy's invitation. A giant electric ghost in the sky. The wind is a caress. He could float in the air. Or zoom down a single shaft of air as if on a giant pool-slide, keep his eyes fixed on the yellow glow of the City Hall clock . . . He could try it.

No . . . God, no.

He inhales sharply and blinks his eyes against the coursing air, checks his footing. No, his is not a life that, like The Stranger's, he can allow to flicker out. His life is starting anew.

All men are condemned to die, that's true enough. But why hasten the process?

The trip down will be easy.

The rest of the night passes for him as it always does, fitfully.

"You mean you lost your job?! How did you manage that? God, Richard, what's the matter with you?"

Only the hour, ten a.m., prevents his mother from reaching full shriek. He has finally gotten around to telling her. Friday morning, a good way to start off her weekend.

"Don't bother waiting for an explanation," Richard says, and is immediately sorry for his sarcasm. But Evelyn doesn't miss a beat.

"What are you going to do now? I hope you're not under the impression that we—"

"I'm working on a murder case." It has just come out of him, that's all. Naturally. No sarcasm, this time. The truth, as he feels it.

"What?!"

"I'm getting close."

A frightened note creeps into Evelyn's voice. "Richard, what's happening to you?"

Richard's chin is cradling the receiver as he sits at the desk in his bedroom. He is doodling on a legal pad on which he has written a checklist of steps he must take to solve his case. "I'm balancing the books, that's all." He's still being honest, but can't resist being cryptic for his mother's sake.

"What does *that* mean?"

"It's long overdue, Mother."

"Richard, I can't talk to you when you're like this. Do you want to talk to your father?"

"No, you tell him."

"Tell him what?"

"Tell him I got laid off and I'm looking for another job, that's all."

"Is that the truth?"

"Sure."

"What about the other thing? Richard, are you still talking about Herb Dempsey and all that? That's making you sick, you know that? It's not healthy."

"I know, Mother. I'm trying to cure myself."

"You're not talking sense, Richard. You can always call one of the doctors, you know, who was the one you really liked? Doctor Jenko . . . what was it?"

She can't talk about it any further. Neither can he. When Evelyn gets off the phone, she makes a beeline for the den, where Marty is watching television, with the volume booming. Since he retired from Dobbs Publishing, where he was a production editor for a line of automotive and construction trade magazines, Marty watches a lot of television. Right now, the business news is on full blast. There's a lot of chatter from investment analysts spouting "long-term" and "disconnect" and "value-driven." Marty follows the market, worries about his diminishing holdings, the money that no longer seems as safe as he thought; Evelyn is oblivious to such threats.

"He's lost his job," she shouts over the TV. Marty just looks at her. She walks to the television, bends over and searches for a button in a recessed row below the screen. "Where's the one to turn this down?" She's twisting her neck to look at him as he reclines in the Barcalounger. "For godsake, you'll wake up the dead, Marty." She finally hits the right button, pokes it several times, and the sound relents. "Good god," she says, straightening, pressing a hand on her hip to steady herself.

"What's wrong?" Marty asks.

"I can't take this noise anymore, Marty. You've got to do something."

"It doesn't seem to bother anyone else," he says.

"That's because no one else lives with you . . . Well, guess what? Now your son can't do the hearing test for you—he just lost his job. I want you to call him, Marty, and talk to him. I can't."

"Lost his job?"

"That's what I've been trying to tell you." She sits on the rattan couch, settling in for a semblance of a discussion.

"What happened?"

She knits her brows and searches the wall, as if a Tele-PrompTer might beam the answer. "I don't know, exactly; he didn't go into detail. But he said he was 'fired.' That's exactly how he put it."

Marty nods knowingly. "Maybe he was laid off, lots of layoffs these days." He gestures toward the TV. "Take a look at this market. Terrible."

On-screen, a young woman with a salon shag is reciting the details of a gory market selloff.

"He said he was fired. That's not a layoff, is it? Marty, I think he's coming unglued again. I want you to call him."

Marty turns away from the shaggy market skid and looks at his wife. "What's wrong now?"

"Have you been listening to a word I'm saying? It's that Dempsey thing again. I think he's fantasizing. I'm telling you, he needs help."

Detectives Pete Burnside and Ricky Alvarez are standing before the door to Davis Braun's apartment. Oliver dispatched them with a warrant wrangled just this morning from Sara Leibowitz, a judge who somehow still trusts his reputation for fair play, and the only judge in town who would grant such a warrant, given the evidence at this stage of the Eleanor Carson case.

It's a veteran–rookie pairing, Burnside a seasoned cynical

twenty-five-year man, Alvarez lithe and sharp-eyed with the cut
of a halfback. Burnside's knuckles hammer the burgundy door.
Braun is in the bathroom, scraping a Gillette Sensor blade over
his stubble, hot water running, door half-closed. He hears the
knocking and wonders what the hell's going on. He turns off
the spigot, puts down his razor, leaves the lather on his cheeks,
and walks out of the bathroom. A bath towel is wrapped around
his middle, and that's it. He looks through the eyelet and sees
fish eyes belonging to Burnside.

"Yeah?"

"Davis Braun?"

"That's me."

"Police, Mister Braun. We have a warrant to search your
apartment."

The door flies open and Braun stands there in his sensitive-
skin shave cream and enveloping bath towel before the two
cops. "You gotta be kidding me."

"No, sir," says Burnside, brandishing his badge and the warrant.

"This is about Eleanor, obviously," Braun says, as Burnside
and Alvarez brush past him, the younger detective's ear missing
Braun's lathered cheek by a whisker.

"Sorry for the inconvenience," says Burnside, opening a bifold coat-closet door in the living room.

Braun's fair skin has reddened beyond the shade raised by
hot water. "I'm the one who's looking for her, and you guys
come *here?*"

His visitors don't say anything, just go about their business.
Braun follows Alvarez into the bedroom, and when the detective slides open the top drawer of the dresser, says, "That's
right, I put her pinkie in with the socks."

"This is just routine," says Alvarez.

"Well it's not my routine," Braun says. "Mind if I finish shaving?"

"Not at all. I'll tell you when I'm ready to come in the bathroom."

"Great. Would you do that now so you don't interrupt me?"

Alvarez stops peeling through the lower drawers and looks up at Braun. A toughness gathers just below the young detective's smooth square features. "No problem," he says, shouldering past Braun and into the bathroom. Braun stands there, shaking his head then scratching it. "Unbelievable," he says to himself. He hears the medicine cabinet door creak open and steps over to the bathroom's open door. Alvarez is fingering a vial of little white pills.

"Miss Carson has plenty of stuff in here, I see," the young detective says.

"She does live here," says Braun.

"What are these?" Alvarez rotates the vial between his thumb and forefinger.

"I don't know. Allergy pills, I think."

"How come she didn't take them with her?"

"I think she switched medications or something."

They return to the bedroom, and Alvarez goes through the closet and the large drawers of the bureau, sees mostly female garments and underthings. "Looks like she's crowding you a little," he says to Braun.

"I travel light."

Burnside has checked the living room and kitchen, and is going through the trash under the sink. He didn't expect a body to be gift-wrapped, but little things can provide the clues that turn an investigation, and the trash is a repository of such things. Not that this is a full investigation yet, but Oliver has a pretty good nose and doesn't waste warrants on pure exercise or cover-your-ass maneuvers.

Alvarez finishes up in the bathroom and bedroom, and wears a blank expression as he waits for his senior partner to complete the trash survey. Braun drifts back in, still wrapped in the towel, showing lots of tan and muscle, almost posing, it seems to Alvarez, who figures a shot to the floating ribs would deflate things in a hurry. Something about him Alvarez doesn't like.

"We're clean back there, Pete. Her stuff is still here."

"Let me know if you find any money down there," Braun says to Burnside, who shovels the small plastic trash can back underneath the counter and stands. Braun backs off from being the wiseguy. "Sorry," he says, "but this is just so unbelievable."

"Like my partner said, 'routine,' " Burnside says. Alvarez fires off a little smile of acknowledgment.

Braun seems to have some hurt in his voice when he says, "I was the one who filed the report. Remember?"

"We know that. Thank you for your time, Mister Braun, sorry for the interruption," Burnside says, and he leads Alvarez out the door, his young partner giving Braun a final glance as they go.

"Guy don't look like a nut, does he?" says Burnside, as they pad toward the elevator.

"I don't know, Pete, what's a nut look like?"

Burnside smiles as he presses the down button. "Good point, kid."

While Burnside and Alvarez are checking Braun's hosiery, Richard receives a call from Frank at the front desk. A large UPS box has arrived for him.

Richard leaves his apartment immediately, looks up and down the hallway to make sure Braun is not around and waiting to pounce on him, and elevators to the lobby. Frank has the box—about four feet high and two feet wide—propped against the wall just to the side of the counter. Smaller packages are stacked on the counter itself.

"That mine?" Richard points to the big one.

"Yep, that's yours, my man," says Frank, tapping a pen on his UPS delivery sheet. "General Motors . . . Whatchyou got in there, a giant carburetor or something?"

"No. I'll tell you about it later."

"I can't wait."

Richard bends his knees and wraps his arms around the middle of the box.

"Handle that?" asks Frank. "We got a wardrobe cart back there, you know."

"That's OK, thanks." Richard grunts as he sways his back and hefts the box, but it's not all that heavy, which is as he expects. He totes it to the elevator and gets on alone. "Here we go," Richard says to the box, his traveling companion, as the elevator lifts upward. The ride is uninterrupted. When he reaches the twenty-second floor, Richard looks furtively about the empty hallway and drags the box out, lifts it again and carries it to his door. Moments later, he has the sturdy cardboard flaps unclasped and opened on his living-room carpet. The note inside is from Terry Runnels: "I probably broke about fourteen corporate bylaws to get you this, so make the most of it." Good man, Runnels; Richard doesn't see much of him anymore, but he's one of the few human beings he's ever relied on. Seems that Lori Calder has joined that small circle, Richard muses, as he pulls out a skull, then a neck, torso, appendages, all the makings of a crash-test dummy. This one, once assembled, will be going on a vertical ride. And not in an automobile.

An assembly instruction booklet is included, a single sheet of paper folded four times over. Richard spreads it open on the floor so that all sixteen rectangular facings are visible. He kneels and studies the diagrams, which are not very complex; parts identified, arrows showing inserts into sockets, screws to secure, etc. Richard feels confident he can put this thing together. His Boy Scout training enabled him to develop reasonable mechanical aptitude.

Braun has stood under the shower's hot water for a full ten minutes in an effort to chase apprehensions and renew his customary optimism and feeling of well-being. It's not every day that the police toss your apartment. He can live without that kind of intrusion.

He turns the water off and steps out of the tub, yanks the bath towel off the rack and flings it over his back with the panache of a matador. Just then, the rapping. It takes him a minute or so to realize that it's not coming from the pipes or from some other apartment but from his own damn door. Again.

"You've got to be kidding," he says to himself, then hollers, "Be right there," before slipping on a pair of gym shorts. He drapes the towel around his neck as he walks to the door and opens it without prescreening, ready for anybody by this time. One of those days.

"Lori." Some surprise in his voice. "Need something else for the pantry?" he kids.

She smiles sweetly. "As a matter of fact, yes."

"Come on in."

"Thank you," she says and steps past him, the door drifting closed behind them. She turns and faces him. She looks like she wants to pose a question to him, and is mulling over the word selection.

Braun smiles down at her. "So? What's doing?"

Lori checks her distance and unleashes a haymaker, a roundhouse-right that smacks Braun's left cheek. He is a full head taller than her, so she has reached high for her target. Braun recoils, looks perplexed. "What was that?"

"What the hell is going on?" Lori's left eye is twitching and the right is a burning charcoal nugget. In that instant, Richard would not recognize her. Neither would her parents. Braun does, barely.

"With what?"

"With you?"

"Are you all right?" He reaches out to her, but she swats his hand away, as if countering an attacker in karate class. "I'm fine," she spits out. "How is *she?* Is she here? I'd like to meet her."

"Who are you talking about, Lori?"

"Your new girlfriend. You move fast, I'll give you that."

She's got him, he realizes. How to smooth it over, duck and cover. Hey, there've been no promises here. What's the big deal?

"Girlfriend?"

"Babe named Janet? Nice body, huh?"

"What?"

"Or just nice handwriting?"

"Lori, what the hell are you talking about?"

"She good at balancing a checkbook? As good as me? How about at wearing disguises? Are you planning to use her next time?" Lori is twisting her mouth as she speaks, and wormlike tendons mar her usually milk-smooth throat. "Your boy Richard has been watching you."

Braun narrows his eyes.

"Right in the building," Lori says. "You're pretty blatant, aren't you?"

Braun leans against the half-wall at the kitchen threshold. "Janet Kroll? Is that what this is about?" Lori's eyes would zap him if they were laser guns. "She's a friend of mine," Braun says.

"Please." Lori looks like she wants to spit.

"Believe what you want to believe, but that's the truth. Anyway, what are we talking about? Did I commit a crime here?

It's not like you and me are married, is it?"

"That's true enough, Davis." She is turning her anger, but not sure in what direction. "But, you see, I'm an old-fashioned girl."

"Yeah, right."

"No, I am, in a certain way. That's the difference between us, evidently."

"You've got it wrong, honey."

"I don't think so. Richard might be a stooge, but he gets the details right."

"Oh really?"

"Did you kill her?"

Braun's face freezes and something twitches in his neck. "Of course not."

"My god," Lori says, not taking her eyes from his. "I was fooling myself, wasn't I? Thinking you were the aggrieved party and were just ripping her off, or 'getting back what was owed you,' as you put it."

"You're wrong about this, Lori."

"What I want to know now is, was it an accident?" She takes a step toward him, closing any gap of fear. "Or are you some kind of homicidal maniac?"

Braun's smile seems to be one of relief. "I hope not."

"Tell me the truth, I'm a big girl."

"I'm not."

"Either way, I think the police would be all ears, don't you?"

His face tightens again. "For what?"

"If I paid them a little visit."

"Why would you do that, Lori?" His voice sounds hurt.

"Because I'm not into sharing."

"Sharing?"

"You."

She's right on top of him, head at his chest. He takes a half-step back, but now Lori tugs playfully at the elastic waistband of his gym shorts, and he is no longer retreating. She slides her hand inside the shorts, and it doesn't have to go very far before her squared-off polished nails tease him, and now she is saying, her voice in a lower register, "No sharing?" and Braun is smoothing her hair back from the temple, as her tongue goes to work on his breastbone. "Hardly," is his answer.

"Dick Tracy says otherwise," Lori breathes into his chest, stroking as she tests him. "Said you two were pretty chummy. But maybe you're colleagues or something, huh?"

Braun grabs her shoulders and lowers his head. "Exactly."

The kiss is hard, consuming. Lori's hands spring free and dig into the small of his back, her wrists slender, a gold-and-ivory bracelet on the left one already making its imprint on his flesh. Their bodies press against one another. The towel slides off of Braun's shoulders and to the floor like a serpent.

Eight feet away, the refrigerator lurches into a cooling cycle and its humming fills the space. It is this drone that Lori hears the instant that Braun's hands shoot to her neck. Her own hands fly up reflexively, as she understands in a shockwave of horror that her strategy has gone sour, and there's no reversing the situation, no chance for a second strategy. She has miscalculated. The drone is her dirge.

Braun's large hands form a vise around the small woman's neck, and his thumbs press inward as if intent on plunging through tissue and bone to meet the fingers wrapped behind. Lori's eyes bug out and the desperate cry she tries to summon cannot escape her throat and, instead, turns downward into her system like something swallowed by mistake. She steps convulsively to her right, and her shoulder mashes against the right-angled ridge of the wall opening to the kitchen, but she can't even feel it, won't ever have to worry about a splotchy black-and-blue mark on the upper arm, an eyesore by the pool or on the tennis court.

Tiny blood vessels spiderweb the whites of Braun's eyes, as he unsneers his mouth and lets Lori's limp figure slump against the wall. He guides her to the ground, first in a sitting position, then places her on her side. Full control all the way. No slip and thud this time. He takes a step back to appraise his handiwork.

Beneath the beachboy locks and anatomically perfect skull, Braun's brain is in overdrive, simultaneously computing a series of steps to be taken to resolve this matter, weighing them against alternative actions, calculating the necessary provisions, movements; his circuitry is buzzing in a neural-electronic frenzy. He knows the drill—this is the third time around, and the other two disposals were successful—but this one is the first spur-of-the-moment termination, the other two being thoroughly planned. The key variable, he realizes, is the 42s trash pickup schedule, which leaves him out of synch. It's Friday, early morning pickup has come and gone; the next is Monday. He knows the schedule, maybe the only tenant in the building who knows. Who else would care?

But a decomposing body, even if sheathed in a body bag, left for seventy-two hours will betray itself, even down there in the garbage heap. Hence the probable need this time to keep the body at bay for a while, which means, of course, that it must be embalmed.

13

As a boy, Richard Keene was always on the run from the noise of the universe, looking for shelter, some safe space where it all became less oppressive and he could breathe. As he matured, the act of running literally became an outlet, the air whistling about his ears creating a kind of white noise to diffuse the harsher sounds always on the attack. He grew wise to the doctors, who could never find anything abnormal about him and attributed his symptoms to neuroticism. He learned to tolerate a level of discomfort and discovered new channels of partial escape afforded by technology and music-makers, earphones and Walkmans and sound conditioners and his own humming or chanting to spar with the world's rude unceasing cascade of decibels. He learned, of a fashion, to exist.

Cindy Dempsey made his early existence bearable, gave him a sense that, in her presence, he could be a human being and show his feelings. There was something precious in the understanding that was theirs alone. She had an Earth Mother's sensibility sifted in a precocious child's body, a wisdom far beyond her years, a caring that thrilled Richard in its lack of demand. They were children and didn't pretend otherwise, but instinctively knew that their bond was special and unbreakable.

Then she was taken from him. Yet the bond remained.

She refused to give more than a hint of the trouble in her life. But her father had always unsettled Richard. And then Herb Dempsey's madness flared that awful night, an unaccountable demon. But no, that wasn't it, it was more than that. There must have been something dangerously wrong all along. Was Richard the only one to see it?

Cindy's mother knew, she had to. Did nothing.

Ever since, Richard has tortured himself mostly over his failure to react that one night, but also for missing, or not acting on (what could he have done?), the clues, the evidence, that preceded the horror. For he was always enormously uncomfortable around Herb Dempsey, always sensed something off-kilter with this man. His dark recessed eyes under darker brows, the way he'd call Cindy to come inside when she was playing in the street, "Let's go, Cindy," the way he said it, a command suited for a dog, a hurried almost contemptuous summons, an assertion of his ownership. But more than that, there was that unmistakable undercurrent of jealousy, something sick, the unwillingness to share her with the kids on the block, the boys on the block, with Richard. That's what six-year-old and seven-year-old and eight-year-old Richard Keene sensed about this man, with the same exactness that his aural antennae received the world around him.

The mother? She was Penny Dempsey, Aunt Penny, so sweet with a tiny voice and a bashful smile, a shyness about her but a warmth, wonderful to the kids on the block, to Richard. No match for her husband, grown-up Richard would conclude. Rendered useless by training and temperament, but hardly blameless. A mother, after all, must protect her own. No match for the horror, the worst kind of violation of nature, the hell on earth brought by a twisted man like Herbert Dempsey. And Richard knew it, knew it as surely as his own heartbeat. Knew it then, knows it now.

Davis Braun, like Richard Keene, is an only child, but while Richard grew up with relatively normal if baffled parents (a self-absorbed mother, to be sure), Braun had only a mother—the father gone in two years, never to return—and a mentally unstable one at that. Dolores Braun, whose vitriol and explosive temper had chased her husband, from then on cultivated a revulsion toward men, and directed some of the bitterness toward her son. In unconventional ways. First, she dressed the toddler in girls' clothes and let his blond hair grow long to feed the illusion. Long after he was toilet-trained, it was routine for her to walk past him naked, going from tub to bedroom after taking a bath; the natural way of things among girls, after all. By the time he reached age eight or so, she continually called on him to zip her up, to button this or that, inhale her fragrances, fetch moisturizer cream from the vanity, and brassieres and panties drying on the shower rod.

When Leonard Braun ran out on her, Dolores had left his hometown of Milwaukee with her two-year-old son and moved back east to Philadelphia, using inheritance money from her father to buy a little brick house in the western suburb of Havertown. She worked at little, secretarial jobs that she'd quit after a few months. Fortunately, her father's estate was sufficient to sustain Davis and her. Neither the work world nor the prospect of family life held much appeal for her. With both her parents dead, her son had no allies, no harbors for retreat.

But in a way, he fooled her. He grew up to be quite masculine, handsome, athletic, smart . . . deranged.

Dolores did have some men, of course, mostly sales types with easy patter and a forced laugh and absolutely no interest in her young son. Dolores was an attractive woman with a great shape right into her forties, so she could be as selective as she wanted, particularly since she didn't give a damn anyhow, except for a diversion, a physical release and, most important, a chance to dominate, toy with affections, maybe break a heart. She'd make a big fuss over getting dolled up for a night on the town, give her son a peanut butter and jelly sandwich for dinner, braceleted wrists fumbling with the Skippy jars, dusky perfume announcing her entry into a room and trailing her leaving it. The doorbell would chime, and there in the threshold would stand the evening's turkey gussied up with slicked-back hair (sometimes not a lot of it) and cologne potent enough to neutralize her own augmented scent, two force fields meeting in a compact living room of lifeless furniture. Davis took it all in, and when he reached his teens, began to challenge the male visitors with pointed questions about their livelihoods and about themselves. They resented his tone and his smarts. He was too sophisticated for his years. Dolores, though, was attracted to this developing quality in her teenage son, his brashness and physical maturity and precocious cynicism. The number of gentleman callers diminished, as she began to prefer Davis as an escort. She had forgotten about her early bid for emasculation, her dressing him like a little girl. Now she took him to dinner at fancy restaurants, first flaunting her handsome young son (how could she have a son this old? patrons and maitre d's gushed)—at forty, Dolores was trim and curvy and unwrinkled and rather stunning in form-fitted gowns and ensembles—then, at other night spots, trying to pass him off as her date, always out of earshot of Davis, but he was perceptive and felt the vibes, the looks they got.

For his fifteenth birthday, Dolores had a special treat. She made an elegant little dinner at home, complete with wine and a chocolate cake sporting fifteen burning candles that Davis extinguished with one gust from his athlete's lungs, but only after shutting his eyes and making a personal wish (that Sheree Ditmar, a college sophomore who lived at the corner, would take him to her bed). After cake and coffee, Dolores gave him two professionally wrapped presents: a cologne/body talc and spray set of some imported brand, and a patterned silk tie with muted colors. She sat with him on the living room couch and induced him to talk about school, sitting close to him and angling her legs so that the smallest movement would cause them to brush against his chino pants. She wore a light intoxicating scent and just a bit of makeup and a calico dress that rose and bunched nicely above the knee when she sat and crossed her legs. At some point, after the wine and the chocolate had commingled in his blood, and the heady vapors enveloped him, he realized where the evening was headed. He'd read scenes like this in steamy novels, seen them enacted in R-rated movies to which his mature looks gained him easy admittance. He knew the score, this kid.

She walked into her bedroom, not even bothering to take his hand. He followed neither trancelike nor like some curious kid, but like he knew where he was going. In her lavender bedroom smelling of hairspray and fresh-cut flowers in a bud vase, she sat on one side of the bed and patted the mattress, the spread halved and creased, exposing a salmon-colored blanket and cool color-splashed sheets. When he sat down next to her—not quite obediently but not resisting, either—she placed her hands on his chest, then on his back near his shoulder, made little caressing circles with her palms. Her cheek nuzzled his neck, and her chin perched on one shoulder like a playful cat. And from that point and that pose, as her hands migrated across him, and her lips parted and found his, he felt powerful and powerless, loved and hated every second, ownership and servitude, diving off the highest dive and into a pool without a bottom.

Lori Calder always had an appetite. She was a wee young girl who outdid her older brothers at the dinner table in their cramped house in Pennsauken, New Jersey, just across the bridge from Philly. She was a welter of paradoxes: a tomboy for whom tears came easily, equally impelled to dive into trouble or her schoolbooks, then a blossoming teenager of enchanting sweetness and startling anger. Two people inside of her were constantly battling for supremacy.

The rest of the family seemed normal enough. Joe Calder worked construction and made good money during the Atlantic City casino building explosion in the 80s, enough to raise three kids and send two of them to college. His wife, Margie, took charge of the household and family finances; she was smart, organized and calm, a tempering influence on her husband, who, while a solid enough citizen, sometimes preferred a scrap to a rational discussion. Lori inherited her scrappy genes from her father.

The boys were athletic and standard high school youth: wrestlers, footballers, average students, prom attenders. Lori was all A's, a cheerleader (as the smallest and most energetic, always out front), a gymnast until the school disbanded the sport, then a basketball player, the team sparkplug. One thing, though. She tended to fall rather hard for guys, but that was hardly a unique predicament among high school girls.

There were two high school loves for Lori, and they both ended in acrimony, at least on her part. As a sophomore, she dated a senior who stopped speaking to her after she had the audacity to question the accuracy of something he was spouting off; he was smart, a member of the debating team and the legal society, self-absorbed. Affronted, he just picked himself up and walked away from her, and that was that. In time, Lori found it amusing.

Then, as a senior, she lost her virginity to a jock, a three-letter man who dumped her for someone taller and more coveted only weeks before the prom. That wasn't so amusing. Lori considered fashioning a Carrie-like revenge, but settled for writing a letter that said she "felt sorry for him." She stuck the letter in the narrow space between the metal edge of his end-of-the-row locker and the tile wall. An orange happy-face sticker topped his name on the envelope.

They graduated and went their separate ways. She didn't really feel sorry for him, but knew the value of biding her time. That summer, at the swim club, she sat down at the foot of his deck lounger as he was taking the sun and made him an offer he couldn't refuse, led him to a semi-enclosed alcove behind the clubhouse, peeled his swim trunks down and went to work. Poised on the roof ten feet above them, her best girlfriend trained a minicam on the action. The boy's girlfriend received a copy. Labor Day Weekend, he died in a car crash, legally drunk and permanently crushed, football shoulders and all. Lori was dry-eyed.

In college, she was active socially and sexually, a smart girl who nonetheless dug mindless fraternity parties and guys who offered muscles rather than intellect. In the adult world, as a career girl interested in men and money, she was drawn to Davis Braun. He reminded her in some ways of the jock who jilted her, senior year. Some unfinished business there, but she didn't quite know what.

14

Braun is sitting on his living-room sofa, a futon he purchased at Ikea and assembled in less than an hour. He is sweating and still in nothing but his gym shorts, an angry scratch at his shoulder blade. Lori's twisted, motionless body lies near the door. A broken rag-doll.

He shut off her oxygen, then broke her neck. Efficiency.

Now he must clean up the mess, and is swiftly calculating his moves when the phone's rude ring sideswipes him.

"Yeah," he says into it, annoyed.

"You really know how to make a girl feel welcome," says Janet Kroll.

Braun smiles self-consciously, out of hell and back into the earthbound normal, hopping dimensions. "Sorry, I was expecting a callback from someone."

"Someone you're not too crazy about."

"Trying to straighten out my cell phone account."

"Roaming charges?"

"Something like that."

"Well, guess what? Instead of Nextel, you got me."

"I'll take it."

"Good. Other than cell phone bills, are you busy?"

"Unfortunately, I have to go in to the hospital."

"I didn't think you were on, today."

"I'm not, usually. Something special. Sorry."

"You'll miss a delectable lunch . . . and more. How about tonight?"

In the moment, Braun is thinking only of Janet and how good she might make him feel. But he does have some business to take care of, and the timetable is uncertain. How long, for instance, will it take for a first-timer to prepare a body?

"I drew an extra shift," he says to Janet. "How about tomorrow? If it's nice, we can get some sun up on the deck. About one o'clock?"

"I'm game if you are, mister."

"You talked me into it." He hears her laugh. "See you then."

He hangs up softly and the moment passes. The next impulse comes from another region of his brain. He must get to the hospital. The things he needs are at the hospital, and he will take them.

When Braun strides out of the elevator, he sees that Mike is at the front desk, big awkward not-too-bright Mike.

"Regular trash pickup Monday, Mike?"

Mike nods his head like it's on puppet strings. "Far as I know."

Braun is in motion, pondering how he'd explain his questioning Mike on this point in the unlikely event that an investigation reached that far. No sweat; he'd come up with something palatable, and chances are huge that Mike would not remember anyhow.

Braun stops at the Wawa and buys a quart of ice tea and a copy of *Philadelphia* magazine. A few months back, some bullet-headed writer interviewed him down at Metropolitan for a story about area med schools; Metro public relations had offered up Braun for a student's perspective, good copy, photogenic. The article should be in this issue, October. Just hit the stands.

Next door, Jay is in the booth at the parking garage, and Braun gives him a healthy wave and smile en route to the elevator. He knows his car is on "L" level, six floors up, on the 16th

Street side, where he parked it after returning with Janet last night. It's a different spot each time, nothing reserved, so you need a great memory unless you write it down on a scrap of paper and stick that in your wallet. The latter is Richard's technique; Braun relies on memory, and it never fails him.

He usually walks down to the hospital on Ninth Street, but he's planning on bringing back a heavy load this trip, so the Acura is pressed into action. The zippered, army-green duffel bag is already in the trunk, where he keeps it. His timing calls for him to get to the hospital during lunch hour, when the morgue is . . . like a morgue.

Metropolitan Hospital, the same one where Richard Keene lost his most recent battle with an MRI machine, is a brick pile sitting behind a well-tended lawn that slopes toward the street and a formidable enclosure of iron spears anchored to concrete knee-high retaining walls, a tall brick pedestal at each of the four right angles. Braun pulls in the main driveway and parks in the subterranean garage, his ID gaining him admittance there and into the bowels of the hospital itself. His canvas duffel bag is scrunched up under his arm. Through broad swinging doors, as if to a hotel kitchen, a dank corridor leads to the morgue on the right, marked in simple lettering on the door, holding tank for bodies headed south. Braun is through that door and, as he anticipated, anything living is at lunch. The metal drawers are shut, oversize safe deposit boxes, double-oversize mailboxes, an embedded geometric array. The supply room is locked, but Braun has the antidote, a slender annealed pick that he won from some juvenile offender in a card game on the beach in Wildwood, New Jersey, many summers ago and that now finds its way to the heart of the tumbler for a delightful click. The knob turns.

The light switch is soundless, and the shelves are stocked with liter jugs of all the necessary fluids. They don't employ inventory specialists from the Wharton School down here, Braun figures; they'll never miss a few items from their stock. He puts into his duffel bag one of each: formaldehyde, mercuric chloride, zinc chloride, borax, glycerine, a few others. Then he takes a snap-shut kit of sharp, steel, specialized instruments and places it among the fluid containers. Plucks a folded body bag from a stack and adds to the booty. Zips up the duffel.

He's back at his car in minutes without passing another human being, this even in a big-city hospital in the middle of the day. It's a question of knowing your terrain and moving swiftly in the creases. The day has come up fine and sunshine-sweet, earthy smells filtering even to the oil-stained depths. Braun keys open his trunk and deposits the duffel. Before leaving, he sits in the car for a few minutes and quaffs some ice tea while trying to locate the med school piece amid the magazine's body contouring and hair removal ads. There's the story, a nice spread beginning on page 72, and there he is smiling in his scrubs outdoors in the greenery, one foot up on a courtyard ledge, forearm resting on the knee, casual-cool, the caption identifying one Davis Braun, Metropolitan Medical School resident, and the caption: ". . . They allow you to be creative."

While Braun is raiding the morgue, Richard is having some difficulty assembling his crash-test dummy. The shoulder sprockets don't seem to be sprocketing quite right. He knows this doesn't have to be perfect, that it's just a simulation, a demo, after all. But he doesn't want to send Venus de Milo down the chute. He's determined to do this without calling Runnels for coaching over the phone.

Thinking ahead, he envisions a court order to dig up a section of landfill where Eleanor Carson surely is buried. Without him, without his prompting, it never gets that far; her body is never recovered and Braun roams free. Of course, he realizes it may *not* get that far, but not for lack of effort on his part; he won't let go this time. It must come to that. He was placed at that spot at that time—the moment of murder—with his special abilities, to right a wrong, balance scales. He could not prevent it, but can redress it, avenge it. The universe may not be indifferent after all, but regardless, man must not be indifferent, man has a choice.

The diagrams can be maddening: part A into socket B, simple enough, but is "socket" in Figure #1 the same as "receptacle" in Step #3? Consistency of terms, come on. And why use both "socket" and "sprocket," but to infuriate? He wonders who makes these things for GM.

Sure, there's still the possibility that Braun disposed of his victim, disposed of Eleanor, somewhere other than the landfill via the Dumpster and a city sanitation truck, but Richard is beginning to believe as strongly in his theory of the disposal M.O. as in the murder itself. Right down the chute into the giant pile of moldering rubbish and floppy discards. Just like a cardboard pizza box.

Lori Calder, dead and discoloring, is naked and stretched out in Braun's bathtub, as the apartment dweller of record draws her blood out through slender plastic tubing taken from a cleaning-fluid spray can straight into the drain, the makeshift intravenous hookup so deft (the tube is pinched at the point of insertion at her throat by a pencil's metal eraser band) that, so far, hardly a drop of blood has escaped. Her bracelet, its little ivory faces encased in gold, still clings to one wrist.

The straw-like, spray-can tubing is necessary because Braun found himself shy one hookup and had to get creative. He does have a long stainless-steel tube through which to draw her cavity fluid, and has made the puncture just below the breastplate. Another tube inserted at the carotid artery forces the aqueous solution of chemicals, including rubbing alcohol, into the cavities and tissued reaches of her body. The tart smell of the chemicals mixes with the now muted stink of the corpse. Lori's normal clean scent of soap and understated perfume has long since evaporated. During the entire procedure, Braun has avoided looking at her face, which is turned downward and resting on the inside tub wall so that only a cheek and her still lustrous brown hair are visible.

Braun has both the dexterity and the apparent fortitude for this task, though he doesn't really have the stomach for severing heads and limbs and discarding them piecemeal. He is not crude, after all, and such acts seem revolting. No, he will not descend to that level of barbarism. It is too messy, gruesome. And, in these instances, unnecessary. Stick to clinical workmanship and a clean dispatch.

So he leaves her to her bloodletting, washes his hands with antibacterial soap pumped from a pyramidal canister at the kitchen sink, and slaps some Swiss cheese and slices of tomato between two mitts of Stroehman's potato bread; dabs with some mayonnaise. Takes a healthy bite and chases with Nantucket grape-cranberry juice. He finds that he's hungry as hell.

He pops the remote and the twenty-seven-inch TV screen fizzes into a visual. Somehow CNN is on. Braun doesn't know how that happened. Must have been an inadvertent stopping point when he last switched it off after surfing. He never watches any news stations or reads a newspaper or listens to KYW all-news-all-the-time on the radio. He lives outside of the world at large and concentrates on his personal pathways.

He jumps off of CNN and on to a premium movie channel. Some teen comedy with all the girls mindless and midriffed. Nice talent there.

After a dish of fruit cocktail and a generous helping of Sara Lee pound cake, he gets back to Lori. By now, a large volume of her bodily fluids has been removed and is spiraling into the city's sewage infrastructure. There is a moment, as he hovers over her, when a shudder runs down his spine. It is a shudder of self-doubt, a split-second hesitancy, as powerful as electric current. In the instant it happens, it possesses him, is all-consuming. But then it passes, and in the immediate aftermath of arrogance, he knows what he must do, what he will do, to survive.

While Braun has his hands full, Richard is still struggling to piece together his hard-plastic dummy for its downdraft ride. He has a call in to Lori, who has pledged that she'll witness the test. By late afternoon, he ankles the feet into place, and has himself a complete unit, a "female adult" model, as he requested from Runnels. He jams it into a four-foot-long suit bag, curling the head down and shifting the lower legs sideways; zips up the vinyl bag and ties it tight with string at several spots top to bottom so that the overall shape is more of a cylinder than that of a broad, flat, wardrobe bag. Close enough, he figures.

He's ready to go, but wants to wait for Lori as planned. He calls her apartment, knowing she's still at work; just a reminder for when she gets home. Her taped mellifluous voice clicks on: "Hi, this is Lori Calder. Sorry we're not speaking at the moment, but leave me a message, and we will be soon."

"Lori, I've got Eleanor X rigged up and ready. Call me as soon as you get in."

Meanwhile, Braun's project is taking longer than expected due to the physics of gravity and the resistance of the spray-can tubing he's jury-rigged for the occasion. He's never performed an embalming before, only observed one.

He calls Janet on her cell phone number and her voice message comes on after several rings. Just wants to tell her he's looking forward to seeing her tomorrow and relaxing in the sun. A short break here at the hospital and he was thinking of her.

Nice voice. She has a nice way about her. None of Lori's flash temper or Eleanor's critical barbs. So far, at least. If redheads are stereotyped as volatile, this one is calm. Sexy, for sure. And sweet and giving. So far.

By five o'clock, anxiety has gripped Richard, causing him to rock and flex his shoulders and nip at his cuticles as he sits with the loaded-up dummy at his feet. He knows that he must contact Janet and warn her about Davis Braun, about the danger she may be courting. But there's a greater concern, a growing fear.

There's been no return call from Lori, and a dark whorl of uneasiness is eating at him. His mind races. He's put her in this position. She got too close to Braun, asked the wrong question, the wrong way, tipped her hand.

He stands, takes a bottle of filtered water out of the refrigerator and drinks. Calms himself. So she's a little delayed, held up at work. So what? What's the hurry? Settle down.

He can't. He leaves his apartment, eyeing the hallway in both directions, still wary that Braun may jump him like some sneaky kid in a schoolyard. He walks to the fire staircase and up one floor, moves silently across the carpet to Lori's apartment, one door from Braun's. He presses the doorbell button and it sends a nice rounded chime into the unit and out into the hallway. He looks toward Braun's door, fearing that it will open, ready to dash away if it does, then hoping it will open, ready for confrontation, ready for anything, damn him. He rings a second time, and it is apparent that Lori is not in, or at least that she is not answering.

He takes the elevator to the lobby and hurries to the Dumpster room at the rear of the building. The room soaks in Halloween orange-yellow light and has a faint smoky scent that seems to rise from the greenish-gray concrete floor. Trash droppings flutter from the overhead chute into the monster Dumpster. The whir of hidden machinery and the pulsing of embedded pipes clot Richard's ear, then clear like a swallow's pop on an airplane changing altitudes.

Richard stands on the eight-foot-high Dumpster's lower ledge, reaches high to grab the top one and manages to hoist himself to a jackknifed view of the contents, head and torso bobbing over the top, legs dangling down the side, hands maintaining a grip. The huge Dumpster is loaded with refuse, about three quarters-full. Scanning the broad pile is insufficient; he must explore hands-on. He rolls his legs over the top and lets himself fall onto a thatch of cardboard and paper and plump plastic bags. He slides off of that tenuous platform and into the heap, his sneakered feet pedaling for traction.

He is like a kid in a McDonald's bubble-ball playpen, only there is no joy in his immersion. He digs and burrows and uplifts and tosses aside, feverish and spastic, changing the shape of the mass with his two-handed tunneling. He has about six-feet-deep worth of shit to search through; thankfully, it is mostly bagged and dry. He spends nearly an hour at this task and doesn't spot anything, no suspicious packages, no human appendages.

He climbs out, a bit of rancid orange juice dripping from his sleeve. His knee throbs as he presses it against the top ledge of the Dumpster and rolls his body over and out. He hangs there for a moment, then eases himself down the side. He is rank and dirty.

He avoids the elevator and walks the full twenty-two floors up the fire stairs to his apartment. On the way, he remembers something in a flash, jerks his hand onto the side pocket of his pants and feels the reassuring, metal edges of his keys. Lucky he didn't lose them in that mess.

The hallway is clear—he continues to be leery of Braun surprising him—and he's back at his apartment. He showers and puts on a clean T-shirt and shorts, and for a moment he feels like the little kid he once was, snuggling into a pair of freshly laundered flannel pajamas and sliding into the warmth and protection of bed; the kid he was before it happened, before that night when the walls whispered to him, screamed to him. From that moment, there was no safety. Everything closed in on him, the world turned into a closet. Even the shelter of bed became a trap, no soft release of comfort but steel belts pinning him to the rack. And all the other compartments of life equally oppressive, except for the heights, towering and open to the onrushing air. From any peak—hiking in the mountains as a teen, from the observation deck of the Empire State Building visited with his parents, the tower at Gettysburg, the ancient Mayan staircase—he was free and in command of his nervous system.

And now here he is, twenty-two floors up but feeling hemmed in and scared. Yet with that, somehow a newfound determination, some kind of rod at his spine that won't let him collapse this time, a gift that arrives with the realization of last chances.

He's got to work out. What else is there to do? He won't be able to persuade anyone to barge into Lori's apartment. Or Braun's apartment.

Or this may be unjustified panic on his part, he concedes. Take a breath and step back. She's all right, Lori's all right. She's just a little late, that's all. Or she forgot, had to do something on a moment's notice. Forgot even to call and leave a message. A simple explanation.

The dummy-test can wait.

Janet Kroll. He'll catch up with her at the fitness center. Warn her. She'll be there, it's that time of day.

He laces up his cross-trainers, takes a business card from the upper-right desk drawer and scribbles his telephone and apartment numbers on the back, places it along with his apartment key in the back pocket of his shorts, and goes to the elevator. She'll be there, Janet will be there. And Lori will be all right.

Janet Kroll is there. She's on a treadmill, her sleeveless athletic top cutting a deep "V" down her bare back. She is running like an anchor for a relay team, accelerating toward the finish line. Richard settles onto a stationary bike that provides a perfect view of Janet, her smooth back and fluid running form. He doesn't want to lose her when she completes her run and steps down from the treadmill.

Richard pedals lazily on the bike, conserving energy. Ten minutes later, Janet slows her pace, then walks the final minute, towels off her neck and forehead, and leaves the treadmill. As she makes her way to the weight room, Richard intercepts her. He keeps his voice low but distinct.

"Janet?"

She looks at him, curious, recognizes him. "Yes?"

"Can I speak to you for a moment?"

She doesn't look annoyed, but says simply, "I was just going next door."

"It won't take long. It's very important."

She gauges him, puzzling it through. "How do you know my name?"

"Oh, I don't know, I asked someone. I hope you don't mind . . . Mine's Richard Keene. Anyway, we're not strangers, right?"

She moves into the doorway of the weight room. "Well, come on in. I'm listening."

"No, please, in private, just give me two minutes. Believe me, it's extremely important."

The intensity comes through his eyes, and Janet can feel the understated emotion in his voice. She can make only one guess about his subject. "Over here," he says, and leads her out of the fitness area and into the deserted banquet room. Almost deserted. A young woman, collegiate and studious, is sitting on a ledge above a heating vent as she uses a yellow marker to highlight a thick text, her back pressed against the window. Richard and Janet walk to the other side of the large room, well out of earshot.

"Please don't get mad or think I'm spying on you or anything like that," he says.

She looks puzzled, tense. "All right."

"Last night, I saw you out with Davis Braun."

A twitch in Janet's side.

Richard holds up his hand. "It was completely by accident, I wasn't following you or anything. I was coming into the lobby and the two of you were walking out."

"So?"

Richard lowers his hand and slices the air with it for emphasis. "I believe that you are potentially in danger if you spend time with him . . . alone."

"Really?" She appears composed, but her heart is beating faster than it does when she's at full throttle on the treadmill.

"I believe," Richard continues, "that he's a murderer. He murdered a girl in this building . . . The girl he's been living with."

Janet struggles for a breath. "OK, you've got my attention." She runs the towel over her face again, chasing fresh perspiration. "How am I supposed to believe this?"

"Did you know he was living with someone?"

"Yes. It was . . . no big deal."

"She's disappeared. Ten days."

He can see Janet counting backwards in her head.

"Well, have you gone to the police?"

"Yes. They're investigating."

"This is pretty wild, uh . . . Richard?"

"Yes, that's right."

"How are you involved?"

"I heard the murder take place. I was passing his apartment. Strictly random."

She is blinking, trying to focus her eyes. "You heard what, a gunshot or something?"

"He strangled her." He taps one ear. "I have very good hearing."

Janet shakes her head and a strange smile shows up. She searches for balance. "This is . . . Excuse me, this is . . ."

"Please—"

"Aren't you worried I'll think you're kind of crazy?"

"Do you . . . think I'm crazy?"

"I don't know." She looks right into his eyes. "Aren't you worried I'll tell him all about you?"

"He already knows. He knows I know."

"This happened ten days ago?" There's a trace of anger in her voice, maybe directed at herself.

"That's right." Richard finds himself staring at her neck, its slope and smoothness. He looks beyond her at the college student slouched against the window, then back at her. "Stay away from him, Janet."

She looks like she's falling through space. "I know what this sounds like," Richard says. "I have no reason to make it up."

She places two fingers on his wrist, a nice gesture. "You seem like an honest guy."

He tells her more, the way in which he heard it happen, how he believes the body was disposed via the trash chute. He doesn't mention Cindy Dempsey or his worries about Lori, that would be too much, overload. He reaches into the back pocket of his gym shorts and withdraws the business card. The business of crime. Sgt. Robert Oliver's card.

"Look, if something happens to me," he says, handing the card to her, "here's the policeman handling the case . . . He's an honest guy, too. I think."

He looks into her eyes. "My number's on the back."

They walk out of the banquet room and back to the fitness area. Richard doesn't feel like working out anymore. "Stay away from him, Janet," he repeats, then stands silent at the elevator as she turns from him and walks into the weight room. He watches her, through the glass walls, adjust the seat height of a Nautilus machine.

He does not hear from Lori all night. He tries to sleep, puts on his earplugs as usual, but finds no respite under the covers. There are no rest stops for the mind, as it spins out its excesses. Lori is dead, he fears, he thinks, he convinces himself. She got too close. Her body is somewhere in that Dumpster pile, he missed it, missed it because it's been carved into small pieces.

Or it's still in Braun's apartment, primed for disposal.

Janet Kroll is at risk.

Oliver. He must call Oliver.

What the hell will he tell Oliver?

Eleanor Carson. Her body. The law's corpus delicti. Must find it, will find it. All the other elements will then assemble themselves in sharp relief in the light of day, the case built and certain. Her body must be located.

He falls asleep, or at least into what passes as sleep for him. He floats into an out-of-focus pastel world . . .

the old row-house neighborhood tented by summer sky, small canvas kiddie pools on front lawns. Kiddie pools for little kids. They are no more than four or five, splashing in the delicious cool water, both of them in the square pool on the Keene lawn, their mothers gabbing on the patio. The heat rises in waves from street and sidewalk, and the air is breezeless and furnace-like, but the two kids in the pool don't feel it. They have the water to distract them, and each other to engage. The little girl sits in the one-foot-high water and smacks it with her palms, punctuating with a squeal of delight. The little boy slaps the water in response, but then keeps silent, letting her be the attraction. They alternate spraying drops and water-feathers into the sunlight, agitating the pool water, then allowing it to settle and gather at their shins or waist, he standing, she sitting. A playful alertness to her, a knowing anticipation in her dark brown eyes even at this age. She is both unsettling and captivating, and as they measure their distance and speak with their eyes, and their mothers' words stay within the awninged shade, and boxy air conditioners rattle and drone from second-story windows, and hundreds of other little dramas unfold elsewhere in the neighborhood, adult barely-sleeping Richard does not want this picture to change shape, does not want the dream to end. It is the hazy drift of the mid-consciousness, the dreamer aware that he is dreaming but powerless to alter or stop it. And then Richard falls out of his pastel world and through a white void, a realm beyond reason and memory, what he imagines to be the flip side of the universe, and from there he lands in some kind of hellhole of desperate murmurs and gasps, struggling and thrashing, a sudden shaft of light from above like a beacon from heaven, and he is fighting gravity as he climbs, panicked and clawing his way toward the light growing broader and brighter. The taste of ashes on his tongue and the cylinder narrowing and twisting like a giant snake as he moves, and he trapped in its tract, its fanged mouth opening wider, the light streaming in now, but he is slip-sliding as he nears the top, fingernails scratching the sooted metal in a disturbing shudder of sound as if on a grade-school blackboard. With a convulsive thrust, his arm feels wrenched from its shoulder socket, yet the first digits of his fingers make it over the top of the open flap-door of the chute. But he is cut off; the flap snaps shut, smashing his fingertips, unhinging him for the long tumble down, not through a cushioned air pocket but bang-ing against the hard metal all the way into the yawning darkness, and screaming, screaming, screaming . . .

The digital clock glows 9:06. A lot later than he usually awakens when he has managed to fall asleep at all. Richard is sitting up in bed, gulping air, sweat lines on his T-shirt. He rips off his earplugs and reaches for the phone; the pad lights up. Punches in the numbers. C'mon Lori. C'mon Lori, answer. Water pipes groan through the walls. Her voice greeting. Richard's pleading message which she will never hear, but the police will: "Lori, it's Richard. Where are you? Please tell me you're all right."

He is still tussling on a sweatshirt as he fast-walks to the elevator. A two-minute wait and a full boat. He annoys them by getting on, nudging the bellies and pocketbooks. He takes a deep breath and closes his eyes as he faces front and waits.

Now Richard is running through the lobby past the mail-room and outside and into the Dumpster room, but he's too late. Minutes earlier, the Dumpster sent its castoffs into the jaws of the city sanitation department's biggest vehicle after be-ing wheeled onto the loading platform. It was lifted and tilted and emptied in a deluge of paper-plastic-garbage-throwaway human exhaust. Richard bursts into the room, looks into the Dumpster, and sees that it has been picked clean.

Trash pickup on a Saturday?

He races onto 15th Street, hears a trash truck's whine-and-grind nearby, but just stands there, aggravated at himself for not getting here earlier, though he had no reason to believe that this Saturday morning would bring a trash collection.

What he does have is an unreasoning fear that Lori Calder's body is in that load.

What to do? He's certainly not going to stop and inspect a city trash truck, not quite. He missed it, the chance to search the Dumpster, he was late. An overnight dump by Braun and no morning inspection. Impeccable timing once again.

That desperation filling him up. He runs back into the building and, at 9:17 on a Saturday morning, calls Sgt. Robert Oliver.

"The next-door neighbor's missing."

Oliver is working on a sizable mug of black coffee. He's been at his post overnight, filling in for the graveyard guy, who's on vacation. Oliver doesn't mind, doesn't take vacations anymore. "Are you the guardian for the whole building now?" he asks Richard. "How long's she been missing?"

"Since yesterday."

"Come on, Keene."

"I think he killed her."

"And why is that?"

"We were working on this together."

"Who?"

"Lori and I."

"Lori's the neighbor?" Oliver takes a sip. Hot coffee is one of the few remaining pleasures that he derives from life, and this ceramic mug of his really retains the heat.

"That's right."

"You say you were 'working together'?"

"Yes."

"Coupla PIs, huh?"

"She was casually getting more information from him. Maybe she said the wrong thing at the wrong time."

"What does casually mean?" Oliver's tone has shifted from flip to businesslike. It's not weariness that tempers him; it's Keene's earnestness and directness. If it turns out that this boy is off his rocker, it will be a damn shame.

"Just friendly, sympathetic. Nothing else."

"Okay."

"Please . . . Can you check it out?" Richard clears his throat to chase the wiggle of panic that has crept into his voice. He sits forward and digs two knuckles into his forehead right between the eyebrows, trying to ground a burgeoning headache.

"I had my men search Braun's place yesterday. It was clean."

"Of course it was," Richard says softly.

Even that doesn't annoy Oliver, because it's not at all patronizing by some punk, but has the sound of a man's frustration. Frustration, if you don't let it get the best of you, is fuel for action. Oliver is well aware of that; it was his mindset, when his mind was whole.

Now it fully dawns on Richard what Oliver has just said to him, that this police sergeant has taken some real action. Not his fault that the timing wasn't optimal. "You did say you searched his apartment?"

"Yes."

Richard feels energy gathering, feels that someone is on his side. "Thanks."

"You're welcome."

"That was, uh, pretty fast."

"My guys go through it thoroughly. They don't miss anything."

"No, I mean doing it in the first place, setting it up."

"Routine," Oliver lies.

"So, nothing at all, huh?"

"Nope. And by the way, we still have an NCIC check out on Miss Carson, so if we get any hits I'll let you know."

"What's that?"

"NCIC? It's a national computer system for missing persons."

Richard never heard of it. "Right."

"If she surfaces and law enforcement spots her, we'll be notified." And now Oliver decides he'll take a leap of faith and pronounce Richard sane. It's a judgment call; if he's wrong, he really doesn't have anything to lose here, anyway. "Meanwhile . . . Look, Richard, I'm in the 'reacting' business, understand? I need more to go on."

"That's what I'm trying to come up with," says Richard, gratified, almost thrilled that the sergeant has addressed him by his first name.

"Suppose he killed these women right in the apartment like you suggest. What do you think he does with the—"

"Bodies? I have an answer for that. It's so crude, it works."

"Let's hear it."

"He dumps them down the trash chute."

"The trash chute?" Oliver considers rather than belittles the suggestion. During his career in Philadelphia, he knows of no body disposed of in that fashion, but that doesn't mean it never happened. It was, in fact, discussed as a possibility in connection with an apparent murder in a highrise off Wissahickon Drive some years back.

"Like a Hefty bag," Richard says.

"Filled with body parts?"

Richard warms to the subject. "Maybe . . . He's a surgeon, or at least, soon to be."

"I get your drift. That's quite a job for an apartment bathroom."

"True. Your men didn't find any traces of blood?"

"That's right," but now Oliver is thinking of another court order, this one for a full chemical scan of the premises. Needs more to go on.

"Maybe he just sends them down intact," Richard says.

"How?"

"In a body bag. He can get those easily enough at a hospital, right?"

"Too bulky . . . the whole body."

"You'd be surprised what can fit down there."

"A foot in diameter?"

"It's a foot-and-a-half here; probably no government standard for trash chutes, huh?"

"Probably not."

"I measured it."

"I'm sure you did." Sonofagun. This kid shoulda been a cop. Much like Frank Grant did, Oliver is developing a grudging admiration for Richard, but his bears a certain professional weight.

"A slender woman—Lori's small and thin—encased in a body bag can fit just as easily as a big bag of trash," Richard says. "And it's a straight shot down."

"Uh-huh."

"In fact, I'm going to be testing it out today, Sergeant. I've obtained a dummy that the car companies use to, you know, test for impact injuries in crashes. I've got it in a suit travel-bag, which is shorter than an actual body bag, which will make it even more difficult, since the body will group up a little, know what I mean?"

"I get the picture." Oliver is warming his hand on the coffee mug.

"Could the police observe, Sergeant?" Richard senses an ally and wants to cultivate him. "Could *you* observe?"

Oliver slurps some more coffee. He is almost smiling at himself. "Eh, maybe I will. I might even bring a body bag for you. No sense makin' it any harder than it has to be."

"Right," Richard says, and now he's the one smiling to himself. "While you're here, why don't you drop in on Davis Braun yourself, Sergeant?"

Oliver takes it as the compliment it's intended to be, that he might pick up something his boys missed. "I don't know about that. But I will try to make it over there. How's twelve-thirty?"

"Sure . . . good."

"I'll see if I can break away for a half hour."

"You're a good man, Sergeant."

"Yeah, right."

"You ever read any poetry?"

Oliver blinks a couple times. That's a question he's never fielded before. "Not since high school."

"Ever hear of Walt Whitman?"

"Know the name. He's got some things named after him over in Camden."

"You'd like his stuff. 'Look for me under your boot soles,' he said."

"Boot soles, huh? That works for the police beat, all right."

"Well, if it ever comes down to it," Richard says, "don't look for me there."

"OK . . . ?"

"No, I won't be there. I'll be, you know, somewhere up on high."

"What's that mean?"

"You'll know when the time comes."

Oliver scratches his chin. Maybe his sanity verdict was premature.

"Oh, Sergeant, you, eh, know where my apartment is?"

"The 42s on Locust."

"Yes." Richard hangs up. *Yes.*

Oliver hangs up and says to himself, "What the hell."

Davis Braun is in his bathroom, observing the previous evening's handiwork. The tubes, both plastic and stainless steel, are disconnected and stashed in supermarket paper bags ready for disposal. He swings Lori's body around and out of the bathtub, and onto the body bag on the white-and-black tiled floor. One side of the bag curls up against the base of the toilet and the vanity.

He eases the body down, then turns on the hot water in the tub full-blast. Steam rises and cobwebs the room, misting the mirror on the medicine cabinet and wetting the shower curtain. Now Braun is jamming Lori into the body bag, as the tub fills with scalding water.

"Maintenance."

It is a muffled voice somewhere, next door, in the hall, somewhere.

"Maintenance."

Braun stops dead. *The guy's in his apartment.* "Hello!"

"Maintenance."

"Just a minute, I'm in the bathroom," he yells and yanks off the water. "Be right there." He can only shake his head in disbelief, step out of the bathroom and close the door behind him. The wood is a bit warped, and the door doesn't close flush and click shut but wedges itself into the doorjamb.

He wipes his hands on his gym shorts, as he walks into the living room. Good-old Orlando, who fixed the garbage disposal on his last visit, is holding a stepladder. He's a small polite man, lines at his sharp dark eyes, a dozen years on the job at the 42s, knows the place inside-out.

"Orlando."

"Sorry . . . Guess you didn't hear me knock."

"Guess not. What's up?"

"Smoke alarms. You get the flyer?"

"I don't remember, I might have."

"Gotta check 'em. Whole building. Got me working Saturday."

"No kidding?" Braun looks back toward the closed bathroom door and relaxes just a little. No need for Orlando to go in there.

"Just be a minute," says Orlando, who sets up his stepladder and climbs so he can reach the smoke detector on the living room ceiling. He uncaps it, fingers the wiring, pokes it and raises a sharp beep. "New central system. We got to check everything out."

He gets down, walks to the alcove between bathroom and bedroom, and resets his ladder. Braun watches. It stinks back there, but there's no reason for him to go into the bathroom. No reason. Unless he has a sudden urge to use the toilet.

Orlando wrinkles his nose, reacting to the smell, but doesn't say anything, just goes about his business. Lots of different smells in these apartments, and not all of them like petunias. The second smoke alarm offers its short, piercing beep. Braun is still standing in the living room, hands on hips. "Sorry about the stink back there," he says. "I got this new stuff to clean up the bathroom. It's really strong, huh?"

Orlando nods yes, gets down, closes his ladder and walks past Braun to the door. "You're all set," he says.

Braun opens the door for him. "Thanks, Orlando. See ya." With that, the little maintenance man is padding down the carpeted hallway, off to his next destination. Braun closes the door and is left to ponder the ferocious irony of timing, and the apparent ease of hiding in plain sight.

15

Richard keeps trying for Lori, keeps getting her voice mail, fears the worst, knows the worst has happened. He's convinced that either the trash has got her by now or Braun still has her. But Oliver is coming to witness the simulation, maybe even bring a body bag to enhance it, and maybe he'll look up Braun while he's at it. There is no turning back from this thing now; the freight car's in motion, and the track is downhill.

His yellow plastic laundry basket is overflowing, socks and underwear spilled out of it and onto the industrial-beige carpet that extends into the narrow closet. Naked carpet fibers shoot from the imperfect tuck at the aluminum runner for the bifold door. A cup of coffee and a half-eaten piece of wheat toast sit on the desk in front of the window at the opposite side of the bedroom. Richard feels like diving into a shower and transforming himself, stepping out renewed, alchemized, both he and the past purified. If only.

The phone rings and he scoops it to his ear. "Lori?"

"Richard?"

He slumps. "Yeah . . . it's me."

"Who's Lori?" asks Evelyn.

"Friend of mine." What business is it of . . . ?

"Oh," she says. "Hope she's nice. Listen, Richard, your father and I are concerned about you."

"Don't worry, there's—"

"We want to talk to you about your . . . situation."

"Not now, Mother, I'm—"

"If you need some money to tide you over, you can count on us, I want you to know that."

"Thanks."

"Richard?"

"Yes?"

"I've never asked you for much—"

Richard sits on his bed. Here we go . . .

"—but I want you to tell me what's bothering you."

"Nothing."

She raises her voice. "Say something, for crying out loud, give me a clue. What's the matter?"

"Nothing."

Then he fires it like a flare into the sky. "Why did you keep me from saying anything about the Dempseys back then?"

"Richard!"

"Why?"

"How many times have we been through this?"

"Never, really, to tell you the truth."

"Oh, come on! This is madness." Her voice is defensive, nasty, scared.

"No, we've never really been 'through this,' Mother."

"Richard, I'm not going to spend time—"

"You asked me for a clue."

"I did, but—"

"I'm giving you one . . . What I heard that night, it . . . mattered. It should have mattered."

"Nothing was ever proven, don't you understand?"

"I'm telling you that what I heard," his voice quavers and rises a half-octave, "mattered more than anything else in the world . . . to me."

"It wouldn't have changed anything. The imaginings of a little boy, that's all the police would have made of it."

"You don't know that; I didn't have the chance."

"I didn't see any point in stirring things up, in pointing a finger at a man who, as far as the police could determine, was innocent."

"I would have become part of their determination."

"For godsake, Richard, I didn't want to put *you* through that." Silence on the line, then Richard's "Me, huh?"

"What does that mean?"

"Just that I don't think it was me."

"Who was it, then?"

"You."

"I don't have to listen to—"

"I think you were more concerned about what *you* would go through, or maybe you were in denial. That's a great expression I learned when I went away. You just didn't want to believe that such a thing could happen in your neat little world. Right under your nose."

"Oh, I see. It's my fault. If you felt that strongly about it, why didn't you run to the police station yourself?"

"I was eight years old, remember? By the way, where the hell was dad through all this? I can only remember you hovering over me, telling me what to do. Typical, huh?" Richard is rocking at the edge of his bed, a bit of anguish, a bit of release.

Evelyn affects a schoolmarm's tone and rhythm. "I must say this is a fine response from a son to a mother's offer to help. That's why I called, remember?"

"Well, if you must say it . . ."

"I always had your welfare in mind, and I still do."

"Remember the circus, Mom?"

"What? What circus? What does . . . ?"

It was the only time that they were all out together, the Dempseys and the Keenes, two sets of parents and a child with each. Barnum &

Bailey/Ringling Brothers had come to Veterans Stadium in Philadelphia, and the six of them took the subway south to the end of the line at Broad and Pattison. They sat across from each other on the hard orange subway seats that clung to opposite tubular walls near the doors, and Richard and Cindy conversed with their eyes, while their parents shouted occasional words across the aisle and over the din. At one stop below City Hall, an obese woman settled into a vacant end seat by the rail, her bulk pressing Herb Dempsey into Cindy, who was sandwiched between her father and mother. Herb looked uncomfortable, as if the temperature suddenly had risen twenty degrees, or a foul smell had been let loose. A man who had just gotten on the train gripped a metal pole and stood between the two seating rows, a Daily News *rolled up and tucked into his armpit. He partially obscured Richard's straight-ahead view, but with the swaying of the train and some bobbing of his own, Richard could keep an eye on Cindy, and she on him.*

He could also see Herb Dempsey's thigh twitch and give Cindy a little push, what seemed at first like a playful movement. Richard maneuvered so he could peer around the man standing at the pole and saw a flicker of annoyance cross Cindy's face, while her father looked in that moment like a grade-school punk playing a practical joke. The thigh struck again, stronger this time, and Richard had to look through the crook of the man's arm, as the man placed hand on hip, the hand that was not gripping the pole, the armpit still able to secure the newspaper. Now Richard could see that Cindy's expression was moving toward anger, her father's disturbing smirk was more pronounced, and her mother was glancing at both of them in an inquiring but fearful fashion, none of the fear rubbing off on her daughter. Cindy then turned away from her father, expressionless, and he sat still. The train, brightly lit and postered with public service messages and skin cream ads marred by Magic Marker graffiti, rumbled through the dank underground tunnel, slowing and stopping at a platform backed by green-and-white tiled walls and squared columns thick enough to hold up a city.

Richard knew of circuses from books and movies, but this was his first time to see one live. The image of a Big Top was vivid to him, but here they would be in the open air of the huge stadium in South Philadelphia, surrounded everywhere by seats vaulted to a curving roofline rimming the whole structure, as if a flying saucer's giant hatch had retracted. Within the concrete cauldron, the scents of steaming hotdogs and mustard, salty popcorn and roasted peanuts soaked the air. This was Richard's first trip here, as he and Marty had not quite reached the point where it was time for father and son to attend a Big League ballgame.

The high wire was strung across the yawning expanse of stadium for its full diameter, maybe ten stories off the ground. The Wallendas were in town, and Richard knew of this act that bore the automatic label "death-defying." From his seat in the lower level, he had to throw his head back as far as it could go for a good view of the high wire splicing the clouds that hung like upended mountains in the Sunday afternoon sky. Richard was entranced by the idea of a man walking through space like that, high above the throng, where only a single slight misstep could be the agent of his undoing. Yet Richard projected himself onto that high wire, felt altogether comfortable with the notion—not as an expression of daring but of freedom. Cindy sat between him and her father, and when a Wallenda death-defier carrying his balancing rod stepped into that sky, Herb Dempsey elbowed his daughter in her small ribs and said in a smart-alecky way, "Think he'll fall?" Resolute, Cindy said "No" and leaned her left shoulder into Richard, and her right away from her father. When Herb Dempsey sent another elbow his daughter's way, the contact rammed her against Richard, whose forearm reflexively forced Evelyn's off their shared armrest to the left, a chain reaction like a car pileup on an interstate. "Richard," Evelyn said, a startled reprimand, but Richard tuned her out. He was watching and listening to what was happening on his right side, a tiny yelp that had come out of Cindy and her mother offering an equally small "Herb," a caution, Richard was sure, that was not being used for the first time. And through the entire afternoon, through the Wallendas' safe passage and the trapeze artists' swing-flight, through the sad prankish profusions of the clowns and the whipcrack staging of bounding lions and tigers, through the loping rumble of the elephants and their glittering riders almost as pretty, almost as captivating, as Cindy Dempsey, through it all, Richard could not stop thinking about that little yelp and Penny Dempsey's soft warning note.

"Remember the circus, Mom?"

"The circus? What are you talking about now?"

"Remember what I told you that time when we went to the circus? After we came home?"

"No, Richard," says Evelyn, tired of the conversation and tired of her son. "I don't remember the circus. What circus?"

It's the toughest cleanup detail that Davis Braun has experienced, including all of his hospital duty here in Philadelphia and at the New Jersey shore. He has to get rid of the stink in his place, and he doesn't want to use a fumigator and leave a traceable action, a telltale clue. Plus, fumigators don't show up on demand, and he needs action now. He's dumped into the tub all of the cleaning fluid from the container whose translucent spray tubing he utilized in the embalming. In addition, he's put to work some heavy-duty scrub foam and several aerosol deodorizers, and he's scouring the tub with a stiff-bristled brush, and sponging the sink and floor, and wiping dry with rags and paper towels, and emptying cans of Lysol with Outdoor Scent in a frantic effort to chase every last offending malodorous molecule, grounded or airborne, from the premises. Strange visitors have been showing up here, as if they're on to him. How could that be?

Keene. That skinny runt, of all the people to show up at his door at the moment of truth; he has to be the one. Unbelievable. Super Ears, a nerd who probably has no life of his own and nothing better to do with his time than to "investigate" other people's lives, as if it's his personal mission to be a savior or something. To come after *me*. What, is he kidding?

Braun spends an hour-and-a-half disinfecting and deodorizing, and decides he's had enough, that he has olfactory fatigue by this time. He'll let it sit and come back for a whiff after his nostrils have cleared. He washes his hands with the antibacterial pump soap, which he regularly pilfers from the hospital.

The main thing is that all evidence and all traces of Lori be removed. The loaded body bag is on the floor in the living room, like baggage ready for a trip. Braun almost trips on it as he steps over it, then realizes he has stepped on something small and hard on the carpet. His eyes search the area and he doesn't spot anything. Drop something on this carpet and the damn thing disappears, every time. He kneels and inspects, square inch by square inch. There it is, lying flat on the carpet fibers, one of Lori Calder's little gold circular earrings. He rotates it between his thumb and forefinger as if it's a nugget panned from a riverbed. When he unzips the body bag, about ten inches' worth, Lori's purpled lifeless face takes one more hit of daylight. The other earring is firmly in place, Braun notices, and he re-attaches the one he's just retrieved. Her ear lobe feels supple enough.

Something resembling remorse threatens to push tears into Braun's eyes, though his feelings might be more directed toward himself and his burden than the dead girl. He gets rid of the emotion by reminding himself of this certainty: They carry built-in stores of betrayal, women do, and each has enough ammunition to be expended on an unlimited number of men. It isn't that Lori turned stupid all of a sudden; it's a woman's natural urge to possess (without having earned such a right), backed by the compulsion to betray should possession be denied. Yes, that is it in a nutshell.

Maybe he'll be a psychiatrist someday after he gets tired of surgery.

A shame about Lori, because they had some fun together, especially when she toyed with Keene, who had fallen into her lap. She had her bad-girl side and that attracted him in the first place. Of course, she didn't think she was dealing with a murder, just some garden-variety forgery and fraud, and the unsavory thrill of being the other woman. With Davis Braun, there was always another woman.

They were potent together in bed, no question about that. Something about Lori suggested she would help him frisk Eleanor's bank account, and even if she balked when he pitched his plan, he felt certain she would not go to the police. She dug him. Then when Keene happened along, he figured she could beguile him and defuse the threat. So he brought her into his scheme, lied that Eleanor was some kind of monster-witch who was taking advantage of him. He was confident that when the moment of betrayal came, he would be equal to it.

For the eventual betrayal of women is something you can count on.

Eleanor. It was nice at first. She was warm and sensuous, and kind of hip and good-looking, especially for a paralegal. She was brainy and stylish, and had a nice way of touching your hand or thigh to elevate a humorous or intimate remark. And he liked it that she wasn't a high-toned chick. They met at a shot-and-sawdust bar in the shadow of the hospital. He invited her to move into his apartment at the 42s without giving it much thought. Sharing the rent was a prime motivation; Eleanor was making decent money, and he was leveraged to the max with his credit cards and student loans. She went for it in a heartbeat, leaving her nearby studio apartment a month early and writing off the security deposit.

Up close, you see each other's warts, Braun knew that. But with Eleanor, things unraveled even faster than he'd expected. Once she moved in with him, she began to treat him like a roommate rather than a lover. She got a bump in salary and he was still grappling with loans from his undergrad days, but rent always had to be an even split. She enjoyed his stud services, then felt no urge to cook meals or be the engaging, attentive woman who had originally attracted him. Worse, her fault-finding, her identification of his flaws (always misguided, he felt) grew in frequency and intensity almost from day one. He was puzzled, then peeved, then retaliatory.

Eleanor had a way of cocking her head to one side when she was annoyed with him, this movement and the accompanying smug facial expression jarringly reminiscent of his mother. As she launched into her recrimination, or eased down into a mode of subtle mocking, her nose seemed to flare and her eyes flattened so that the overall look of womanly superiority perfectly fit her tone of voice. It infuriated him. The first few times he caught an Eleanor broadside, he felt physically sick—something he'd admit to no one, least of all her—and it took his system a full day to revive, a period during which he and Eleanor would be separated by work and he'd try in vain to regroup as he went through his paces at the hospital. Worse, he was sure that, while he was obsessing about her, he was the last thing on her mind. She was, in a word, unstable. What the hell had he let into his home?

She'd try, or at least seemed to try, to make amends in bed, but he was pretty damn sure that brought her a nice payoff, too. He never doubted his potency in that regard, his ability to please a woman. He had the right physical equipment in abundance, and he'd had one hell of a teacher. Dolores had seduced him, and herself, it would seem, with a meticulous months-long campaign, and none of the neighbors dared dream of what went on behind the brick walls of their Havertown single. Dolores provided the primer, the training camp that made him a sexual athlete. Those months, that year, sophomore year in high school. Dolores Braun, dead these last half-dozen years, the cancer less yielding than her son. He misses her.

After a session of lovemaking several months into their live-in arrangement, Braun decided he was going to kill Eleanor. In the combined muskiness of her sweat and perfume and secretion, she had smelled like Dolores, the memory of smells being everlasting. That was both enticement and sacrilege.

That was her death sentence.

But if the impulse was just that, the deed would be carefully crafted. In the cold, sober light of day.

Just like the one before.

"Richard?" Janet Kroll says into the phone after wheedling his number out of Frank at the front desk. "Janet Kroll . . . I've been thinking about what you told me yesterday. I'd like to speak with you."

Richard is surprised, excited. "Sure."

"Can we meet on the sundeck up on the roof in about forty-five minutes?"

"Sure."

Braun has zipped the body bag nearly shut, when he remembers something and unzips it with a hissing flourish. Just double-checking: the body is naked, except for the attached gold circular earrings and—yes, there it is—the gold-and-ivory bracelet at the wrist. Dressed for the occasion. Nothing left behind; Lori's clothes and shoes are stuffed in a plastic shopping bag tied in a knot. Now he zips the body bag closed in semi-slow motion, so that he sees Lori's face gradually disappear, a kind of final goodbye. He stands and drags the body bag into the living-room walk-in closet, props it L-shaped against one wall. A holding tank.

At Richard's place, the phone rings again. Hopes against hope.

"Lori?"

"Mister Keene?"

Sinking feeling. A solicitor. "Yes."

"I'm with Centennial Cable. We're offering a significant savings to our customers for long-distance telephone service . . ."

Richard closes his eyes in utter weariness, and shuts off his ears. Yes, he can do that when he's overwhelmed to the point of capitulation, a defense mechanism that, regrettably, works only for bursts of time. Fragments from the cable gal: "How much are you currently paying for . . . Wouldn't you like to have . . . ? Can you tell me approximately how many . . . ?"

"I'm sorry," Richard says, ever polite. "I have to go."

The solicitor is firing off an 800 number as Richard hangs up gently. He punches in the three digits for Information and gets a homogenized, unearthly, computerized, vaguely female voice: "What city and state, please?"

"Philadelphia, Pennsylvania."

"What listing, please?"

"The City of Philadelphia Sanitation Department." Long shot.

The next voice is human. Barely. "Hold for that listing, please."

He automatic-dials the Sanitation Department, gets through to a woman he fears may be busy mopping the floor on this fine Saturday, and explains to her that he has inadvertently thrown out a very valuable item. Can he somehow intercept the trash truck or meet it at the landfill and rummage around in the load? He'll be able to spot it readily.

No sir, she says. I don't know any way we can do that. It's kind of like putting a letter in a mailbox. Once you drop it, it's gone. Besides, it would be dangerous for you to do that, plus we're not insured for that kind of thing, know what I mean? What did you throw out?

He calls Oliver and suggests a court order. Keep those court orders coming. Premature, says Oliver, who says he can't make it to the 42s this afternoon to witness Richard's dummy drop and won't question Braun again, at least for now. "If I interrogate him after my detectives have already done that, with no further information, it starts to look like harassment," he says. "But I tell you what. Hold off on that trash chute business 'til tomorrow, and I'll come over when I'm off-duty. Just as an interested private citizen, understand?"

Richard will take what he can get, but he's growing antsy, can't bear to wait around. He hasn't had any strenuous exercise in a couple of days—the ten easy minutes on the stationary bike yesterday while watching Janet was nothing—and that's OK because he wants to give his sore knee a little more time off. Her invitation to meet him on the deck is quite welcome. Fresh air. High altitude. She needs to confide in him. He's excited about that.

And what if he happens to be up there, Davis Braun, so what? Turn the tables on the sonofabitch. Who's pursuing who?

Richard slips on the DisneyWorld T-shirt he's had since his middle-school trip more than fifteen years ago (it was big then and still is) and leaves the apartment, looking both ways like a child crossing the street, as he steps into the coolness of the hallway. He takes the elevator to the top, walks past the fitness center and the banquet room and the glass-domed swimming pool, and steps outside onto the sundeck.

September is almost gone but it is still a day of high heat, as if summer is determined to fight the calendar. The pale-green concrete decking stretches to a barrier of bulky wooden-planked planters hugging a chest-high railing, gaps between the planters wide enough for a person to squeeze through. Azaleas sway and flutter in the highrise breezes, and beyond their dance, the city's forest of glass and chrome looms broad and immovable, and gauzy traces of cloud brushstroke an otherwise clear sky. The sun is welcome against Richard's neck and cheeks and arms, pale skin attesting to his indoor life. There's a part of him that wants to strip off his shirt and drink in this scene of lounging bodies and oiled limbs, but somehow he doesn't trust himself to do that. Instead, he just receives the sun as a dose of health, hoping to store its warmth for recall when the world turns cold. Maybe at some point after Janet arrives, and they're talking and relaxed, he'll take off his shirt and take in the sun, lie back on a lounge chair next to her.

She's not here yet. Sideways, he makes his way through the space between two wooden planters to the metal railing of short column-like verticals attached to a single horizontal top rail not far from the edge of the building. Here, at the heights, like the little boy on the monkey bars or way up on the Empire State Building's Observatory Deck, like the high-schooler on the Gettysburg tower, like the collegian atop the Mayan ruins, he is comfortable and free and somehow safe, as if the city scattered below, and its towers and spires yet above, shield him from harm. To the east, the Ben Franklin Bridge seems to hang above the river, its sweeping lines shrunken by distance, sized for a wall painting. Due south, just a few blocks away, bronze William Penn squeezes through the nouveau giants that now dwarf his amply-brimmed hat, once the highest point in the city. The majesty of the lofty and the scale of metropolis secure Richard's hope for a grand scheme of things. He likes the city when he can view it from a distance. He feels relaxed and powerful, a tingling of invulnerability, however temporary, spreading through him like an analgesic chasing pain.

He props his arms on the railing and looks downward.

"Long way down, huh?"

The voice chills him, but only for an instant, because somehow, he knew he'd be here. Has to be this way; avoidance is yesterday's curse.

Richard turns from the rail and faces Davis Braun, who is barechested and wearing pricy sunglasses that turn his eye sockets into coals. "I don't know how they build 'em this high," Braun continues, moving a step closer. "Can you explain that to me?"

Richard tightens and cowers ever so slightly, not altogether frightened, but no longer feeling invulnerable either. Time to press the issue, confront the monster. Braun is an impressive specimen, a blunt configuration of evil in a photoplay package. He steps back, selects a deck lounger and drapes his towel on the backrest. There are five additional sunbathers up here at this midday hour, four young women and one other guy, capsuled apart from one another, separate magazines and lotions.

"You look familiar," Braun says to Richard, playing with him. "You live on my floor?"

Richard looks at him squarely and doesn't move. "I don't know."

"Wait a minute . . . I got it," Braun says. "Yeah . . . right . . . I saw you at the elevators that time, remember?"

"No."

"What's your apartment?"

Richard keeps silent but moves away from the railing.

Braun sits and straddles the lounger, which is angled toward Richard and the sun. "Yeah, that's it. Aren't you that guy right underneath me, the one who thought he heard some funny business goin' on at my place, isn't that you?" Braun is kneading sunscreen onto his deltoids. "You get off on the wrong floor that time or somethin'? Musta had one too many, huh?" He coats his neck, cheeks and forehead. "Or maybe you were just visiting someone else on the floor, that it?"

Richard is stiff and his voice low in his throat, but he is not super-scared, he can feel that in his extremities, which remain limber. "I don't remember."

Braun springs from the lounger as if ready for a round of horseplay. Richard flinches a second before Braun extends his hand. "Davis Braun."

Richard puts his hand out and Braun takes it, gripping it like a sopping wash rag he wants to drain dropless. "It's nice to meet people in the building," says Braun, as Richard hangs on, worries about crushed small bones at the knuckles. "Sometimes things can be pretty impersonal around here, you know?"

Braun releases him and Richard draws his hand back as if from an electric shock. Braun smiles. "Looks like you got some kind of nervous tic there?" He goes back to the lounger and lies down, a frat boy lolling in the sun.

Richard remains locked in place, absorbing the insult, weighing his actions, his future actions, then the calculations stop and something out of his gut takes over. He steps forward, approaches Braun, hesitates, passes him as if heading out of the area, then stops and turns toward him. "I know what happened," Richard says softly, his words thinned away by the altitude. "To *both of them*. Every bit of it . . . It's just a matter of time 'til all the evidence is in."

Braun doesn't move a muscle. "How's that, buddy?"

A tremor runs through Richard. "You want to kill me, too?" The other sunbathers are too far away to hear Richard's soft voice.

Braun just lies there, luxuriating in the sun. "Soon . . . soon enough," he says between almost-closed lips.

Frozen for an instant, Richard turns and walks away, but another voice stops him.

"Is this seat taken?"

Richard turns back slowly to see Janet Kroll in an aquamarine one-piece bathing suit. Funny he had not noticed her on the deck before right now; her angle of approach, his attention to Braun. Now, though, he sees her. The way she curves above, below and through the high-cut suit.

Braun pats an empty chaise lounge. "All yours."

As Janet sits down, she sees Richard and averts her eyes, covers them with sunglasses. Disappointment shows in his eyes, but he won't let them linger. In a moment, he's on his way. He'll speak with her later. She obviously doesn't want to acknowledge him in Braun's presence. She's playing it smart.

Something stops Richard when he opens the glass door to the banquet room and steps inside. That corkscrew twisting in his stomach, and the breath that dies in his throat. She wasn't sidetracked by Braun, *she came there to meet him and not Richard.* The bathing suit, her cool demeanor, a rooftop rendezvous. Wanted to see Richard squirm, have Braun frighten him off. Served him up on a platter.

No. She could have been wearing the suit for him. Well, if not exactly for him, at least to get some sun while she was up there. To meet with him. Expressly with him.

Richard doesn't know what to think. If he could talk to Lori about it, she'd figure it out. If he could talk to Lori.

He wants to turn back and look through the glass at Janet and Braun, check their body language, maybe catch their expressions from a distance. But he keeps walking.

Stretched out on their lounge chairs, Janet and Braun are close enough to smell each other's breath.

"So," she says. "How's the sun?"

"Outstanding," he says.

Her skin is moist with the Sea&Ski SPF40 she's already applied. Braun can smell it and see its sheen. "You got sunscreen on."

"Sure do."

"How come you didn't let me do the honors?"

"We're not quite ready for that," she says.

"But we're getting close?"

"Close enough for me to cook you dinner tonight."

"I have to go to—"

"Let me guess . . . the hospital. What else is new? Tomorrow night?"

The lounger squeaks, as he sits up and extends his hand toward her. "I'm all yours."

She remains on her back, drinking in the sun, but reaches out and places her hand on his, delicate as a leaf falling onto a pond. "Bring some white wine."

16

Herb Dempsey is pointing an empty sleeve like the Ghost of Christmas Future. His face is distorted and malleable, changing shape like pizza dough. What doesn't change are the eyes, lifeless and milky blue, eyes that you run from. Through the sleeve comes a forefinger-leading extended hand, which has a life of its own detached from his body, an alien's accessory to disengage and hunt down prey, incapacitate and kill.

And through it all, Evelyn provides the overview, a Greek Chorus of fear and uncertainty and self-recrimination. "We wanted to keep you out of it. Nothing was ever proved . . . We wanted to keep you out of it . . . We wanted to . . ."

If she didn't listen to him, didn't heed his warning, add the name of Janet Kroll to the list of people who have paid him no mind, have given his words no weight, for whom he has been invisible. He's offered her his most earnest caution; if she chooses to regard him as a nut and cast in with Braun, that's her misfortune. Lori's situation was different. *He* got Lori involved, and that's eating at him. That this guy could be so brazen as to do it again, in a matter of days, same place, same M.O., the live-in, then the next-door neighbor. Surrounded by people everywhere, side, top, bottom. Unthinkable.

Because that's what happened, Richard knows it like he knows the sounds he heard that night at the door of Apartment

2307, and that night in his bedroom of the row house on Airdale Road.

Something else gnaws at him. What if Braun showed up on the sundeck neither by coincidence nor by Janet's invitation. What if Braun somehow is tracking him, shadowing him. The familiar shudder of fear runs straight up through Richard from his pelvis to his neck, then he forces his mind to leap to another thought, to focus on what he's doing, his mission, the completion of which will take care of Braun and all the demons through all the years. That banishes the fear, that sickening paralyzing dread that arrives irrespective of season or hour. He can deal with it because he sees a way to end it. There is a resolution coming.

Lori's disappearance makes it inevitable. But the original case, the matter of Eleanor Carson, that is everything that Richard must master. No one to safeguard her when she lived and no one else to avenge her in death. Not her father. Not the police (at least without undue prodding). Not her *boyfriend,* for godsake. Her unlikely champion: Richard Keene. Strange casting.

The facts and the suppositions, the weight of it all will tell. The bodies will be in the landfill somewhere, under layers of refuse. If it takes a small army to find them, so be it. If it takes Richard working round the clock with a pick and shovel, like the little kid he once was, dredging wet sand at the shoreline in Atlantic City, so be it.

If Janet was surprised by Braun on the deck, if she believes Richard, she'll let him know, otherwise the hell with her. Meanwhile, the crash-test dummy. Assembled and ready to go. Wait a day for Oliver, the man's on his side.

Richard has just arrived at the door to his apartment and is listening for any strange sounds from within, though he knows nobody's there. He's listening for murderous sounds. He's listening for subtle sounds. Maybe Braun somehow flew down the stairs ahead of the elevator and got inside his apartment with a passkey from Mike. No . . . *no.* Richard is too smart to succumb to paranoia, too stable now, this newfound stability arising from conviction. No, there's nothing sinister awaiting inside, just the ticking of the battery-powered kitchen clock and the refrigerator's drone and all the other buzzing-slicing-swirling sounds that saturate the hallway and the building, all tucked about his cursed ears.

Davis Braun had been thinking about Richard Keene an hour before heading up to the sundeck, thinking about what to do with him, to him. He can no longer ignore him because this Keene is a tenacious little bugger, that much is clear. Probably had a hand in the police showing up at the apartment. He's tried scaring him, thought that might be enough. But evidently sterner measures are needed to take care of the Richard Keene problem.

So when he spotted Keene heedless of danger near the edge of the rooftop sundeck, Braun's first impulse was to grab the skinny sucker by his shorts and boost him over the railing for an unimpeded swan dive to the street. Obviously, the rashness of such an act was off the charts, but so easy had his previous eliminations been that he had grown a bit tipsy on success. Maybe no one would see it. He was unstoppable, undetectable.

The continuation of which depended on his keeping his wits, he reminded himself, as the murderous urge subsided on the sundeck high above the streets of Philadelphia. Disposing of Keene must be as masterful a stroke as the others. The movie . . . with Eleanor . . . now that was a great touch, symbolic and, in its masking of like noises of distress, tactically inspired. *The Boston Strangler* had made an impression on him when he'd first seen it on late-night cable a few years back. He loved the realism of the movie and the fact that it was based on a true story. So when the time came for a well-considered coldblooded murder, why not embellish with a *Strangler* soundtrack and, simultaneously, conceal a struggle of even greater realism?

Of course, he was no serial killer, no mentally disturbed Albert DiSalvo killing at random to quench some compulsive need, attaching a ritual to the act. No, he was not seduced by that, not at all. That was a portrait of desperation, and he was Davis Braun, a man in charge of his emotions, of his life, fully capable of taking decisive action when called for. There were triggers for certain behaviors—he knew that, he'd studied some psychology—but the trick was to recognize them and be rational in your response. Murder could be the most rational act of all. Self-preservation was the ultimate goal.

So the use of *Strangler* in such circumstances was ingenious, he told himself. Eliminating Eleanor was a reprise of his Karen Rodalewicz performance. Same problems with Karen, disrespect, emasculation. That was the first one. Same movie, same outcome, but no one on his trail that time.

Lori a different story. Spur of the moment.

Now Keene, with this crazy hearing of his and a persistence about him, like a flea. And there he was, on the sundeck, standing near the edge of the building, an invitation difficult to renounce. But Braun was too smart for that. Self-control, baby; rational. He flexed quiet intimidation in the mellow sunshine and sent the boy off even more damaged than before, he supposed. Susceptible to a later strike. Not too much later, though.

Some bird-dogging was in order.

As she lay next to him, both of them face-up to the sun, part of her felt cold and sick and hopeless, and part of her remained alert and calculating. Now, back in her apartment, she worries that she's placed someone other than herself in jeopardy. She drew Richard Keene to the deck in order to observe Braun under pressure, induce a reaction that might tell her more, that she might use. She saw enough, and sensed enough, to confirm everything.

"Who's he?" she asked him.

"Nobody," Braun answered. "Just one more disposable character in the big wide world." Then he sort of caught himself and added, "I've seen him around here once or twice."

"He looked upset," she said.

"Could be." Braun smiled broadly and jabbed the armrest of his lounge recliner. "I think he wanted this spot. But I beat him to it."

Of course Richard has it right. As if she really needed more confirmation. God, another dead woman and she did nothing, could do nothing. She knows he was living with her, she's been watching him for a month now. But it's not an easy task in this highrise vault. Private worlds are locked up. The last couple of weeks, of course, she's maneuvered herself into his life, yet still had no inkling of what took place until Richard told her.

She's in her bathroom, combing some coloring through her wet hair straightened and lengthened by the water. She keeps hearing the word "disposable," and the flutter in her stomach is the one she feels when an airplane hits a rough patch. She's touching up with a few lines of Clairol red. The blonde highlights are still there. The hair and the thinned eyebrows and the aerobicized contoured body have been more than enough to fool her audience of one, since they had seen each other only once before, and on the fly at that; a quick introduction from Karen, goodbye, nice to meet you, see you again. A matter of seconds, he never got her last name, barely her first. Still, this has been a command performance for her, fooling him, putting herself at risk, staying with the name Janet. Of course, there are lots of Janets in the world.

She likes the new Janet, a much more provocative version both in appearance and manner. But that's a consideration for another time. This thing can't go much longer, she can feel it, and she is alert to the danger to self and others, and moreover, the overriding possibility of failure, of coming up empty. Richard Keene . . . what a strange story. He comes from out of nowhere with his bizarre but precise account. What else could it be but true? Now Braun has two people coming after him. She must stay on him, step for step, or miss the chance that may not come again.

It will not come again if she becomes the next victim.

Fellow casino employees had noted no warning signals prior to Karen Rodalewicz's disappearance, nothing at all. She was well-liked on the floor and in the front office, a blackjack dealer who kept the cards coming, her balances accurate to the penny, and her cool at all times.

Missing bodies were not a new phenomenon at the seashore. Atlantic City, with its lurid history, its rootlessness, swampy back bays, barnacled piers, and its great lapping ocean, was a place where people disappeared. Like sand crabs.

Karen Rodalewicz had disappeared and it made no sense to her sister. Janet had seen Karen's boyfriend—a medical student, she was told—only once, that quick introduction at their place (actually, *his* place) at the highrise Oasis on the boardwalk, perhaps not even enough to etch her face in his memory. But she knew she'd recognize him again, and she knew he knew something. The instinct of a sister, a close sister.

After Karen's disappearance, Braun and Janet were each summoned to the police station on different days to answer questions, provide information. The police were as baffled as Janet. There was no evidence of foul play, not a mark anywhere. Karen's car was in its reserved spot in the parking garage. Her live-in boyfriend was a well-mannered, well-spoken medical resident on loan from his Philadelphia school to Burdette-Tomlin Hospital in Cape May County. Davis Braun.

Janet tried to reach him for weeks, but he never returned a call. Finally, no sign of her sister, hope fading, the police with nothing, she went to the Oasis to see him in person but he wasn't there. The desk man told her he was scheduled to move in two days. Karen had lived there only a few months.

A Realtor since her early divorce from Philadelphian David Kroll, who placed her second to his investment banking work with one of the old-line firms, Janet liked to set her own schedule, and that flexibility was about to serve her well. On the day of Braun's move, she returned to the Oasis and staked out the moving van for three hours while it was being loaded. There was no sign of Braun. She followed the van as it motored on the Black Horse Pike all the way to downtown Philadelphia and the rear dock of the 42s building on Locust Street. The next day, she applied for an apartment, and moved into her fifteenth-floor unit six weeks later. Her house in Lower Merion was mortgage-free courtesy of the divorce settlement, so for the time being, the 42s became her home away from home.

He'd seen her just that one time at the Oasis, he coming in, she leaving. Seconds. Still, she was taking a big chance. She turned her thick brunette hair red and let it grow, thinned her eyebrows, and attacked the fitness center, transforming her already curvy figure into something sleek and stunning. She found out what she could about Davis Braun. She bided her time, then worked it so that their paths would cross. She would get close to him, get him talking, her microcassette recorder concealed. She'd find out how the pros do that sort of thing. She would risk her life if necessary to turn up something against him.

Outside the parted slats of the miniblinds, Richard sees the somber light of dusk take over the city and slow its pulse. Most of the windowed squares of the office building directly across the way are dark and deserted, though a couple are lit and occupied. In one of them, a man whose white-shirted midsection spills over his belt buckle, is slumped in his chair and facing off with his computer, Saturday overtime at the office. In some shut-down squares, desks and shelves alternate shadow and streaks of dim light; others are dark enough to hide all traces of weekday action.

Richard is pacing in his living room, the rippled soles of his running shoes flexing against the low-pile carpet. He is antsy, anxious to do the demo, make the drop, prove his theory. It is past seven p.m., and though Sgt. Oliver will not be coming until tomorrow, Richard is tired of waiting, you wait and bad things happen. He wants to move now, and just in case he gets only this one chance, he wants a witness. Lori was his original choice. Lori's gone.

Frank. Frank's the one. Frank is ready to join his team. Plus Frank's the only one who can get him into the Dumpster room, locked up this time of day.

"I'm busy down here, man," Frank says to him on the phone.

"You have Mike there."

Frank makes a disparaging noise. "In body only. Without me in the saddle, all hell's liable to break loose, you understand?"

Richard has asked him to witness a little experiment.

"You know Lori Calder?" Richard asks.

"Little girl on twenty-three?"

"Twenty-three-oh-five to be exact . . . Might want to hold her mail." He is forcing himself to get over Lori by being blunt.

"Don't do this to me again, Keene."

"Frank, I'm giving you a chance to help solve a murder in your building. Maybe two. You'll be a hero."

Frank thinks about that and likes his thoughts. Imagines the chief of police pinning a medal on him in a ceremony at City Hall.

"All you have to do is go with me, open the door and watch. Nothing else for now," Richard says.

"Here we go with the 'for now' bit. What comes after 'for now'?"

"Nothing. I'll do the rest."

"Oh, that makes me feel much better. All right, let's hear it. Watch what?"

"Listen, this is it." And Richard explains the whole thing, the crash-test dummy, the drop down the chute, corroboration that it works, the grisly yet almost whimsical disposal right under the collective noses of all of them, of the entire city. Talk about a throwaway society.

"I don't think I can allow it," Frank says.

"What do you mean?"

"How big is this thing?"

"It fits down the chute, don't worry."

"You clog things up, Keene, it's all over."

"It *fits*. Remember, straight down, right?"

"You are too much, Keene. Too fuckin' much."

"It'll take two minutes, man." And Richard is comfortable using the word "man," talking like a real guy, making the leap into a new fraternity of maleness. "Two murders, Frank, I'm telling you. You can feel it that I'm onto something, don't deny it. Come on up, you can't ignore this. If you don't . . . I'll do it anyway, some other time."

While Richard is trying to persuade Frank to witness his chute demo, Davis Braun is sitting on his living-room couch, a cell phone pinned to his ear and Richard's recorded voice filling it. "I am on the line at the present time. Please leave a message and I'll call you back as soon as I'm free."

All right, so he's in his apartment. Good deal. Fastidious little twerp, has his voice-message distinguish between merely "on the line" and out of the apartment altogether; of course, the "out" message could play and he might be taking a crap, so nothing's foolproof. But if it's "on the line," he's there. Unless he's not and someone else is using his phone, which is unlikely. This guy's a loner all the way.

Time for a little surveillance. See what this guy is up to. Get him out in the open, then eliminate him. As they teach in med school, the best cure is prevention.

17

Richard has the assembled crash-test dummy stuffed not into a suit travel-bag, but a longer wardrobe "hanger" that he inherited from one of his mother's cedar closets in the attic. He found it hidden in a corner of the closet, forgot he had it. He has dismantled the squared-off top by removing its metal-spoked frame and wire hanger so that the zipped-up package is suitably rounded and scrunched, and will fit into the chute. Through his closed door, he hears the chime of the elevator and the automatic opening of the elevator door, followed by some static and babbling from a walkie-talkie. Frank has arrived.

Richard opens the door to his apartment and there's Frank with a this-better-be-good look on his face and a black, palm-sized walkie-talkie clipped to his belt.

"Thanks for coming, Frank."

"Yeah, sure. Let's see whatchya got."

Richard reaches down and lifts the wardrobe-wrapped dummy halfway off the floor and drags it into the hallway, right under Frank's nose and disbelieving eyes. "That's it, huh?" Frank asks, as Richard moves ahead.

"C'mon Frank. We're gonna drop it down the trash chute."

"*We're?*"

"This will confirm the feasibility of disposing a body via the trash chute."

"Well that's wonderful, professor, but . . . no way! This is exactly what I was worried about. This thing is too goddamn big."

Richard gives him a level look. "It's not, I checked it."

Frank looks like he has an itch somewhere. "Are you nuts, man? What if it gets stuck?"

Richard is now halfway to the trash room. "It should slide right through; I measured. If it doesn't, I'm not gonna jam it; I'll be wrong, that's all."

"That's all? And I'll have a mess on my—"

"But if it fits through . . . All the way down, right, Frank?"

Frank feels like he's driving on a rain-slicked curve without enough car under him . . . like a crash-test dummy. "I can't let you do this, man. Sorry."

"Look," says Richard, gripping the knob of the trash room door. "I'll just do it on my own later, I told you that. At least now you're here if anything goes wrong . . . and you're part of the investigation."

"That's great, man. That'll look good on my termination notice."

"C'mon. Frank. You're off the hook, it's all on me. I won't say a thing about you if there's a problem."

Frank scratches his chin and the beginnings of a goatee, a look he hopes will project both hip and distinguished, the best of both worlds. Inside the trash room, the smoky-rancid scent trumps the innocuous heat of a nest of electrical wires. Richard opens the hatch. "Give me a hand," he says to Frank, motioning to the back end of the dummy-wardrobe bag.

"No way, it's all yours. I'm not touchin' it."

"I promise not to name you as a co-conspirator," Richard says, but gives up on him after a few seconds and tugs the wardrobe bag into the chute himself, inching it forward by segments, until more than half of it is inside. Then, with a whoosh and a puff of sour air, it vanishes from their midst, down into the depths like a torpedo. Richard bends from the waist to stick his head into the opening and listen to the whistling of the falling object, then straightens and looks at Frank. "Let's go," Richard says, and leads the way out of the trash room and to the elevator, where he presses the down button. "Told you, no sweat."

"I still say my ass could be out of a job behind this," Frank says.

"No it won't," Richard says. "You'll get a raise, you'll be a hero. Just wait."

The elevator arrives and they get on.

Davis Braun has seen all of this from his vantage point by the fire-tower door at the end of the hallway. His cell phone is in one pocket, a handkerchief and a hard-plastic kit containing a vial of chloroform and a hypodermic needle in the other. He had walked down a flight and through the door at the moment that Richard, Frank and what looked very much like an occupied body bag were making their way across the hall, and here he clings, plastered against the closed door to stay out of sight, one eye peeking round the edge of the alcove.

No need for the cell phone to check on whereabouts now. He can see with his own eyes that Keene is on the move. Braun rushes into the trash room to be sure that the body bag isn't there. It isn't.

It's clear what the little shit is up to. Braun needs no more convincing that Keene has become a major threat. The chloroform, more product smuggled from the hospital, no doubt will come in handy.

On the fifth floor of the 42s, Flora Spivack, living the highrise life of a four-foot-ten widowed octogenarian, carries a small bag of trash from her apartment to the trash room. It's a little sheer-yellow pouch that she props in a small metal frame by the sink to hold large fruit pits and rinds that she doesn't want to submit to the garbage disposal and risk a breakdown; the disposal has already received repairs twice in the last year. She doesn't like the little pouch to sit long with such contents, so here she is headed for the trash room from her apartment number 511, the bag tied and knotted by her determined arthritic fingers.

Flora enters the trash room, opens the chute's metal flap with a little grunt and, with her other hand, swings the yellow garbage pouch in a tight arc toward the opening.

But something stops her from completing the full motion and making her deposit.

After eighteen straight hours overnight and through the day at the station, Sgt. Robert Oliver is back at his apartment and sitting on a straight-back chair pulled out from the dining-room table. He is avoiding the recliner angled toward the TV set because he can't bring himself to relax, can't get a grip on how to spend the evening or any evening for that matter. What he's doing, he realizes, in the larger scheme of things, is waiting around to die. He hopes that retiring from the force will speed that process.

He's been here in this walk-up on Pine Street for nearly three years, starting six months after Cassie's accident. When Libby died, after the cancer had spread to her lungs and beyond, after he had given quarts of blood and urged others to give lesser amounts in her name, after she'd been cut open and sewed back up, after he'd taken a leave of absence from the force and spent every waking moment at her bedside, after he'd found a deserted moment and cried for the first time since he was a toddler, after he'd cried some more and then cursed the enemy he could not fight, after all of that, he stayed in their Mount Airy home with the big backyard where Cassie and Robert Jr.

had played, where Cassie ran her treehouse club and dug for gold or oil until her mother told her to fill up the hole, where both of the kids splashed in their little kids' pool, where the sun rose and set and the seasons changed. Then when Cassie was taken from him, that whole world became a photograph bleached by the sun and fading with every minute, and part of him wanted to lie down and die right there, and that part of him was capable of making it happen, but some kind of automatic pilot pushed him forward, set him in motion to play out a string whose end he could not see, a dreary regimen that he had no power to change. Robert Jr. went away to the west coast and some kind of job in films—a creative kid, gets it from his mother—and they haven't talked since. They were never close.

Yes, Sgt. Robert Oliver is sitting on his dinette chair with nothing to do and nowhere to go and no sense of how to change that, with no feeling of even wanting to. He's a man out of road maps and out of gas, but not out of time. Not, regrettably, yet.

Flora-on-the-fifth-floor's problem, the thing that has her standing there, mouth agape, her little trash bag of fruit pits and rinds dangling from her hand, is that a paper bag of trash and dripping garbage has toppled out from *inside* the chute and landed at her feet. As if someone tossed it at her. Her other hand loses its grip on the metal flap and it slams shut.

"Oh my," Flora says, then puts her trash on the floor and opens the chute again. Another bag, this one plastic and copper-colored and bottom-heavy, hurtles out of the opening and plops on her deck sneakers. There are more bags bulging behind, itching to burst. The cylinder is ripe.

After taking the elevator to the ground floor, Richard and Frank made their way across the lobby, Frank motioning toward Mike before turning toward the rear with "I'll be in the, uh, Dumpster room."

When Mike said, "Gotcha covered," Frank frowned and stepped past Richard. "Let's go. See if that thing came apart like a cheap suit or what."

They walked through the mailroom and down a short corridor to the rear exit door that led them outside to the building's concrete apron fringing the alley called Latimer Street. A step away, the door to the Dumpster room. Frank keys it open. Now they're entering; the room is washed with yellow light and smells like soggy cardboard. "Sucker better be there," Frank says.

"Why wouldn't it be?" asks Richard.

"I don't know, you're the genius."

"You're the one who knows the building inside-out."

They go to the Dumpster and step up onto the lower ledge. "By the way, Frank, they usually pick up trash on Saturdays? I was down here this morning right after they left."

"They missed yesterday, so they had to clear it out for the weekend. Otherwise we'd be swimmin' in this shit. I saw those guys this mornin' comin' down 15th Street. Probably gettin' time-and-a-half."

"Hmnh."

They hoist themselves onto the top ledge of the Dumpster, swing around and sit there so they can scan the contents. The first thing Frank notices is the low level of trash. "Not a whole lot here for this time of the day, even after the pickup," he says. "Lotta people musta gone away for the weekend."

They both expect the wardrobe bag to be right on top somewhere, or maybe partially obscured by some other material just fallen through the chute.

But there is no wardrobe bag in sight.

Richard is not fearful, only curious. "Where is it?"

"Good question," Frank says, his puzzlement quickly yielding to anxiety, though his voice doesn't show it yet.

They swing their legs up and around to the outside, step down to the bottom ledge of the Dumpster and off, and stand there and wait, eyes fixed on the chute. Richard remembers a neighborhood restaurant from his youth, a family cafeteria-style restaurant cheap and well-salted and full of pleasant ordinary people. There was an oblong counter wrapped around a conveyor belt that ushered orders in from the kitchen, plates heaped with home fries or hot roast beef sandwiches, small saucers of baked beans, bowls of beef barley, all moving inexorably toward the front, a nonstop procession. That's where Richard always wanted to sit at the counter so he could lean over and look to the rear of the belt for approaching dishes, watch the parade and wait for that moment, which came at least once every visit, when the lineup was too much for waitresses limited by two arms and a collision was inevitable, often spilling contents onto the counter.

Now here he stands in the bowels of the 42s, watching the chute opening with that same eager expectation, that same heightened sense of urgency. But nothing is happening at the chute opening, nothing is coming out.

"Shit," says Frank, which nicely sums up his thoughts at the moment.

To him, the room is silent except for the hornet-buzzing of the overhead fluorescent lights. Richard, however, is captive to remote sounds that sneak into his ears. He hears a medley of noises, his private, hidden, discordant orchestra: a groaning of water pipes, the buzzing of electrical feed lines, the humming of gas furnaces even though the heat's not yet fired up . . .

And something else. He steps closer to the chute on the far side of the Dumpster, as close to it as he can get. Frank follows him, stops, puts hands on hips, impatient. "What?"

Richard's eyes dart about. He realizes what he's hearing. The faint creak and snap of a few chute flaps opening and shutting on different floors all the way up to forty-two. The friction of something sliding on metal, then coming to rest.

"Nothin' since we walked in here," says Frank. "That's just great. I knew this was gonna happen, I just knew it."

"People are using it."

"Using what?"

"I can hear them putting trash in the chute," Richard says.

"You can hear—?"

Just then, Frank's walkie-talkie squawks and sputters like a transatlantic broadcast, vintage 1930.

"Yo, Frank." It's Big Mike, the pride of South Philadelphia, number-two man on the 42s desk, a lifer. Frank rips the walkie-talkie off his belt.

"Talk to me."

"Somethin's wrong with the trash," Mike says.

"*Tell* me about it."

"Fifth floor has got it backed up. That's what they're tellin' me."

Richard is peering up into the chute, listening for clues, trying to divine the source of the blockage.

"What the hell's that mean?" Franks asks Mike.

"The, uh, whadiyou call it? Trash bin? . . . is filled when they go throw theirs out. Y'understand? It's, like, stacked up."

Frank does a little agitated wiggle. "All the way to the fifth floor?"

"Guess so."

"Any other floors call in?"

"That's all we got so far."

"Well, if it's the fifth floor, there must be trouble on the floors below, too."

"Yeah, I guess you're right."

Frank turns to Richard with an accusatory look. "See, what

the hell did I tell you, man? How I let you talk me into this . . ."

Frank trails off when he sees Richard narrow his eyes and cock his head, as if trying to communicate with the contents of the chute.

"What? What is it?"

Richard's lips barely move when he says, "There's something there."

"Yeah, your damn dummy."

"No . . . too soon."

"Too soon for what?"

"We just dropped it, Frank. It clogs up five floors that fast?"

"How do I know? Maybe it's just stuck right on that floor."

"Thought you said straight down," Richard mumbles, standing perfectly still.

"Yeah, for *normal* stuff. I musta been out of my—"

"Ssh!"

Frank glares at him, but Richard is looking somewhere else, he is looking only into the black cylinder of the chute, a horror hatch, another dimension perhaps, like the movie thrillers of ghosts and time warps that always entranced him.

"Frank, you still with me?" Mike's voice is flat and dull and very much of this world. But Frank is tuned in to a different frequency, is mesmerized by the sight of Richard drawing a bead on the chute like a cat on a bug. "What is it, for godsake?"

"Frank, you there?"

Frank snaps out of it. "I'm here. Listen, Mike—"

A hissing "sssh" from Richard, so strong, so authoritative that it startles Frank into silence.

From the chute comes a faint scraping sound that only Richard hears. It stops. "Hold on, Mike," Frank says into the walkie-talkie. Richard clambers onto the top ledge of the Dumpster right below the chute opening and almost falls off as he stands and grabs at his knee in pain. Frank rushes over.

"What the hell you doin', man? Get down from there."

Richard looks up into the darkness. The scraping sound resumes, louder, scratchier.

He is petrified in his bed, unable to move, as if bolted down. The wallpaper is closing in on him. The cowboy on the bucking bronco can offer no help, no sign of reassurance. The cowboy's face is angled toward the wall so that his features are not visible and the top of his head is obscured by his large sand-colored cowboy hat and a red scarf flies out from his neck and one arm is tethered to the saddle while the other reaches toward the ceiling and his boot presses down on the stirrup. But he is of no help, Richard's wallpapered friend, because the gasps are coming from next door, from beyond the wallpaper, coming into his bedroom, Cindy Dempsey's gasps, coming into his bed, an alarm he cannot answer. He could scream, he could get up and rouse his mother, his father. But he can't move. He might be dreaming. He prays that he is dreaming. It is the middle of the night. And the gasps keep coming and now he knows that he is not dreaming and that life must be oozing out of her, the one who means the most to him on this earth, and he knows who is doing this to her and he is powerless to prevent it because he is molded to the warm bed, strapped down by the fear that confusion brings in the middle of the night for an eight-year-old who is smothered by it all, the wallpaper closing on him, the sounds, the sounds. . . .

He is at eye level with the chute opening and he is trembling, looking inside, up and into the dark cylinder.

The scratching persists.

Richard looks around the room. Not a broom or a mop or a shovel in sight.

He must climb in somehow. Defy gravity and dislodge whatever is there. Enter this narrow dark world of mysterious noise, metallic scratching and whistling drafts and muted roars like the inside of a seashell cupped to one's ear, the ocean's symphony embedded there, so goes the tale told to youngsters on the summer beach with the sun a hot lamp from above, pail and shovel waiting in the sand, all carefree scampering, the child that was, that should have been, a child intercepted, aborted.

Richard must climb into the chute, even as nausea and dizziness and panic will throw up a wall to meet him. It is his penance. He must go in there like a groundhog, like a tunneler, like a prison escapee, must go to the source of it and, maybe, just maybe, he *will* escape and be a free man. The other choice is to turn away and that doesn't work. His life has been built on that choice and he knows it doesn't work. The time has come to change that life. No matter the cost. Even if it means ending it.

The scratching.

What to grab onto? Richard believes he sees the outline of something wedged into the chute a few feet up, it's hard to tell. He closes his eyes, takes a deep breath, reaches in with both arms like day-camper Richard Keene springing off the side of the pool in swim instruction, and pushes off from the Dumpster ledge with his cushioned sneakers. He leaps and grabs hold of something, legs kicking furiously to propel him as if he truly is in the limpid waters of a swimming pool.

"Hey, who the hell do you think you are, Superfly?" Frank offers, as Richard fights his panic and wriggles into the mouth of the beast, wedges himself between the curved metal and the trapped trash, and reaches up to grab the next rung. Just like on the monkey bars.

"C'mon, Frank," bellows Mike's voice on the walkie-talkie. "What the hell am I supposed to do?"

The guy's been here twice as long as me, forever, and he still can't think for himself. But then that's why I'm the boss, Frank reminds himself. And true, he's got to admit, this is a first.

Clogged trash chute. Five floors' worth. Maybe more by now. Not a feather has fallen, and Richard, crazy Richard, is climbing up the chute. The best mess yet.

"Sit tight," Frank says to his front-desk colleague. "We're checkin' something here."

Inside the chute, Richard has opened his eyes and is drawing on whatever will power that he can muster. Yet, even as he fends off panic, one small corner of his brain is suggesting how ludicrous his predicament is. What is he doing? "What are you doing?" Evelyn used to ask him when he'd dig a deep hole in the backyard and stick his arm into it, delighted that the rest of him was free of the trap. "Digging for gold?"

Enough fluorescent light from the Dumpster room feeds into the chute to give some visibility right at the mouth of it but not much farther. Richard can't tell what he is among, this apparent wall of trash he has joined. He pats nearby objects to discern composition. Paper, filmy plastic, vinyl, something sharp. He must pull down the wall whatever it is, yank down the clog, human Drano. Which he starts to do right now, while the angle is favorable and he can still hold his position. He can't see it but he knows the answer is there. He reaches into the dark, into the unknown, into a lottery jar of scorpions, or toward a button of release, he doesn't know which.

Toward the sounds he reaches. Chute flaps opening. A pile of trash above him, shifting, mounting. He is inching sideways and reaching upward, straining for leverage, torso twisting and arm extended impossibly from its shoulder socket, and fingers splayed, the little bones and digits of the hand at maximum torque, and just then, something cool and hard and sharp and . . . ow! The hand yanked back with the childlike exclamation, and in the faint light straining through from below, he can tell that there is some bleeding at the base of his fingers. Something sliced him, a metal edge, glass maybe. Then that scraping sound once more, light and scratchy, a tease, a lure. He settles himself into the groove and reaches up—he should have gloves on—and in the instant that he touches and tugs at what feels like . . . like a finger, a human finger, a thread of light drops from above, all the way through the chute, and winds about a bracelet on the wrist of a lifeless arm, a golden bracelet with chunks of ivory clear to Richard in that sudden light, and the shiver that runs up his spine tells him he recognizes the piece of jewelry, the wrist it belongs on, the wrist it *is* on, a quarter-inch from the metal cylindrical wall and bobbing there almost imperceptibly like a specimen in a jar of fluid.

The light dies and, with a convulsive last-ditch surge, Richard grips the hand he cannot now see and, as large, much too large, jagged pieces of glass fall against his shoulders and dirt powders his face, he begins to slide backward, yanking the braceleted arm down with him and dislodging the tower of trash above him.

In the avalanche, Lori's head pops out of a body bag skewered by glass from a broken bottle, maybe a half-gallon of Mott's apple juice collided at some strange angle and happenstance of force and timing, a four hundred-foot drop, but there's too much glass for just that, as if some moron threw out a pane of sheet glass or a sharp square of metal and it raced down the chute like a guillotine. But this is all split-second supposition, as Richard is falling the short distance out of the chute and into the Dumpster, and Lori's visible hand and head are following him though he hasn't seen them yet, and the wedge is broken and it's raining glass and debris, and five-plus floors' worth of trash is tumbling down the chute.

Richard is plopped down onto the Dumpster pile, ass-first the way it turns out, and he has no choice but to sit there and shield his face from the torrent. It is crashing around him and on top of him, but it is mostly light stuff, plump paper bags and skinny plastic ones, no more broken glass. Now he scrambles away from the downpour, backpedaling uphill on the shifting pile. And it is over in seconds, the Dumpster still, the chute unclogged. He shakes his head vigorously and flings his arms outward to cast off whatever flecks and gobs are clinging to him, opens his eyes.

The smell around him, that of moldy cantaloupe and the insides of a vacuum cleaner, is not overpowering but strong enough to get his attention. For the second time in as many days, he is in a sea of trash, a giant playpen of moveable parts devoid of color and mirth.

He looks about, trying to be methodical, steeling himself against the horror he knows will present itself in moments. A few feet away, there's his mother's pink wardrobe bag intact with the dummy inside; she'd never guess it would make such a journey. Richard half-stands and begins to rummage through the mini-hill of refuse, tossing cartons and bags and boxes and glop as he goes. He is careful not to handle several foot-long daggers of glass that look like stalactites. He cups less danger-ous chunks of the pile with both hands and flings away, extracts bulging wedged-in paper bags to create tiny landslides, moves about the heap as he levels it like an archaeologist sifting for artifacts. When he two-hands a layer of Styrofoam packing bubbles and loose grapefruit rinds, Lori's head comes clear, sticking out of the body bag slashed at one corner. So, too, her hand and wrist, decorated by—Richard's grunt is his reaction to both the horror of the situation and its futility—the gold-and-ivory bracelet. And now he is crying because, indeed, the horror is overwhelming.

A new wave of guilt takes hold of him, another young woman he failed to help, placed in jeopardy no less. He looks toward the top of the Dumpster, a couple of feet above his head. "Frank," he calls out, remembering that he brought a partner down here to view this discovery. He has really jumped into something now, he realizes. The Stranger had it wrong. Death makes a difference, the timing and nature of it. Fate doesn't condemn man but throws down a gauntlet. Some make it out the other end, some don't.

"Frank?"

So things don't always go straight down the chute, but then human bodies aren't thrown out every day, either. Richard has a job to do. He slips to his knees and stands again. "Hey, Fr . . ."

He can feel the heat of someone else's eyes on him. He snaps his head around fast enough to pop a vertebra. There, hunched above on the upper ledge of the Dumpster, looking down into his eyes and through them, then looking beside and beyond him to where Lori's visible head and sheathed body have come to an inglorious rest, is Davis Braun. His eyes seem to have a sleepy boredom about them; his forearms press onto the scraped metal and his hands expand a pair of skin-tight surgical gloves. By his standards, this has become a sloppy operation, but he has time to clean it up.

"Looks like you're in up to your neck, Keene."

As Richard moves one leg, the pile shifts beneath him and he sinks so that he's shin-deep. He feels the twinge in his right knee, as he steps up to higher "ground." Fear has been knocked out of him; strange, the specter of Braun is almost welcome. It has come to this.

"Looks like we have a Mexican standoff," Richard says.

Braun frowns and shakes his head. "That's not a politically correct phrase, Keene. A fine fella like you, an upstanding citizen, should know better."

What Richard does know is that Braun intends to kill him right here, right now. There are no other options. Kill him and bury him with Lori. He backs up a step onto a higher section of the trash mound, and now can look out of the Dumpster and see Frank lying facedown on the concrete floor, and a bit beyond, a two-by-four pinioned at an angle between the floor and the knob of the room's only available door at night. The outdoor loading/pickup dock is sealed off by the rolldown garage door. Fact is, the room gets almost zero traffic, especially after hours when it's locked.

Braun has followed Richard's eyes.

"You can't throw us all in the Dumpster," Richard says.

"Why not? This trash removal is better than the witness protection program."

"Mike knows he's here."

"Mike's a halfwit. I'll take my chances."

Richard looks right at him. "What's wrong with you, Braun?"

"Just people like you who clutter up my life from time to time."

Richard is thinking of Lori, Lori's body, and what it's doing here after a pickup this morning. He is sure that Braun killed her yesterday because he was expecting her all night and didn't hear from her. To think that her body was kept in the apartment overnight, like a piece of merchandise to be returned to the department store. Richard scratches his cheek and tries to look casual. A way to rattle Braun. "You didn't know that they picked up the trash this morning, did you?"

Braun looks pissed off. "What?"

"That's right. Special pickup. They didn't get here yesterday. Lori would be long gone by now, wouldn't she?"

Braun smiles at him, conceding nothing. "Well I dressed her up, so I decided to keep her around for a while. You like her, man?"

Richard knows he has one chance to get out of here. Yelling won't work; thick walls, and they are too far back in the building. Once Braun gets his hands on him, it's over. Maybe he can beat him to the door somehow, but he won't have enough time to open it and get out. He looks around the Dumpster for a spray can of Lysol or something to bob out of the morass, but no such luck. Dig for something that could serve as a weapon? No time, no way.

"Actually, I have an alternative plan for you boys," Braun says, as if he's dressing a minor wound at the hospital. "Don't want to leave you here too long; like you say, pickups are becoming erratic. Must be shifting from summer to fall schedule or something."

Richard plays along with this conversation game, buying time. "Yeah, guess that's it. So what's your plan?"

Braun holds up a finger. "Sorry, Keene. They only keep talking in the movies. You'll never know."

Richard will wait for him to make the first move. The Dumpster area is large; he's not in a phone booth. Braun will have to come in after him. Anything can happen, like a muddy football field neutralizing a superior team.

In the instant that Braun hurtles over the edge and inside the Dumpster like a kid in gym class vaulting the horse, Richard sees it, the thing that has been right in front of his face all the time, the red cylinder mounted right there by the door he has been looking at. The fire extinguisher.

So as Braun lands feet-first in the pile a couple of body lengths away, Richard, whose reflexes have always been sharp and whose frame has always been lean, counters with perfect timing, scrambles to one side of the Dumpster, and vaults over top and onto the concrete floor. He yells as his knee takes the impact and transmits the message to his brain, and even stumbles as he rushes headlong toward the door, but there is no time for pain, not now. He doesn't glance toward Frank's prostrate, chloroformed body off to one side. Without looking back, he mashes his shoulder against the door, rips open the extinguisher's black hard-rubber latches, yanks the tube off its bearings, pulls the pin, and wheels to face his foe, his trigger finger in position. Twice, he's let loose with a foamy blast in his apartment, salmon drippings and then ground round igniting in the oven's broiling pan. He knows the implement.

Meanwhile, Braun, rather infuriated by anything that makes him look or feel at all foolish, has torn over and out of the Dumpster and made a direct line for Richard, meaning to knock him senseless with the collision. But his arrival is met by Richard's sharp pivot and a propulsion of phosphates and sulfates that blinds him, stuns him, and throws him off course so that he crashes into the wall rather than his intended target. Richard takes the moment to kick free the two-by-four, and promptly exits the room. He knows that the rear door to the building is locked—Frank was his way back in—and pauses for a fraction of a second before he turns and runs down the alley, starting to feel the pain now in his knee.

Within seconds, Braun bolts out of the Dumpster room and into the alley, looks up and down Latimer Street. There is Richard, running toward the end of the block at 16th Street. And now Braun is going after him, Frank left behind unconscious and out for hours in a spot that should remain undisturbed, the door locked from the outside, Mike with a key and under the impression that Frank is attending to emergency business away from the site, that's what Braun forced him to say into the walkie-talkie after he'd pounded on the door to gain admittance, hammer-locked Frank's arm and taken his keys. Frank's a bystander, but now he's got to go, too. Richard, though, is the prey right now, to be knocked unconscious, brought back and properly eliminated.

Put Lori in a fresh body bag and leave her where she is, let the accumulation of trash bury her, no one looking. Even over the weekend, little risk; she's embalmed. Monday's trash pickup will cart her away, no one paying attention on either end—it's just a landslide of trash, after all—and no one to finger him, no damning evidence. As for Frank and Keene, make the chloroform dose lethal, load them in the trunk of the Toyota, dump them in the Schuylkill somewhere, maybe below the banks of the picnic grove on West River Drive where he and Eleanor went one Sunday afternoon before she moved in. Steam-clean the trunk.

No, too risky, far too risky. Too much movement. Don't want the bodies discovered, period. Stay with the program. Body bags for both and have them join Lori in the Dumpster, three-for-the-price-of-one. Take your chances with no embalming, let them molder over the weekend. Can't take two bodies all the way to the twenty-third floor. The fire stairs, the elevator, the hallway? Can't do it. Can't do two more embalmings. Anyway, enough of that. Take your chances. It works out. The Dumpster has been golden.

Braun considers all of this in seconds, in motion. But he's getting just a little bit tired now. His mind is getting tired.

First things first. Richard Keene.

Braun is on Latimer Street, legs churning. His eyes did not take a direct hit from the fire extinguisher's onslaught and are functioning well enough for the pursuit. He has Richard in his sights. This will not last long.

18

Her mounting anxiety sends her to the telephone. She's used Richard as bait, and bait is something that gets snatched away before you can even react.

She's more than willing to put herself in harm's way but the last thing she wants is yet another victim. What else can she do? Camp outside his door? Call Oliver? And tell him what?

It rings four times and Richard's voice comes on, polite, apologetic even, asking the caller to leave a message. She leaves nothing, hangs up, rushes out of her apartment and takes the elevator seven floors skyward. Rings the bell at apartment 2207. Bangs on the door. Waits.

Back in the elevator and down to the lobby. No Frank at the desk.

"Do you know Richard Keene, the tenant in 2207?" asks Janet Kroll.

"Not sure, ma'am," says Mike. "What's he look like?"

"Oh, thin, average height, dark hair . . ." She struggles to think of some defining phsyical trait but comes up empty.

Mike looks at the ceiling and thinks hard. "Can't say. Sorry."

"Where's Frank?"

"Oh, he had to leave."

"Damnit," she says to herself.

"Oh, wait a minute, I'm sorry, ma'am. What's the matter with me? I know who Richard Keene is." He smiles. "Yeah, he's been a pretty busy guy around here lately."

"Really?"

"Absolutely."

"Has he been by here tonight?"

Mike scratches at his temple. "Sure, him and Frank had to go in the back. What floor you on, ma'am?"

"Fifteen. Why?"

"Were you hit by our little trash problem?"

"What?"

"The trash shot, er . . ."

"The what?"

"Trash sh—, uh, the thing that, ya know, takes the trash all the way down and—"

"Chute?"

"Yeah, that's it. It was stuck for the first time in history, far as I know."

"Stuck?"

"Yeah, somethin' got stuck and it was clogged up to the fifth floor. You believe that?"

"So it's unclogged now?"

"Far as I know. Frank said so."

She has begun to move away but now stops. "Frank said so?"

"Yeah, he checked it out. That's what they went to see."

"When?"

" 'Bout half hour ago. But then he had to leave right away."

"How come?"

"Some kind of emergency at home. But I'm here so we're OK. Don't really need two guys here most of the time anyways."

"Can you tell me where they pick up the trash?"

"We lock that up at night."

Janet puts her arms on the counter and leans toward him. "I'm sorry, what's your name?"

"Mike."

"Mike, I have to get back there. It's very important."

Mike's eyes seem to swim a little. "OK, ma'am. I guess it won't hurt for me to leave the desk here for a second."

Janet has never been in the Dumpster room and doesn't know what to expect, but she's sure as hell going to have a look. On second thought, she fears she does know what to expect. A clogged trash chute. Clogged with what? Richard Keene had this pegged, all right . . . She doesn't remember a specific reference to a Dumpster room in the official report of the Atlantic City police, but they searched the entire building, that's what it said. And found nothing. No Karen Rodalewicz. Nothing incriminating.

They leave the building by the rear door. Mike fetches a ring of keys from his pocket, selects one and opens the door to the Dumpster room, and they walk into the yellow light. At first, that's all that stamps Janet's retinas: the garish numbing light.

Then she sees him, a second or two before Mike does. Frank Grant, twenty-five feet away, facedown. "Oh, geez," Mike says, his voice unsteady. He approaches Frank, kneels and touches his cheek; it is warm. He puts two fingers to Frank's throat and feels a pulse, sees that he's breathing, looks up at Janet and nods. "I don't get it . . . What . . . ?"

Janet yanks her cell phone, a wafer-thin Nextel, out of the hip pocket on her jeans and calls 9-1-1 to report the scene and request an ambulance. Then, from another pocket comes her wallet and, out of that, Sgt. Oliver's card. She runs through her mind what she'll say to him, how she'll say it.

"This is where Frank and Richard Keene went earlier?" she asks Mike.

"That's right."

The police desk sergeant tells her that Oliver's off-duty. She must speak with him, and only him, it's an emergency. The sergeant balks, suggests alternatives, but she's persuasive. He offers to call Oliver at home. She leaves her cell number.

Richard is on 16th Street and, though he's running with a limp, he's mindful of keeping a comfortable distance away from Braun, who is in pursuit and moving easily, as if out for a brisk evening jog. Braun is gauging how fast he must go to catch Richard before they reach the entrance to 42s, for that is surely where Richard is headed. He'll catch him in a few moments by turning on a burst of speed, maneuver him into the shadows, and smother him with a chloroform-doused handkerchief. It's past dusk now and not enough people are around to figure out what the hell's going on. No one pays attention anyhow, that's what he counts on. Braun almost smiles to himself, as the warm stale evening breeze slides past his cheeks and he runs in the half-light, closing the gap.

At the corner of 16th and Locust, Richard does not make the turn toward the 42s. Instead, he continues north on 16th Street across Locust, running hard but laboring, favoring his right leg. Every couple of seconds, he glances back to see if Braun is drawing closer. Something inside of him has resisted going straight to Mike at the front desk, as if reporting this improbable matter, going through proper channels, is no longer an option. This time, he will take it elsewhere. This time will be a different story. It will be decided in the open, in the broad arena of the city, in the gaze of the public eye and perhaps the heavens above.

Braun is mystified. Where the hell's he going? He expects Richard to stop someone on the street and blurt out his story like a scared little boy. He has his hypodermic needle primed and ready if Richard tries his luck with a passerby. Excuse me, sir, I'm a doctor, this man is my patient, he's troubled, in plunges the hypo and an armlocked Richard is whisked away.

But Richard is simply running past people: a shining well-dressed couple headed in the same direction toward Walnut Street, a young woman in tattered jeans coming the other way, a haggard man in a thin suit and necktie from yesteryear. Past the black statue of a man holding an umbrella against ever-threatening skies. Richard is running faster than Braun would have guessed, fast enough to maintain the distance between them, the little sissy. The light is green at Walnut and Richard continues straight across, and now Braun picks up his pace, and Richard shoots backward glances and picks up his. Richard doesn't bother turning back to look again. He senses that Braun will soon be running flat-out, so he accelerates yet again, turns the corner sharply and takes off down Walnut toward 15th. The sudden change of direction has knifed into his knee and cut a jagged swath of pain to his ankle.

"Richard said you were the one to call, that he could count on you."

"To do what?"

"To do the right thing."

"And what's that?"

The return call came in less than a minute. Janet is standing there, still swallowed by the Dumpster room's awful light, Frank lying on the concrete a few yards away, Mike wearing a blank expression. The cell phone is pinned to her ear. No Richard in sight. She's afraid to look in the Dumpster. "Investigate and . . . bring Davis Braun to justice," she says.

"What's your connection with this, Miss?" asks Sgt. Robert Oliver.

Janet doesn't hesitate. "He killed my sister."

She tells him the story, the abridged version, because time is short, with a mixture of urgency and control that registers on Oliver. He is the first person she has spoken to about this, and the emotional strain of the past months, all that she has borne alone, comes through her voice though there is nothing hysterical in it. To Oliver, it somehow mandates a response without commanding one. Not unlike the quality he found in the voice, the presentation of Richard Keene. Two of them on this same case. It's enough to grab Sgt. Oliver by both shoulders and lift him out of the quicksand. These are people who need help, young people, and what are the police in business for? And this case is just quirky enough, interesting enough, to pique whatever intellectual curiosity is left in him.

There was a car once, and a boyfriend at the wheel, a young man who meant little to him but could have meant nearly everything in the reach of time, who knows? Nearly, because *everything* was in the next seat, and, of course, there was nothing that he could have done to save her, there was the utter helplessness of it all, the infuriating helplessness. And just like that, Cassie was gone, and he was left with himself, a husk of the father, the husband, the police officer who had gripped life as a muscular challenge and hid his tender regard for it.

But maybe a crueler outcome awaited his daughter, had there been no accident. Who's to say that young man would not have done to Cassie, eventually, in some apartment, in the unseemly glare of the kitchen at some mad nether-hour, what Keene alleges this fellow . . . Davis Braun . . .

Oliver is up off the dinette chair and on his feet.

He feels like he's floating down Walnut Street, though he realizes, of course, that he's running hard, just about as hard as he can but leaving a little something in reserve. Faces startled or amused pop up in his viewfinder, but to him they're as lifeless as the mannequins in the tony shops that flank them. Richard knows that he can run fast, even injured. He knows that Braun is maintaining the distance but is having trouble closing, and doesn't bother looking back. He has run through the pain in his knee, reached the point where he can't even feel it anymore, and right here, as his legs churn and the sidewalk treadmills below them, the world slows down in front of him and grows silent, nullifying not just the sounds only he hears, but all sound. He does not know what to make of it. An eerie prelude to death or a sublime gift of relief.

When he reaches 15th, plants his right foot, and pushes off to turn the corner, it all comes back, the pain in his knee, the din of the night. Pain, as a foe, is something to battle, but as a warning signal, it must be heeded. It is accompanied now by a squishiness in the knee, as if bone and softer tissue are beginning to fragment and float in gelatin. Richard gets the message, but cannot turn off the machinery now; he'll go until the wheels come off.

The light is red at Chestnut Street, but the closest car coming toward him is a half-dozen storefronts away and cruising, and his crossing is short. He bounds to safety with three loping strides and resumes the choppier gait on the north side of 15th. Now he does glance over his shoulder and sees Braun a hundred feet away, pumping his arms and puffing out his cheeks in textbook exertion. Richard calls on whatever's left in his tank, and accelerates to a sprint. The light is red at Market Street and it's six lanes across, but he checks the traffic and gauges that he can make it, an instantaneous instinctive bet on his life.

As they run on street and sidewalk, the city towering above looks down on them, two ants in a mad chase worth everything, the one struggling to break free of a lifelong straitjacket, the other intent on his own survival and puzzled, almost panicked, by this sudden unraveling of his life, this man of prized conventional assets compromised by terrible impulses. And as the chase persists, the one chasing, the other choosing to be chased, other people in the city go about their nightly business of digesting dinner, sitting in movie houses where giant celluloid images transport them from reality, shouting to be heard in noisy smoky bars, most of them reaching out for connections, impelled by need or routine or ego, but not by the same desperation that drives Richard Keene and Davis Braun through the streets of Philadelphia this insane night.

Richard escapes the moving cars on Market Street, missing a fender in the thigh by a yard and a stopwatch fraction. Nobody has even hit the horn. He sprints across 15th into Dilworth Plaza in the lap of City Hall, where dank, urine-tinged air rises in shafts from the subway. He moves toward the courtyard, looking back to see Braun crossing Market, waiting for Braun a second or two now so as not to lose him. What has drawn him here he cannot precisely name, but he thinks he must have had it in mind all along. He runs into the courtyard tunnel swallowed in shadow.

Braun is ten seconds behind him. At the outset, he thought that catching Richard would be a snap, and he was wrong about that but didn't panic. Now he's regaining the confidence that he has the stamina to prevail. If they sat together and had a civilized, man-to-man discussion, Richard would tell him that confidence is the most fragile of human commodities. But Braun feels his building. The true test is how you perform under pressure—not when everything is going your way. This goddamn Keene can really run, but he'll get him. It's a matter of time.

Braun follows Richard into the mouth of the tunnel. Twilight filters downward about a hundred feet away where the straight-away is interrupted and the space broadens into City Hall's courtyard of statuary, benches, and flower beds brightening and softening the grim gray confines. Another hundred feet and the arched concrete tunnel resumes, emptying finally into Broad Street and the swirling traffic that encircles City Hall. Braun, with the twenty-fifteen vision that has always enhanced his tennis game, can see all the way through to the street, and there are only two people in that long passageway at the moment, one coming toward him, the other walking away, neither of them Richard. No way Richard ran fast enough to reach Broad Street, impossible. At the courtyard, which seems lit as if through an indoor skylight, the flowers' brilliance reduced to black-and-white, Braun spots a door leading into the century-old French gothic building. The door is propped open by a pail that is dripping water. He runs right up to it and steps over the pail.

Inside, it's non-gothic, nondescript. Yellow adhesive strips mark a pathway on a swamp-colored concrete floor. A sign on the wall says "City Hall tower elevator" and points visitors along the yellow-strip road. Another sign sends footwalkers down an intersecting corridor to Public Works and Engineering. Braun hears the whir of an elevator.

He sprints over the yellow adhesive strips, reaching the elevator alcove just when the door is sliding shut.

When Sgt. Oliver pulls his rattling Dodge Coronet into the alley-street at the rear of the 42s, uniformed officers summoned by Janet are already on the scene at the Dumpster room, and at the front desk where they're talking with Mike, who opened the rolldown garage door before returning to the front desk. While paramedics attend to Frank and load him into an ambulance at the base of the loading platform, two policemen are grappling with something in the Dumpster. Janet is standing on the driveway below the platform, waiting, when Oliver's dinosaur comes to a stop and he gets out, the driver's side door squealing closed.

"Janet Kroll?"

He looks sad and tired, and there is something trustworthy in his face. "Hello, Sergeant."

Oliver watches the paramedics close up the rear of the

ambulance. "That's the front-desk man you were tellin' me about?"

"Yes. They say he's been knocked out with chloroform or something."

"Uh-huh."

"They say he'll be OK."

One of the patrolmen comes over. "Hey, Bob, Miss Kroll here told me you'd be coming. Understand this is one of yours."

"Yeah," says Oliver. "Another one as slippery as an eel."

He looks beyond the young cop. A split-open body bag is being hoisted and tugged out of the Dumpster. A head is visible. Oliver's jaw ripples. "Who's the young woman?"

"We don't know yet."

Oliver looks at Janet, who has her back to the Dumpster. "Do you know her?" he asks. Other than a small shake of her head, she doesn't budge. No force on earth could make her look at that body again.

"Nobody else in there, right?" Oliver asks the cop, praying that's the case.

"No."

Oliver breathes.

"These two guys'll show up sooner or later," says the cop. "Neither one's around right now. We got our eyes peeled."

"Where do you think they are?" Oliver asks Janet.

She just shakes her head again.

He turns back to the patrolman. "You know, Rog, I'd really like to get this guy."

"Which one?"

"This Braun fellow, the medical resident."

"That what he is?"

"That's right. He's the one we want. The other fella's the good guy."

Beyond the platform, the Dumpster sits there like a giant

crypt-on-wheels. Janet's hand shoots to her mouth and covers it, and her whispered words are exhaled through and around her spread fingers. "Oh God."

Up through the steel-girded, spiderwebbed innards of City Hall tower rides Richard, climbing to the heights. The luminous golden clock dials slip into his field of vision and then recede below the floor of the elevator as it rises, the distance above ground level increasing by twenty feet per second. When the elevator stops and the door opens and Richard steps onto the narrow, circular walkway of the observation tower, a night sky greets him, dark and coarsely clouded, transformed from the tepid overhang of twilight. Planes crisscross in the southern sky, and below, a prairie of lights stretches to eyesight's limit. Richard looks at the massive statue of William Penn above him, folds his arms and waits. He has the luxury of waiting now for a couple of minutes or so, time for the elevator to complete its descent and then return. All of his internal arteries are quiet now, all the neurological circuitry unblinking; he is at ease, no heartbeat thumping the chest, no constricted throat, no grinding stomach. He is as relaxed as if he were taking a hot bath and had settled into the water's caress, a slap here, a soapy swirl there.

From the bowels comes the elevator's wheeze, the faintest of sounds, something only a Richard Keene could pick up at this separation. Still, his nervous system does not rebel. He is calm, an almost dopey serenity, yet his senses keen and his resolve certain. He hears the elevator climbing, feels its vibration through the rubber soles of his sneakers and his instep and up his ankles to his shins. The rider is his nemesis, and it is here at the top of the city, still its symbolic zenith despite taller and more modern buildings, where Richard will make his stand. Up on high in the rippling crosswinds, the city's ultimate perch.

This time, he will go all the way to the top. But there is a treacherous route to the brim of William Penn's bronze hat. For Richard, it will be carpeted with hot coals, studded with razor blades. On the other side of the thicket, though, is freedom. A free sweep of sky and the floating kiss of eternity.

Consciously making it up as he goes along, or drawn to it like the proverbial moth to the flame, whichever, he is here.

He flexes his knees, the bad one complaining but game, and primes himself for a powerful spring upward, the kind of lift he needed for a successful high jump in track-and-field competition when he tried out for the middle school team and didn't make the cut. The top of the glass enclosure that fronts the base of the statue is within reach, but will require a healthy leap to get there. There is no room for a running start. Richard feels the thrust in his calves and the meatier cable-like muscles of the thigh, as he revs up his breathing and windmills his arms like some big bird ready for stationary takeoff. When he leaves the ground, the bad knee does not balk, or if it does, his will overrides it. No extraneous noises—no sounds at all, in fact—clutter his senses. There is only his body and its capacity, and the space between it and the top of the glass barrier. And when he flies up and his fingers curl over the top of the glass, and his nose and forearms flatten against the smooth cool surface, again his concentration is such that no sounds are allowed to intrude, even as he elbow-thuds and scrapes his way upward . . . and over, keeps his grip and twists his body and slides down the other side, lets go and falls dead weight to the concrete. He finds his footing. He's on the other side of the action, like at a hockey rink. The thick door to this off-limits area is just off the elevator and locked. Here at the very end of this inner, curving corridor, the base of the statue yields to an opening like a rounded, hidden fold at the mouth of a cave or an amusement park funhouse. It leads to the statue's interior, a narrow hollow through which a ladder rises more than thirty feet up one of the massive legs and the torso and the head, all the way to the narrow—wide enough for one reasonably trim man to crawl through—hatch that opens Billy Penn's hat to the elements. Richard knows all this because he's read about it in an article somewhere, maybe in the *Inquirer*'s Sunday magazine.

He waits on the other side of the looking glass.

The elevator arrives and disgorges Davis Braun, who eyes the empty space and walks halfway across the observation deck. Richard knuckles the glass with three taps and Braun whirls to face him, snaps his head upward to gauge the top of the barrier, then brings his eyes down to meet Richard's once again. He smiles through the glass at Richard, an I-got-you smile but also one of recognition that Richard is a fellow lunatic (if of a different stripe) and even a worthy adversary. It's a smile that has all of Braun's potent charm in it, a poison Tastykake.

Richard turns from him and walks leisurely toward the entry at the base of the statue, disappears into it. Inside the thirty-seven-foot-high bronze giant, he grabs a rung and gets his footing on the ladder. He brushes against the cast metal as he ascends, and it becomes blacker than tar. Dread seizes him, the sweats of closed-in fear, but he fights it on equal terms now. He convinces himself that the darkness is his ally because he can keep his eyes open and imagine himself to be on a beach whose ocean hugs the horizon, or he's drifting in the sky, caressed by clouds. And now he begins to gather strength from each step up, the altitude recharging him like water aerating the gills of a landed fish tossed back into the ocean.

He knows that Braun will be coming after him. They'll finish this thing, at last.

He hears him, feels him, on the ladder, twenty feet below. Richard runs out of ladder and fits himself into the hatchway, which is snug as an MRI scanner or a blanketed bed. But the dread is gone, all gone, adrenalined away. He places both hands on the metal surface above him—the hatch itself, he knows it to be; the very top of the structure—and feels about for a handle or latch but locates none. So he pushes for all he's worth and feels it give a bit. He lowers his hands a few inches, then thrusts them upward so that the heels hit first, and the palm and fingers complete the impact.

The hatch flies open and the night rushes into the space. A refrain of wind, a sky of primer blue speckled with early stars. Richard pokes his head out and breathes in the sky-cooled air.

Below, Braun is climbing, hand over head.

Richard eases himself through the hatch and onto the top of William Penn's hat, now on his knees, palms down, and then up on his haunches. Rears up, gritted teeth pulsing his jaw, to a full standing position. A mountain climber at the summit. More alive than when viewed from the enclosed observation deck, the city spreads before him, a platter of shapes and angles and lights, and now he feels a literal part of the tapestry rather than a spectator. This is no oil canvas or planetarium display, no mere scene, but a fabric that has stitched him to its center.

Braun is in the hatchway and at the top.

Richard senses him and steps onto the brim. This is where intrepid city workers drape giant, sheet-like logos of the town's sports teams when a championship has been won. Bright colorful symbols the populace can rally round. Up here, at the peak of dreams.

There is precious little maneuvering room. Braun stand six feet away and they face one another through a dancing wind surrounded by a dizzying panorama. But they notice neither. Braun has the chloroform in his pocket but has no need for it now. The perfect suicide, he thinks. No one can see them up here, no one is watching. What he has been relying on: the indifferent, the oblivious. He takes a small step toward his prey and Richard holds his ground.

"You're a crazy one," Braun says, another small tentative step, his conversational words chasing through the wind to Richard's ears, and Richard hears them as if through a megaphone, for his senses are ultra-sharp, every nerve and corpuscle strung to the limit. Braun is just about an arm's length away, and in the fractional second that it takes for him to lunge at his target, Richard sidesteps with perfect economy and the bigger man is swatting at air currents that tease from head to toe. Richard is in his element, surefooted at the apex, but does not counter even though Braun is off-balance and ripe for a shove.

They square off again and Braun sees something in Richard he has not seen until this moment. Power, a palpable resolve in him; it's a revelation. And Braun realizes, his self-delusion decomposing, that *he* is just as crazy as Richard. Crazier. It's a magnificent insight. "I'll take you with me," he says and prepares to charge. Below the two of them, the broad visage of William Penn surveys his real estate, unmoved by their dance overhead. Radio-tower lights on a neighboring building blink at the sky.

Now Braun is on him and, this time, Richard avoids the brunt but not all of the short charge. They are both down after a Braun shoulder has collided with the left side of Richard's flat chest, football-style. Braun is floundering on the mild slope as he scrambles to stand. Richard has already gotten to his feet and is standing there, silhouetted against a mass of night-white cloud. He is not far from the hatch and could try to run away and take the elevator back down, but he has no intention of doing that. There is no safety in that. He has his monster on a limb and wants to cut it off.

Braun sees bodies lying and rotting everywhere, yet his mind still calculating, remembers that he's left a warm one back at the 42s. The unbidden image of his mother takes hold of him at this precise moment, and he isn't sure what he is feeling—some curious mingling of embarrassment and arousal—but he does know that it's something he wants to extinguish and fast. He has Keene in his sights and figures he'll climb back up and nail him with the next charge, but he is overheated and sweating beyond the cooling powers of the unrelenting wind. He is leaking, juices ebbing out of him.

Something is coming for him.

A gust leaps out of the river of wind and takes him as he stands up, moves him like a piece on a chessboard, slides him as if he were on ice, right off of the bronze brim and into open space on a cushion of air. Richard twitches forward at the sight, but there is nothing to do. Braun hangs there a frozen moment like a bird seeking direction, a puzzled look on his face. And then he is gone, and the gust is gone, its trailing breeze just a flutter whispering unintelligible secrets forty stories above the pavement.

19

The news about a jumper off the statue of William Penn comes over the police radio, and Oliver is the only one to make a connection.

Good God. What he said that time. Under the boot soles. Up on high.

"I hope that's not our boy," he says to Janet.

She is leaning against a strip of brick wall next to one end of the loading dock. She imagines Karen's lifeless face sticking out of a body bag an instant after she realizes that Oliver has said something to her. She looks at him. "I'm sorry, what was that again?"

"Someone just jumped off the top of City Hall."

"What?"

"I'm hoping it's not . . ."

She needs a couple of deep breaths. Oliver places a warm hand on her shoulder.

Lori Calder has joined Frank on the ambulance for the ride to the hospital; they'll be going to different departments. The horror of the discovery in the Dumpster clings to Janet. For the police, it was part of the detail; they've seen bodies in Dumpsters before, though not necessarily ones that have fallen through highrise chutes.

"Do you think . . . ?"

"I'm gonna check it out," Oliver says. His intuition is back. His sense of the world is returning, he is becoming a human being again. He walks over to a squad car, braces himself with one hand on the roof, and leans toward the driver. "I'm gonna see what's up with that jumper, Rog," says Sgt. Robert Oliver.

"Busy evening, huh?"

"Yeah."

The patrolman starts the engine and eases the car into the alley; a second blue-and-white follows. Oliver goes back to Janet, who hasn't moved from her spot in about ten minutes.

"Why don't you get some rest," Oliver suggests, feeling there's little else to say.

"What will you find there?"

"At City Hall?"

"Yes."

"Well . . ." All he can do is look away and shake his head.

"Who will you find there?"

Oliver looks right into her eyes, beautiful hazel-colored eyes, he realizes, a woman about the age that Cassie would be, maybe a few years older. "I don't know," he says evenly. "But I think our guy's comin' out of this one whole. Just a hunch."

"I want to come with you."

He balks. "Well . . ."

"Please."

What the hell. This kid can take it. Just like Cassie. Tough young lady.

His eyes tell her to come along before his words do. "Let's go," he says, turning toward his battered Dodge in the alleyway, almost smiling to himself. "I'm off-duty anyway."

The police barricades are up in Dilworth Plaza, squad cars and TV-news vans angled just outside of them, a crowd gathering. Big doings, film at eleven, big-city swan dive to the pavement.

Braun's once Grecian body lies crumpled beneath a sheet right in the middle of the plaza, lined up with the tunnel leading to the courtyard, eerily in keeping with Mr. Penn's preoccupation with symmetry. The police are interrogating a grizzled homeless man in his sixties, who, so far, is the only eyewitness at ground-level.

The 9-1-1 call came in from a janitor in a highrise office building facing City Hall, one of the Penn Center buildings right across 15th Street on Market. He was Windexing the tall windows and had a dead-on view. That's it, apparently, for the entire city; no other calls. If anyone else caught a glimpse, either it didn't register or the random onlooker refused to believe his eyes. A daredevil's final flight and not much of a gallery for oohs and ahhs.

There is, of course, one other eyewitness. Richard Keene has been sitting on William Penn's hat for some time now, sitting there with his arms bracing hiked-up knees, at first glance relaxed and carefree as if on a beach or a high-school gymnasium floor, but on closer inspection, holding onto himself, taut and inward, primed for an eruption. The winds continue to snake-dance on high, funneling up from below the hat's huge brim and spinning off into the mist of the night.

He stands and a shiver seems to run through him and out into the air. The surface of the great bronze hat is getting slick with the light rain. Five hundred feet below, a mad world scrambles about. Richard hunches at the precipice, looks up at the phantom sky and back down at the hard level ground, the city's very first town square.

Behind his grimace is a silent cry of triumph. After a while, he stands and slips himself back through the hatch and down through the gullet of William Penn.

Meanwhile, Sgt. Oliver has checked with the detectives on the scene. "One of yours?" they ask him. "Could be," he says. They've already retrieved a wallet, keys, a hypodermic needle, and a shattered vial and handkerchief, each with traces of chloroform.

"Interesting stuff he carries around," says one of the detectives, a fortyish man with a pinched face and thick wavy black hair.

"How the hell'd he get up there, don't they lock this place up?" Oliver asks.

"Janitor left the door open," says the detective.

Janet stays outside the barricade, waiting, looking almost shell-shocked now, but still striking enough to generate some admiration from a couple of the officers. Oliver is looking right at her as he walks across the plaza after seeing the sheeted corpse. A smile would be inappropriate, but he wants to do something from a distance to reassure her, settles for walking fast and letting his words-in-motion do the job. "It's Davis Braun," he says, as he nears her on the other side of the yellow sawhorses.

Janet takes it like a smack across the cheek, a stinging jolt of relief and wonderment at Oliver's intuition, her own doggedness, the end of her travail, the unplumbed tangles of personal lives. And she begins to cry.

Richard appears out of the darkness of the courtyard tunnel like a ghost. Oliver's been waiting for him.

"Look who's here," he says to Janet, and she stifles her crying, looks up and sees Richard moving toward them, limping. There is something reverential in his eyes, as if he has gone into the wilderness and returned with a truth that will anchor him forever. They both realize that he is looking past them, an almost hypnotized gaze about him. Then Oliver shifts so that he is directly in front of Richard, who is now thirty feet away. A flicker of recognition and Richard's trance falls away. He walks right up to them and Janet moves to him and hugs him, her chin on his shoulder and her eyes full of turmoil. Startled, he hugs her back. When they break, Oliver asks him, "What happened up there?"

Richard jerks his head back toward City Hall and looks up the steel-stone clock-tower to the sky. "He chased me," Richard says simply. "He wanted to kill me."

Oliver nods, directs his eyes skyward then back to Richard. "All the way up there, huh?"

"All the way up there."

"And?"

Only truth can come out of Richard and Oliver knows it. "He went after me and . . . he slipped . . . He was gone."

"He's gone, that's for sure," Oliver says.

Richard turns to Janet. "I'm sorry."

Her cheeks are tear-streaked and she'd almost smile if she could control her facial muscles. "Thank God you're all right."

Oliver places a hand on Richard's shoulder, and points to the sheet-covered body and the huddle of police, none of whom are aware of Richard's presence or relevance. "Time to tell them your story."

Richard takes in the scene, revolving red lights and hot white floods for TV, the machinery of accountability, of public display, the energy of it all. They move toward the barrier, but Janet stops them in their tracks. "He killed my sister," she says to Richard.

He looks at her.

"Atlantic City," she continues. "Another highrise. They were living together. He was never even arrested."

Their silence unleashes the squawking of police-car radios and competing media voices carving out slices of the story. "I've been after him ever since."

Richard can't hide a note of disappointment. "Why didn't you tell me? We could have—"

"I wasn't trusting anybody, and I didn't want to endanger anybody. But you had it right, Richard, all the way." She shuts her eyes. A derisive puff of air sneaks out of her. She opens her eyes and looks through the drizzle toward the sheet-covered mound. A near whisper: "Goodbye, you bastard."

"You might as well come with us," Oliver says to her. "We're gonna take lots of notes tonight. Make a call to Atlantic City while we're at it." He leads them through the barricade.

"What about you, Richard?" Janet asks, walking next to him. "What was this about? What was it really about?"

Richard doesn't break stride and he is looking somewhere beyond the corpse and the plaza when he answers. "Freedom."

20

Three days later, a day after Richard learned that First Federal Bancorp has implicated Lori Calder in Braun's brazen scheme, news that would have torn out his heart if her death had not already done that, he is standing in front of his bathroom mirror. When his reflected form stares back at him, he figures he's real enough, as tangible as his toothbrush.

He has told the police an amazing story, every bit of it true, and they have no reason not to believe him. They have an embalmed Lori Calder, a chloroformed Frank Grant, Frank's testimony and that of Janet Kroll, a still missing Eleanor Carson. They have Sgt. Robert Oliver backing Richard's story all the way, and a nice find by detectives Burnside and Alvarez on a return visit to Braun's apartment: traces of embalming fluid. They did ask Richard repeatedly why he raced Braun through the city and drew him to the top of the City Hall clock tower instead of seeking the protection of others, calling the police. It was uncertain whether he could find immediate sanctuary with Braun coming after him, he told them, and even if he could and contacted police, Braun might have had time to cover things up yet again. Furthermore, why endanger others, with a killer on the loose and on the attack? So he took it on himself and devised a strategy on the fly. He went where his legs and heart and lungs, and perhaps his mind carried him.

The telephone is ringing. He walks into the bedroom and picks up the phone. Evelyn on the line, breathless.

"Richard, Herb Dempsey committed suicide."

Richard lets the news seep into his skin.

"Did you hear me?"

"Yes, I heard you."

"Two days ago. It happened in the building where he was living . . . in West Philadelphia somewhere . . . I thought you should know."

His eyes are shut. "How?"

"What?"

"How did he kill himself?"

"Stuck his head in the oven."

A strange, slow nodding from Richard. "What took him so long?"

Nervous laughter from Evelyn.

Richard's eyes are open. He hopes he isn't dreaming.

Several floors below, Janet Kroll is in her apartment and reordering the pivot points of her life. She's clearing out of here fast and going home, she knows that much. The job is done, the investment has paid off. At the seashore, her sister's disappearance is back on the police front-burner.

Meanwhile, she has learned some things about herself. She's a tougher person than anyone had suspected. In dogging Davis Braun until he selected his own death, she became a different person. To avenge her sister, she became her sister—the actress, the personality, even the morals—and she leaves the crime scene with altered chemistry.

Across town, Sgt. Robert Oliver is feeling better about himself and the world around him, or at least the immediate four walls of his apartment. Feeling this way for the first time in years. This morning, he could taste the sweet-sour tang of his orange juice and the fresh-brewed flavor of his coffee, elevating those beverages from rote offerings to pleasures. He shaved close and smooth, and slicked a skin-conditioning gel over the sagging pouches of his cheek and neck; it smelled great and soothed the scraped skin, even if it did nothing to firm the contours. If he's not exactly a man with a new lease on life, he is at least one whose outlook has risen above that of a galley slave. There are lots of people on this planet, he reminds himself, and he's still among them. People of strength like Richard Keene and Janet Kroll. He hasn't stepped into a church since Cassie's funeral, but may change that.

Last night, he even retrieved the photo album barricaded at the top of the closet and looked at the old photographs. Cassie at four with her blond hair cut short, giving the camera a big gap-toothed smile, her nose wrinkled and eyes squinting under a sky radiating sunshine. Libby raking leaves in the backyard. Robert Jr. standing in his crib, clutching and smiling through the wooden restraining bars.

Call him tonight.

In another part of town, flat desolate acreage stretches out under a tame sky like some ancient riverbed deserted by its waters. Big birds issue predatory squawks, as they circle and observe from on high. The stink of decay rises as if to fend them off, but serves only to entice them.

A broad pit of earth receives its payload, as a trash truck rears and lets slide, then pivots and roars into traction like a tank on a battlefield. Two hundred feet away, a steam shovel is unearthing heaps of trash, a torrent of dirt falling away between the huge metal teeth. At the edge of the site, their backs to the highway and the traffic that flies past, police stand aside their squad cars on the hard-packed dirt.

Fifty-five miles east, Atlantic City police will go through a similar exercise designed to recover a body, probably encased in a body bag, possibly embalmed. And no doubt buried beneath many more layers of trash.

ABOUT THE AUTHOR

Jim Waltzer is a veteran newspaper and magazine journalist in the Pennsylvania-New Jersey-Delaware region. He has written two books about vintage Atlantic City: *Tales of South Jersey* (Rutgers University Press) and *Monopoly: The Story Behind the World's Best-Selling Game* (Gibbs Smith). His short stories have appeared in several fiction journals. *Sound of Mind* is his first novel.